BRAYDEN

MELISSA BELLE

ALSO BY MELISSA BELLE

Boston Boys Series

BOSTON BILLIONAIRE

BOSTON LOVE

BOSTON ESCAPE

BOSTON ROOMIE

WILD MEN Series

WILD MAN

COLTON

DYLAN

AYDEN

JENSON

BRAYDEN

CAMERON

Sign up for Melissa's Newsletter to receive alerts and updates on upcoming book releases.

ABOUT

A contemporary love triangle romance:

Leleila

Brayden Wild was my first kiss. The Montana football star with the cowboy boots and sexy tattoo. He salvaged my heart from a bad choice I wish I never made, on a night I wish I could forget.

But that was twelve years ago. And since then, I've been wise enough to play it safe. Certain. Risk-free.

Until I go to the store and spill granola all over...Brayden Wild. He's still rocking a wild mess of blond hair. He's still sexy as hell.

My smooth reaction? I trip and fall on him. And then I run off like a frightened deer.

Because I still WANT him.

But I'm getting married in a month.

Brayden

Leleila Wills. The bookish, teenage girl with the sad, beautiful eyes and killer body who electrified me at first sight—is now a grown woman living here in Mountainview. I finally know her name. I finally have a second chance to ask her out. But I can't.

Because I DON'T go after women who are taken. Ever.

I try to focus on coaching my football team and on taking care of things at the ranch. So why can't I get her the hell out of my head?

I tell myself it's because she needs a friend. I mean, what kind of tool stands up his wife-to-be before their wedding dance class? But the truth is...

I like Leleila's awkward, quirky personality. And I can't deny how my body's on fire whenever she's nearby.

I've got one month to get to know her the way I wanted to twelve years ago, even if it's only as her friend. That will have to be enough.

So what the hell will I do if it's not?

STAY UP TO DATE WITH MELISSA

Do you want to stay up to date on awesome sales, upcoming hot releases, and giveaways? Sign up for my VIP List and get access to frequent freebies!

For wild Montana

CHAPTER ONE
Twelve Years Ago

Leleila

The dark strobe-lit basement is filled with wall-to-wall high schoolers getting wasted at their self-titled Football Is Paradise and Cowboys Are Cool Party, and I don't fit in. But I push forward through the loud country music anyway, moving away from the bass coming out of the corner speakers and determined to find the center of all the fun. I grab an empty red solo cup at the table, and get in line for the keg.

Since this is the county-wide football party held every Christmas season, teams come from all over the area. And in our part of Montana, that's a lot of teams.

But I have my sights set on one player in particular. He's the reason I talked myself into coming tonight. I push my glasses up on my nose and shift awkwardly from one leg to the other as I look around for him. I see Stella waving at me, and I smile in relief when she comes over and hugs me.

"You look amazing, Leleila!" she says as she touches my fitted red knit sweater with the outline of a heart on the front. "I love your top! I couldn't see it at the game; it was too cold to take off our coats!"

"Thanks," I say. "It's like the only thing I could find in my closet that didn't make me look like a total dork."

"Did your parents say it was okay to come here?" she says. "Mine think I'm at the movies with Delvin." She points to her boyfriend across the way. "He'll cover for me."

"My parents are so disappointed in me for not acing my science exam that they didn't really care where I went to tonight," I say sadly. "As long as they didn't have to look at me. My A in art class didn't count for much."

"You got a B- in science! That's like perfection in my book." Stella squeezes my arm. "Let's just forget about school for a night, okay, and enjoy our junior year for once. Oh look, there's your cowboy crush," she adds in a whisper. "Remember our pact; tonight's all about being sixteen and free. You're going to follow your heart, and try to ignore that brilliant brain of yours for the night."

Before I can answer her, Noah appears next to me. "Lei, I'm glad you decided to come," he says, slinging an arm around me. "Thanks again for letting me cheat off your math test yesterday. Can't believe you're only a junior and taking the class with all seniors. You know I can't afford to get kicked off the team. Who would catch the big passes then, right?"

I smile at him, wishing I were brave enough to reach out and touch the cowboy hat perched over his wavy brown hair. "Sure. Math's easy for me, so no big deal."

He offers to fill up my cup. I look underneath his hat at his bloodshot hazel eyes and resist at first, but his smile is focused only on me. I relent and give him the cup. Stella hugs me and says she's going to make out with Delvin. I watch her go, half-wishing I could turn around and go home.

While I wait on the fringe of the crowd, I nervously fiddle with my hair and glance over at the beer pong contest in the corner.

Two guys in cowboy hats are going at it hard with the winner walking away with his arms in the air victoriously. He looks back at me over all the girls draping themselves on him, and our eyes lock. I freeze when he gives me a quick nod. I have the urge to walk over to him, but I hold my feet where they are and don't move.

He tosses his cowboy hat onto the nearby couch. His dirty blond hair is messy and he keeps his gaze on me as he peels off his Keep Montana Wild t-shirt, revealing glistening tanned skin and muscles on muscles. The tattoo on his bicep stands out even from a few feet away. I can tell from his body and the way he carries himself that he's a football player, but he's not from our school. No way I'd forget him. His worn-out jeans hang low on his hips, and I swallow as he pushes the girls away and starts walking in my direction.

I don't know whether to be disappointed or relieved when Noah returns to my side, and I shift my attention to him.

"Full of good beer," he says with a grin as he hands me back my cup now filled to the brim. "Drink up."

I send one last glance at the Keep Montana Wild guy before letting Noah lead me over to a corner where he pushes the cup to my lips and props his arm against the wall over my head. I take a look at him, wanting to feel his arms around me. But then, I glance down at my cup, and I know Stella was wrong. I can't ignore my brain because all I can hear in my head right now is, "the date rape drug is odorless." And something about this drink just feels off.

"I don't think I'm thirsty," I decide before dumping the cup of beer into the nearby trash can and walking away.

Noah follows me and takes me by the arm as we pass an open doorway. Before I can react, he drags me through the door and slams it shut behind us.

I gasp. "Wha—"

He pulls me toward the bed and throws me onto it. I take one panicked look into his eyes that are glazed over with alcohol or something stronger, and fear hits me so hard I feel sick. I lurch up off the bed and bolt for the door. As soon as I put my hand on the doorknob, Noah twists me and presses my back hard up against the wall. Keeping me still, he shoves his tongue down my throat.

I struggle against his heavy weight, but he grips my waist so tightly it hurts.

"You're not getting out of here that easy," he mutters as he pulls back and reaches for the button on my jeans. "I asked you here tonight for a reason, and you know it, you tease!"

"No—"

He tears my pants down to my knees and rips my panties as his fingers reach for the place I never gave him permission to go, a place where no man has been before.

Terror slices through me. I'm way out of my comfort zone without a book or a brush in my hand, and Noah is far stronger than I am.

My panicked mind reaches for something, anything, and I flash back to the self-defense classes my parents signed June and me up for last fall.

"You're Montana girls!" the instructor would shout. "I'll make sure you know how to rope a wayward steer!"

I take my right forearm and slam it across Noah's left, causing him to momentarily lose his grip on me. He grunts, and I take my free right hand and jam the base of it into the bridge of his nose. He cries out and steps backward, his hands finally leaving my body. I hear knocking on the door, and I bring my left knee into Noah's groin with as much force as I can muster. He topples to the ground, and I kick him in the stomach before I pull up my underwear and jeans and then hurry for the door.

It bursts open as I stumble forward, and I go barreling through the open doorway, landing straight against a solid, masculine chest.

All the adrenaline drains out of me as the truth hits me of what I just narrowly escaped. My legs buckle underneath me, and I start to topple over, grasping at anything to keep me upright.

Strong arms wrap around me, and I raise my head.

Shaking, I come face to face with the Keep Montana Wild guy, cowboy hat back on his head.

"Are you okay?" he asks gently.

I manage a quick nod.

His shirt's back on his body, and his sparkling blue eyes are feral as he looks past me into the room.

"Stay here," he says. "I'm going to make sure that asshole doesn't get up again for a while."

But I grab at his soft, cotton t-shirt. "No. Just..." *Don't leave me yet.*

Without another word, Wild guy lifts me off the ground and carries me a few feet down the dimly-lit hallway until we're completely shielded from the party.

He slides me back down his body until my feet hit the ground. He reaches out and touches my cheek. "You're bleeding."

I shiver at his gentle touch. "I'm okay. I'm sorry for landing on you like that."

"No apologies. You have nothing to be sorry for." He hesitates, and then reaches for his cowboy hat. "Here." He puts it gently on my head, tilting it to the left. "This will help hide your cut."

"Thank you." I feel my face flush with shame as I hurry to rebutton my jeans.

He helps me adjust my sweater so that both my shoulders are covered.

I jerk back from him. "I have to go."

He keeps his hands on my arms to steady me. "Hey." Concern fills his handsome face.

I need to get out of here.

I step past him and hurry down the hallway, but he follows me.

"What happened in there? Did that bastard do something..."

"Nothing I couldn't handle."

I head for the stairs. If I can just get out of here, I can go back to my homework waiting for me in my bedroom, lock this whole night up inside my heart, and never think about it again.

"Are you sure you're okay?" he says quietly from behind me. "I can call the police or take you to the hospital."

The terror, which had somehow disappeared for a few brief seconds, is back in full tilt, and I spin on him as I reach the front door of the house. "I'm okay, I swear. I can take care of myself."

He takes a deep breath as he peers underneath the brim of his hat I'm still wearing.

"Your eyes look so sad," he says softly. His tone is low with an attractive timber to it.

I adjust my glasses nervously. "I hardly know anybody in there," I say with a shrug. "I never should have come tonight."

I turn away from him again and step outside the front door. I'm sure he won't follow me out into the cold in just a t-shirt, but apparently he's immune to the chilly Montana air because he walks right out with me, and he doesn't even have goosebumps. I stare at his tanned, muscular arm, wondering what his tattoo means.

A pair of wings with a crescent moon behind them.

"So why did you come?" he asks me as he continues to follow me down the front walk. "You don't look like you belong here."

"Thank you," I say. "I don't need any more insults tonight."

"It's not an insult," he says. "You just look … like you're a lot better than that." He gestures with his thumb to the loud-ass party still raging inside the house.

I stop abruptly by a row of bushes and throw up my hands. "I guess I just...wanted to feel something real for once. Outside of a textbook."

He nods like he understands even though I don't see how he can.

"You're a football god around these parts, right? You probably have tons of friends."

"People who like you because of what you do on the football field aren't usually real friends," he says simply. "I always try to remember that."

"Oh."

He touches my cheek again. His hand is warm and comforting. "You should put something on that cut."

"I will."

He goes to remove his hand, but I reach up and keep it against my cold skin.

His clear blue eyes trap me in place, but not in a threatening way, and he runs his thumb gently across my jaw.

"Sweetheart, are you hurt anywhere else? Somewhere that I can't see?" He holds my gaze tight with his, and I can't possibly look away.

I know what he's asking me. "No. I'm..." My voice comes out raspy. "I'm okay."

I swallow hard as I lean into his hand, and he inhales sharply like our connection has surprised him too.

Our gazes lock onto each other like nothing can tear us apart, and I take a step closer to him until our shoes touch. His eyes widen, but he doesn't move away.

I feel raw and unguarded like I could snap from the intense energy coursing through me.

And I don't know what it is about this boy with his kind blue eyes and mess of blond hair, but I feel the most powerful desire to be closer to him. To inhale him, and maybe then I can feel safe again in the world.

Without thinking about it, I stand on my toes and press my lips to his.

His hands go to my arms, and he holds me still, almost like he's trying to stop me. But I cling to his mouth for several seconds before pulling back.

Emotions flicker across his face like he's warring with himself.

But then, he tugs the hat back so my face is exposed, tilts his head, and brushes his lips to mine. So tenderly, the most tender touch I've ever felt.

My first real kiss.

As an introverted girl who puts her studies first, second, and last, this moment feels beyond crazy. I react to his touch by kissing him back with an urgency and a desperation that I don't understand; I just know I need more of him. I can't make sense of the way my stomach is clenching and my heart pounding, so I grip at Wild's shirt like an anchor.

He kisses me slowly like I'm a fragile bird he doesn't want to hurt, and I let out a soft moan when his tongue lightly touches mine. He's soothing me and sending away my demons at the same time.

He curls his hand around my hip and draws me flush to him. The feel of his growing erection against my stomach jolts me back to reality. Fear once again overwhelms me as I remember what almost happened in the house. The lust that had taken over my brain disappears, and I go rigid in his arms.

He lets me go immediately. "I'm sorry; I shouldn't have done that."

I wish I could tell him yes, he should have. It was the most alive I've ever felt in my life.

Instead, I take off his hat and try to give it back to him. "Thanks for lending me this."

But he pushes it back to me. "Keep it. You can return it next time we see each other."

I stare at him. "But..." *I don't even know who you are.*

"Please let me help you," he says. "I can take you home."

But I back away. This guy is obviously not Noah, but he's a football player and a cowboy all the same, and I clearly have proven myself to be a terrible judge of character. If I had any clue at all, I never would have come to this party or crushed on Noah in the first place. And to kiss a total stranger like I just did? I cannot trust myself. Not anymore.

"Don't worry about me." I take one last look into his sapphire blue eyes that are so bright they nearly blind me. "I'll be okay. You'll never see me again, anyway."

Carrying his cowboy hat in my hand, I run to my car as fast as I can, turn the key in the ignition, and drive away from the ranch.

And for the next twelve years, I was right—he never saw me again.

CHAPTER TWO

Present Day

Brayden

"Fweet!!!" Standing in the middle of the ranch I plan to buy one day soon, I blow hard on my whistle, and the pack of animals—otherwise known as a high school football team—stop running laps around the field I've designated for informal practices.

All fifty-two players, plus the other assistant coaches, turn their heads and look at me. The head coach is sick and left me in charge for the day.

"One more lap," I say.

A collective groan goes up through the team, but they comply and start jogging past the wire fence separating them from the cows grazing nearby. Due to heavy spring flooding, Wilcox High's athletic fields are out of commission for a while. So even though Big River Ranch is a town over from Wilcox, it was the best available option, given the fact that I live here and could offer a safe, solid field to practice on. Between my brother, the Wilcox coaching staff, and myself, we had the field chalked and ready to go in no time. For me, less travel has meant more time to ride the ranch and look after everything.

My life is full between riding, herding cattle, and coaching, but I was a player once too. Star wide receiver for Wilcox High. I played alongside my cousins, Colton and Dylan. They're both now successful stars in the pros.

But most of us don't make it to the professional level. Some, like me, don't want that kind of grind and stressful lifestyle, so we never plan for the draft, and some don't have the talent to make it past tryouts.

Either way, the simple fact is—the vast majority of high school athletes need a plan for when they leave the football field. And that's really why I coach these kids. I try to be a resource to them, to help them find tutors if they need to pull up their grades, help them figure out what college is best, and make sure they know that most of us aren't Dylan or Colton Wild.

The other assistant coaches keep talking amongst themselves, and I give their conversation part of my attention, making sure to keep my focus on the players.

As they pass the makeshift end zone on the left, a movement behind the wire fence catches my eye.

I take a step forward.

A woman is bent over at the waist as she picks something up only a couple feet away from the small group of cows hanging out by the fence.

She's over fifty yards away, but something about her causes my gut to twist in a strange way, and I suck in a breath. Her high heels are no match to the rough terrain, and she stumbles as she digs at whatever the hell she's doing. Her long chestnut hair covers most of her profile, but her body...it's perfection. Curvy and tall, and when she stands up straight, I get a look at her face.

She's...intense. Serious. Almost like she hasn't smiled in a long time. Her dark cat-eye glasses give her a sexy librarian look.

And she's...familiar somehow.

Without thinking about it, I raise my hand in a hello, but she's already turned away. She waves at the cows, and I chuckle as she ducks underneath the ranch fencing and turns the corner.

The trespasser is gone.

"Hey, Coach Wild!" Wes, the captain and starting quarterback for Wilcox High, calls out to me. "We done yet?"

I glance at my watch. Right on time for me to go for a quick ride before heading to my new part-time job, one that will hopefully help me to accomplish the two things that stir my soul: live on my own Montana ranch and still be around football as much as possible.

I need my own land. Having been raised on a six-hundred acre ranch, room to roam is essential for me, and sharing the family ranch with my siblings, especially my oldest brother, would never work. One of us would end up killing the other. Luke and I love each other, but we've never lived together well.

I give Wes the thumbs up. "All done for today. See you tomorrow after classes—if you're late, you know what that means!"

As soon as the players and coaches have taken off, I head for the barn. I need my daily ride.

I tack up Blazer quickly, and within minutes, I'm in the saddle and trotting through the first field to the open pastures beyond. With the Bitterroot Forest on my left, I urge Blazer into a gallop. He's my favorite horse for a reason—we both like to pretend we can fly.

Blazer follows the southern edge of the hundred-acre property, and as we reach a section of the ranch with an open view of our neighbors, my gaze catches on a truck disappearing down the makeshift dirt road at the back of the property. Going that way, he would never pass the main house.

I know that truck doesn't belong to the Eastons, the family who's owned the ranch next door for four generations. Chuck Easton's been having some health issues, and I try to keep an eye on things for them when I can. I pull up on Blazer, watching until the truck disappears out of sight.

A shiver of cold dread shoots down my spine. Something doesn't feel right about this, and I make a mental note to check back when I have more time.

"Come on boy." A light tug of the reins, and Blazer turns around, taking me back to Big River.

Time to get to my new job.

———

Leleila

I hustle away from the field where I collected my sample of cow dung for Save the Soil. The owners of Big River called and asked for us to take a specimen, but they're out of town, and I don't know who's in charge while they're away. Most likely, the information wasn't passed on, and I don't want to run into another ranch hand convinced I'm trying to steal his cows.

I've made it about ten feet when my cell rings. Phillip wants to confirm that I'm okay going to the Galapagos Islands for our honeymoon. He thinks the Galapagos is the sensible thing to do.

I want to tell him it's supposed to be a honeymoon, not a science project, but I hold my tongue.

"Phillip, the Galapagos is fine. And since we can't go to Africa next year like we planned on…"

He cuts me off, sounding excited for the first time since I failed my dissertation. "Don't worry, honey. I have a new idea. One that could still get us to Africa right after the wedding."

"What? How?"

"I'll tell you at home."

Phillip's always been superhuman in my eyes—brilliant, handsome, and opinionated. He swept me off my feet back in high school biology, and I don't know that I've come down yet. He aced all the tests, and I leaned on him to miraculously pull off an A minus. But more than that, he was there—constant and reliable—when everything in my world felt dangerous and black.

Now, he's still kicking ass out there in the world of academia, and I don't know if it matters, but there's something about being with a hero that feels…lonely.

Like my parents, he never stops trying to heal the planet. At twenty-nine, he's the youngest tenured professor ever at the University of Montana where he focuses on the fragility of ecosystems. And his latest research is for a paper he hopes will be published in the *Scientific Ecology Journal's* winter issue. He's my parents' ideal man for me, and I'm pretty sure they can't figure out how I got so lucky.

As Phillip rattles off all the perks of the hotel he found for us in the Galapagos, I cut across the empty lot until I reach Main Street. I walk down the street of our small Old West town of Mountainview and turn into the parking lot of Big Sky Natural Grocer & Ranch Supplies. He continues to talk while I duck inside the Save the Soil suite that's adjacent to the grocery store and drop off the soil specimen I'd collected.

I'd left my car in the parking lot when I went to collect the soil, but before I drive home to sit by myself, I decide to pay my sister a quick visit.

As I walk the few steps to the grocery store and enter through the front door, I call out a hello to June working the counter over by the bagels.

Through the phone, Phillip says he needs to secure our hotel room today, and I tell him to go ahead and book it. "Just get a nice room," I say. After all, we only get one honeymoon.

We finally hang up then, and I let out a long breath. From her register, June raises her eyebrows at me in that annoying way she has of expressing her constant disdain for my fiancé. I get it. My younger sister doesn't like Phillip. We've gone around in circles over this for years. And because she doesn't know the whole story, I cut her slack. I head over to her, tugging my suit jacket down where it keeps riding up on my hips.

Before I can comment on her still-raised eyebrows—

"June, you want the squash put into the far bin, over by the lettuce?"

The low, sexy tone of voice gets my attention.

I shift my stance and swallow as I stare at the attractive, muscular guy holding a carton of squash in his arms.

A tattoo peeks out from the cuff of his shirtsleeve. Just a hint of wings but enough to give me pause.

I raise my head so I can take in all of him.

Hotter than sin body.

A strong jaw and kissable mouth.

Sapphire blue eyes that are focused right on me.

He's more mature and has a shirt on, but I'd know him anywhere.

I'm face to face with the Keep Montana Wild guy I kissed and then ran away from twelve years ago.

CHAPTER THREE

No way.

As our eyes lock, I jump. Shock waves shoot through my body.

I push my glasses up on my nose and keep unabashedly looking at him.

His wavy, dirty blond hair is still shaggy and untamed, and he's still dressed casually but perfectly, this time in worn blue jeans and a t-shirt that says "Ranch Life." His cowboy boots are...really sexy, and his muscled body is trim and tanned.

He keeps his intense gaze directly on me as June answers him in the affirmative, and I surprise myself when I maintain the eye contact. He looks down my body slowly and then back up to my face where his eyes linger on my red lipstick. By the time he pulls his gaze back up to meet mine, I'm shaking.

He gives me a quick nod and then walks away with his carton. I watch him leave, my gaze trained on his ass. He's got a nice ass. And nice—okay, fucking amazing—blue eyes that still sparkle.

Did he recognize me? I can't be sure. He didn't give any indication that he had. Well, he's certainly more memorable than I am. And it *was* twelve years ago.

Without thinking why I'm doing it, I reach for my tight bun and undo it, letting my hair fall past my shoulders.

I turn back to June, hoping she won't notice how much I'm shaking. "Who is that?"

She smiles as she counts her drawer. "That's Brayden Wild. He just started working here. I thought you might notice him."

Brayden Wild. All these years, and I never knew his name.

"What? Why? Why would I notice him?" I say it in a low voice in case Brayden has super-good hearing. But when I look over toward the squash bins, he's no longer there.

"Just a hunch." June's finished with the ten dollar bills and has moved on to the fives. "He lives on Big River Ranch right behind the store. I met him when I relocated Big Sky Grocer here last month."

"I was just at Big River collecting a sample. Isn't that the ranch you've decided to get a lot of your meats from?" I ask.

"Right. We're also going to buy eggs and organic produce from them. And Brayden needs extra cash right now, so he's going to help me out part-time with extra stocking and other things. I guess he's saving up to buy the ranch from Phil and Betsy. Now that they're in Florida most of the year, they want to sell it."

"Brayden's going to buy it?"

"That's his plan. He's also an assistant football coach for Wilcox High."

"The state champions one town over?" I nearly gasp like some sort of swooning fan. I wonder if Wilcox is the school he played for.

"Those are the ones. He's been coaching them for years. His body's sure built like a football player, huh?"

"Sure is," I say without thinking. *Always was.*

She glances up to wink at me teasingly. "Good thing you look so hot today. Did you have another job interview?"

"Yep." For good luck, I dressed in my best business suit and black heels to match. I even applied mascara and lipstick—a rarity for me. It was all in an attempt to feel professional and grown up. I should feel grown up all the time, I suppose, since I'm twenty-eight years old, but chronological age doesn't always equate with maturity. "I don't think the interview went well. No surprise there. Overqualified, blah, blah, blah."

"Don't give up hope yet, Lei. You'll get something."

"I better."

"I'm sorry you failed your dissertation, as you know. But I have an idea."

"No," I say.

June's nose wrinkles in that way it does when she's momentarily stymied. "You don't know what I'm going to ask."

"And yet, I can already tell I won't like the idea."

"I think you should work here for me."

I burst out laughing. "Ha, ha. That's funny."

"Seriously. You know how a lot of the professors stop in. Working here will keep you connected to the university while you're banned from the department..." She stops talking when she sees the look on my face. "While you're working on your thesis from home," she rephrases.

"I wasn't technically banned. I know Gerry said I have to take a break, but I doubt working here is what he had in mind."

"Just while you're figuring things out," June says. "I can even pay you."

"I write your monthly store newsletter for free," I say. "And I'd do this for free too, whatever it is. I'm not going to be your employee, believe me."

"Fine," June says. "No money exchange then. You can start with something small like the sign out front that's so faded. You have a painting portfolio, Lei. Or have you forgotten?"

I flush. "That part of my life is a closed book, June."

"Right. I forgot," she says even though I know she didn't even remotely forget. "Let's circle this conversation back to more important things. Like the hot cowboy who just got you to let your hair down."

"June..." I warn her. I never told anyone in my family about that night in high school, and I don't plan to start a confessional right now.

Flustered, I head down aisle four to pick up breakfast for the week.

I walk quickly until I reach the nine-grain granola bin, which June inexplicably keeps at nearly eye level. I grab the plastic spoon from the tray above my head and then open the cereal bin and dig in. As soon as I've filled the spoon, I realize I forgot to grab a plastic bag to put the granola into. I don't want to put the spoon back down because then the granola will start to slide off the spoon, and I'll have to start over. I'm lazy that way. So I keep my left hand on the spoon inside the open bin and stretch my body as far as I can to the right so I can rip a bag off the holder with my other hand.

It takes a few seconds to separate the perforated lines from the next bag, and when they finally do come apart, the effort sends me off-balance. The spoon comes out of the bin, and granola spills everywhere.

"Shit!" I say loudly.

Still holding the now-empty spoon, I step back, and that's when I see Brayden squatting below me just to my left. He's got a cardboard box filled with cereals next to him and, courtesy of me, granola all over his head. His blond hair comes down past his ears and stops in a wavy style on his neck. It's really nice hair, hair that I've now messed up with granola.

"Oh, God." I stand awkwardly with the spoon in my hand. "I'm so sorry. I didn't see you there."

Brayden stands up and brushes granola off his hair. "I think I'll live," he says with a smile.

Laying the spoon on the shelf, I step forward to try to help clean up my mess. As I do, I slip on the granola coating the floor.

"Oomph." I pitch forward, arms flailing as I grasp at anything to keep me from bashing my face on the ground.

What I find is Brayden's nice, solid chest. My hands grip at the soft fabric of his shirt at the same time that his arm curves around my waist and keeps me upright.

"You okay?" His voice is still low, like super-sexy low.

My face is buried in his chest, and I don't know why I'm not moving. It sounds crazy to say, but I feel more at peace in this one moment than I have in years.

Brayden's hands go to my shoulders, and he gently rubs my back. "It'll be okay. It was just surprising is all."

Yes. Surprising. To run smack dab into a man I haven't seen in years, a man who's not my fiancé and yet who's making me feel something. Something big.

I jerk to awareness and pull back from him quickly. Not making eye contact, I murmur, "I'm sorry. Again. I'm not usually this clumsy."

His callused thumb and finger take my chin and tilt it slowly, forcing me to look at him. His expression is filled with genuine concern and interest, two emotions that haven't been directed my way in a long freaking time.

He's taller than I am but not by a lot, and he looks so relaxed I suddenly realize just how stressed out I am.

"Need some help with anything?" His question is innocent, but the words come out heated, and our gazes clash.

"No, thanks."

I break away from him, from those sapphire blue eyes that look even more alive and sparkly than I remembered.

And I've remembered him a lot over the years. As much as I've tried to forget that night, I could never forget the Keep Montana Wild boy who gave me my first real kiss.

And now he's a man, all sexy and mature and standing right in front of me.

Emotions—and needs—that I'd stuffed away into the recesses of my heart come flooding back.

The way I wanted him that night when my lips clung to his.

The way he held me.

The way I ran away.

I swallow and reach to put the spoon back into the proper bin. I suddenly don't feel hungry, at least not for granola.

He extends his hand. "I'm Brayden."

I take his hand and feel how strong it is in mine. I shake it quickly and then let it go. "Leleila."

"Nice to finally put a name to the face."

I clench and then unclench my hands together. "You remember."

"Of course I remember. I never forgot you."

"It's just...it's been a long time."

"Sure has." His eyes are warm on mine. "You're all grown up now."

"So are you," I say without thinking.

He chuckles. "I think I saw you earlier today. At Big River Ranch? I didn't make the connection then, but something about you was familiar."

I startle. "Oh! Yes, I was collecting a sample of cow dung."

His eyes flash with amusement. "Cow dung?"

I nod. "Phil and Betsy requested it. My parents run a foundation called Save the Soil. We focus on teaching people about ways to protect the soil from contamination, such as the dangers of pesticides. Mountainview is working to increase its organic fertilizer options, but it still has a ways to go. Sometimes the ranches get hit with pesticides from surrounding properties, and it shows up in the cows' waste. Sometimes the ranchers are grateful, and sometimes they hate us." I laugh nervously. "I didn't know you lived at Big River Ranch. That's the first time I've collected from you, I swear."

"I think that's cool what you're doing." He tilts his head. "So you work in the environmental field then?"

I blow out a breath. "No, my parents do, but I'm actually a psych major. I'm supposed to have my PhD but...I didn't pass. Not yet. So I don't currently have a job. Not a paying one, anyway. I help my parents with their foundation as much as I can." I fumble with the bag I'm still holding. "I didn't see you. At the ranch."

"I know. You were too busy looking at the shit." He grins. "No matter. I got a second chance to meet you. Or I guess I should say a third chance."

Our eyes clash, and silence fills the space between us.

I open my mouth, but nothing comes out.

Brayden breaks the eye contact and gestures at the empty plastic bag in my hand. "You going to try again for the granola?"

I shake my head and back away from him. "No. I have to go, actually. I have..." To go home to Phillip. "I have a prior engagement."

That's not exactly what I planned to say, but it couldn't be more truthful.

I turn my back on him and nearly run through the aisle.

I hear June calling to me as I pass by the registers, but I don't stop.

I keep running all the way to my car, and then I jump into the driver's seat, turn on the ignition, and floor the gas, not letting up until I'm safely in my driveway.

———

Brayden

I stand frozen in aisle four, staring after her as she makes a fast track away from me.

What the fuck was that? This whirlwind of a woman, all green eyes and an amazing mane of dark brown hair, just slammed into my chest and knocked me so off-kilter I'm still catching my breath.

Just like she did twelve years ago.

My heart is doing triple time as my brain tries to play catch up.

The woman with the emerald eyes and barest hint of a smile—the kind of tension-filled smile that makes me want to ask her why she's so unhappy—has me all sorts of thrown off.

We're total opposites. You don't have to be a genius to pick up on that. We always were.

I was the football jock who grew up on a cattle ranch, and she was clearly a smart girl who didn't normally frequent the kind of parties I was used to. The moment I turned away from the ping pong table, her eyes were stuck to me like I was the first half-naked guy she'd ever seen. Maybe I was.

I frown as I remember what happened next that night.

After I lost sight of her at the party, I went looking.

When I reached the empty hallway, I heard banging coming from one of the rooms. My gut tightened, and fear cut through me.

I rattled the doorknob and pushed the door open.

When Leleila crashed into me, I instinctively wrapped my arms around her. I glanced over her shoulder at the guy laid out on the ground, and my fear turned to rage.

But she clearly didn't want a scene. She also didn't want to be left alone.

And that kiss between us...I run my thumb over my bottom lip as I continue to stand in the middle of the cereal aisle. She was inexperienced but passionate, and it felt like she gave me everything with that kiss.

And now?

We're still total opposites. She was rocking a fancy business suit, and I'm still dressed for manual labor. Her body filled out her suit nicely, and her jacket kept riding up on her ample hips. Her blouse was undone at the first two buttons, just enough to reveal a hint of cleavage.

I was drawn to her all over again. All of her, not just her body.

I run my hand down my face.

I want her.

I want to ask her out.

Christ, Brayden. Let it go.

I'm in the middle of a crossroads in my life. Being a high school football coach is great, but it's not enough to keep me living at Big River. If I want to buy the ranch I live and work on, I need to put all my energy into bulking up my savings. Any woman would—and should—probably run from me right now.

But for the first time in a long time, I met—okay, I remet—a woman I want to get to know better. And...I'm going to follow through.

I finish putting away the final cereal box, and then I head to the front of the store, stopping at June's register.

She looks up with a smile. "Her name's Leleila," she says before I have to figure a way to get it out of her.

I cock my head. "I know."

"Well, color me surprised." June's eyebrows shoot up. "My sister's not exactly the social type."

"Leleila's your sister?" I say, not able to keep the disappointment out of my voice.

I may be working for Big River when I'm here, but asking out the store owner's sister is a level of complicated I can't do.

But June just smiles wider. "You won't get any pushback from me. I think you should go for it. My sister, on the other hand..." She trails off, but something in her tone makes my heart lurch.

"Is she...involved with someone?" I ask.

Please, please, say no. Please say she's single.

June hesitates, and that's when my chest starts to ache.

"She is." I stuff my hands in my pockets.

"There's somebody else, yes," she says in a pinched tone like it pains her to have to admit it. "Although I'm far from convinced it's a forever thing. So I would still go for it if I were you."

I shake my head. "I won't get in the middle of someone else's relationship. Ever."

"That's not what I meant." June purses her lips, looking like she's choosing her next words carefully. "Let's just say that I think you and Leleila could be good for each other. At least get to know her, Brayden. As friends. My sister acts like she doesn't need anyone, but the thing is"—another long pause as she appears to again search for the right words—"Leleila could really use a friend right now."

"I don't..." I rub the back of my neck. "I don't do female friends."

"Well, maybe Leleila can be your exception." June turns away from me, and I realize the conversation is over.

But as I go back to work, the words play through my head, and I can't get them out—*maybe Leleila can be your exception.*

CHAPTER FOUR

Leleila

I've just barely stopped shaking by the time I walk in my front door. Grateful Phillip's not home yet, I race upstairs to our bedroom.

When I open the closet door, I reach inside to the far back corner until I feel the firm brim I know so well.

I wrap my fingers around it and pull it onto my lap.

The cowboy hat Brayden gave me so long ago when he was trying to shield my cut face from the room full of partying drunk kids.

Through all my years at college, and graduate school, and moving in with Phillip, I never let go of it. I go to put the hat back, and my hand brushes something else long forgotten. My portfolio and my easel.

"Lei! Are you there?"

I shove the easel back into the closet and toss the hat on top, but I tuck the portfolio under one arm and plaster a smile on my face as Phillip walks into the bedroom. He's wearing blue spandex bike shorts and a helmet.

"Hi!" I say. "How was your ride?"

Phillip shrugs as he takes off his helmet, revealing dark hair plastered to his head with sweat. "Pretty good. I got up to twenty-three miles per hour this time. Oh, and I entered the Keep the Forests race next weekend. It's only a fifty miler, but it will be a great tune-up before winter comes."

I walk closer and look up into Phillip's dark eyes. He's six foot three, so it's difficult for me to see his face well when we're both standing, but it looks like he hasn't slept in days.

I stand on my toes to give him a kiss. "I'll come to the race and cheer you on like I always do."

"You sure you don't want to bike it with me? It's great exercise for a great cause. The proceeds go to the conservation of Montana's rural forest lands."

"Yeah, I'm pretty certain. Biking's not for me. But it is a great cause, and it's very noble of you to want to help."

"Your parents have done about thirty years more work helping the environment and animals than I have," he says. "This must feel like nothing to you."

That last sentence gets me.

I stare at Philip's windburned face, his tight jaw, and the layer of tension that always seems to hide the shine in his eyes, and I exhale.

Phillip leans down to kiss my neck. "I know we haven't had a lot of time alone together lately..."

More like any time.

"And I miss us. In bed."

Oh.

He looks at me. "Honey, I know you and I have different needs."

Right.

The couple times I've tried to talk to Phillip about what I like, he brushed me off and said he didn't need an instruction manual. And I haven't been able to tell him about what happened in high school with Noah.

"What's wrong?" he asks me. "Are you okay?"

"Phillip..." I begin.

He snaps his fingers. "I forgot I offered to host the wine and cheese get together tonight. For Dr. Lucas's visiting colleague."

I freeze. "Here? At our house?"

Phillip's eyes soften. "Lei, nobody's judging you."

Right.

"Is Professor Hammond coming?" I say casually.

"I don't think so."

"Were you at Big Sky Grocer with her the other day?"

He furrows his brow. "Yes. We grabbed lunch before my afternoon classes. Why?"

I bite my lip. "Because June mentioned someone was touching you. A lot."

Phillip's eyes crinkle with amusement. "It was nothing. I can assure you, honey, that Elsa Hammond and I have never...done anything inappropriate. You don't have to worry about her. Okay?"

I don't feel okay, but the sharpness in Phillip's tone tells me this topic is closed for discussion.

As he goes to sit down on the bed, I reach for his arm.

"Honey?"

He turns. "Yeah?"

"Dance class is tomorrow night at June's. Are you in?"

Long pause as Phillip frowns.

"I'm not sure I can swing it. You know how busy I'm going to be leading up to our wedding. I've got that ecology conference down in Boulder, and I have to finish reviewing my data."

My jaw tightens. "Will your research be done by our wedding?"

"It has to be. I want to take the findings on our honeymoon so I can review the notes and maybe add to them with anything extra I find there. It would just be gravy for this paper, but I'm not complaining. It's not every day you get to test your theories in the Galapagos, right?"

"Okay, how about a compromise?" I suggest. "I know we're just having a low-key gathering with our immediate families after we marry, and that we're not dressing up or having a real wedding cake or anything like that..."

"Complete waste of money," Phillip interrupts me. "Total commercialization by the wedding industry to get paid for something that shouldn't empty anybody's wallet."

"Right. And I agree with you on all of that. However, I think it could be fun if we had a wedding dance. You know, to introduce us as husband and wife, and it would be fun to learn a dance together. Class is only once a week, on Tuesdays, and you don't teach that night. June says the instructor will teach the basics to everyone and then fine-tune each couple's dance to fit them."

Silence for a minute. Then—

"Sure. I'll take the class with you."

I throw my arms around him, and he chuckles.

"Now that that's settled, let's get ready for tonight," he says, pulling back from me. "I need to make sure Dr. Lucas backs me on this paper submission."

"I miss having time alone together," I say suddenly. "It's been a while."

"It has," he agrees, sounding like he's already distracted. "I think I may meditate before I shower, get myself in the right mood for tonight. Do you mind getting everything ready?"

"Don't you want to talk?"

He kisses my cheek, but he's already turning on his iPod. "I'm trying to unwind from a long day of research, Lei. So if you don't mind waiting to chat until I'm finished here, it won't be too long."

———

I stand awkwardly at Phillip's side, feeling like I don't belong as he holds up a glass of champagne and solemnly toasts to his colleague's recent publication. The small circle of five professors, plus their spouses, all raise their champagne glasses in unison, each one just as gravely as Phillip.

Phillip and I met in front of a microscope junior year of high school in AP Biology lab. We were the only two juniors in the class. Phillip was granted approval because he's brilliant, and I was granted approval because my parents are both brilliant biologists.

Having barely made it through Honors Biology the semester before, I was in a panic, not having a clue what I was looking for on the slide and certain I was going to let down my parents. Phillip slid over from his spot one desk over and offered to give me a hand in figuring out the specimen.

I accepted his offer gratefully, and he walked me home afterward.

When I introduced him to my parents, I could practically see the lightbulb switch on over my father's head. It turned out that my dad and Phillip's dad were former colleagues and had published a scientific paper together. My father enthusiastically hired Phillip to tutor me in biology. Phillip asked me out two weeks later. I was still reeling from my attempt to socialize at the football game and afterparty the month before, and Phillip's serious nature and focus on scholastics appealed to my scared, wounded soul.

He was safe.

I said yes to the date, and that was it. We were a couple.

I can still remember the look of pride on Dad's face the day I told him Phillip and I had started dating. He beamed and said he couldn't have hand-picked a better young man to be my partner— in life and in school. His approval of my decision to date Phillip is the most proud of me I ever remember him being.

The toast for Dr. Lucas comes to a close, and Phillip puts his arm around me. "As you all know, Leleila has been going through a rough patch."

Dr. Lucas frowns. "Psychology professors don't know anything. It's a soft science, Leleila. Don't let them bring you down. I'm sure you'll pass next time."

"We've all been there," Dr. Gray says to me, her brown eyes shining with pity.

"You didn't pass your dissertation the first time?" I ask her.

"Oh, I did," she says. "But the hard sciences are black and

white. That's what's wrong with the field of social sciences. No clear answers."

Backhanded compliments as usual, but I keep my chin up as I nod.

"The good news?" Phillip says. "I have the perfect solution to our problem."

"How did you come up with a fix so fast?" I ask him, my guard immediately up.

"Because I realized everything doesn't have to change just because you don't have a career," he says.

I cringe at those last six words.

"Yet," he adds quickly. "You will eventually, but in the meantime, a new grant just became available. It's brand new, doesn't require us to both be professors, and will be super competitive. But I think I can pull it off, especially if my latest paper gets published. That will really help to put me ahead of the competition. It's for tenured professors only, and if I get it, we can still move to Africa after we marry. In fact, you not playing into the mix could actually free us up to do even more location-based work in the future." He looks over at Dr. Lucas eagerly. "I've always wanted to go to Costa Rica and study the rainforests there, you know, how to salvage rainwater and perhaps..."

"Phillip," I say. "I'm not sure about this. I mean, we were going to be living on two salaries, and if I can't get a job abroad..."

"But we're only living on one now," he says. "That's a big improvement from when we were both in school and relying on our parents' help. So what will be different?"

I don't know how to tell him everything will be different if I'm sitting around in Africa or Costa Rica with absolutely nothing to do except help my husband collect data for his future book.

I exhale slowly. "I want to get my PhD still, honey. And I have to be here to do that."

"But you can't even try again for a year," he says. "So if we leave for Africa in January, we'd be back just a couple of months after that timeframe. What's a couple of months in the scheme of things? You could stand on your head and spit pennies during that time."

I think I'm going to throw up. I shift away from him and turn to face the rest of the group.

"Who wants more wine?" I say brightly.

When I get to the safety of the kitchen, I reach for my phone to call my advisor.

It goes straight to voicemail.

"Gerry, it's Leleila. I would like to talk to you about my dissertation. I think the panel may have acted hastily and that my research is more complete than you all thought it was. I will be spending some of my time at Big Sky Grocer, and I know you get your lunch there sometimes, so..." I pause, not sure how to avoid sounding desperate. "Please come see me so we can figure this out."

I end the call and immediately press another number.

"June," I say when she answers. "I'm in. I'll start tomorrow."

CHAPTER FIVE

The next morning, I walk into Big Sky Grocer and immediately head for June's office. As I round the corner in the produce section, I run straight into Brayden.

"Hey, granola girl." Brayden grins at me. "How are you?"

I freeze, a half-smile on my face.

Good Lord.

Brayden's eyes are beautiful. And he looks directly at me when he's speaking to me. I'm so not used to that.

He's wearing a fitted t-shirt, a pair of sexy jeans, and those sinfully-hot cowboy boots again. He's athletic and fit, but he smells so good, like cologne and soap. I don't get it. Phillip sweats like a dog from biking, yet Brayden doesn't seem to suffer at all from lifting all those boxes.

Powerless to break the eye contact, I stand there like an idiot and stare back at him.

"Do you work here every day?" I eventually get out.

Brayden winks. "It bothering you?"

I open my mouth to answer him, but I can't think of what to say.

"Leleila. How are you?" he says more softly.

I definitely need to start walking again. I turn on my heel but call back in as friendly a voice as I can muster. "I'm great! I'll see you later!"

When I reach June's office, I shut the door behind me.

"Hi," I say in a strained voice.

"You sound all breathy," she says. "Did you run here?"

I laugh. "Right. You know me and running don't get along."

"Well, what's the matter?"

"How many hours a week does he work here?" I ask her.

"Who?" she starts to say, and then she looks at my face and laughs. "Ohhhh." She goes back to looking at her schedule.

"June!" I put my hands on my hips. "How many?"

"Every hour that he drives you wild. Get it?"

"Ha, ha."

"He asked me about you," she says in a softer tone.

My damn pulse goes haywire. "What do you mean?" *Did he tell her we'd met before?*

"I mean you caught his attention."

"But he didn't say anything..." I try to sound nonchalant when I add, "about high school?"

June wrinkles her nose. "High school? Why would he have brought that up? You guys went to different schools."

"I know. Of course." I exhale in relief.

Luckily, June is distracted.

"I'm a pretty good matchmaker, you know," she says, a mischievous gleam in her green eyes. "You really should trust me on this Brayden and you thing." Now her eyes actually glow with excitement.

"I. Am. Engaged." I let out a deep exhale after spitting out those three words. "You can't play matchmaker to someone who's taken. Don't forget."

"Not possible," she tells me. "But I want you to be happy."

I struggle to shift the conversation back to a comfortable place. "Have you heard from Mom and Dad?"

"They sent an email this morning. Some cruise ship passing by gave them Internet access where they were both anchored off the coast of New Zealand. They said they tried to send the email to both of us, but yours got spit back for some reason. Dad called it electrical sputterances. You know him. Making up words as he goes."

"Well, how are they?"

"They're fine. Everything's going smoothly and according to plan."

Of course it is. No bumps in the road, no doctoral issues or Braydens for them.

"They're worried for you," June says. "They feel badly about what you're going through." She glances at my outfit. "Speaking of, are you planning on dressing for your dissertation for the rest of your life?"

I look at her outfit. Jeans and a flannel.

"You look awfully casual," I say defensively as I tug at my blazer and look down at my black pants.

"I look the part of a natural grocery store owner," she says. "You look like a student interviewing for her first job."

I sigh. My sister may be younger than I am, but you wouldn't know it the way she talks to me. She's always been a little bossy, and she's never stopped pushing my buttons.

"Okay, truce." I head for the door. "Just tell me what you need done, and I'll get started."

———

I end up outside the store on a twelve-foot ladder. June asks me to just trace over the faded sign, but I take one look and decide it needs a major facelift.

Before I can get started, a voice calls to me from the sidewalk.

I look down into the eyes of Brayden. "You're not scared of heights, are you?" he says teasingly.

"Not unless I have to keep looking down."

"Well, June asked me to spot you on the ladder," he says. "So no wobbling."

I pick up a paintbrush and dip it into the can of white paint propped on the top of the ladder.

"That was a joke," he calls up to me. "A bad one."

I glance down at him. His face is in shadow, but I can feel his bright eyes on me nonetheless.

"No worries," I say quickly. "But you really don't have to stand there and wait for me."

He gestures to the wheelbarrow of pumpkins next to him. "I'm going to arrange these by the window while you paint."

"That will look nice and autumnal," I say.

Autumnal? I face-palm myself in my head and then turn away from any further eye contact.

Distracted by the fact that Brayden is below me, I hastily paint over the faded lettering with white paint and then tilt my head as I stare at the blank sign.

"I can pass you more cans of paint if you need them," Brayden calls up to me.

"Thank you. I've got a can of red up here now. This old sign just really needs a change. I can't believe it attracted anybody off the street." I don't know why, but I keep going. "This building is a real relic from the Old West. They don't make them like this anymore. It's on the registry of historic buildings in Montana."

"It's a cool building," Brayden agrees. "I can't believe there's an empty suite next door to June's store. You'd think it would be a prime retail spot."

It really would. And chatting with Brayden gives me an idea for June's store sign.

I pick up the brush again and start painting.

———

A while later, I hear my name.

I glance down at June standing below me with her hands on her hips.

"Leleila, when you're finished, can you paint a mural on the big wall inside?"

"Um, I'd have to have something to paint."

"I'm sure you can think of something," she says confidently. "Anyway, the lunch crowd's going to be here any minute. Can you take a quick break so you're not blocking the front?"

"Sure. I'm about finished anyway." I nod at her just as my advisor walks briskly by and heads for the front door.

"Gerry?" I start down the ladder. "Gerry! Hold up, please!"

In my hurry to get to him before he disappears, my high heel catches on the third to last rung. I try to shake my foot free, but the ladder comes loose from the wall.

I let out a panicked squeal.

Brayden quickly grabs hold of the ladder and calmly pushes it back against the wall so I can safely descend the rest of the way. But I'm so flustered I fall into his arms as my feet hit the ground.

"You okay?" he asks as he puts his arms around my shoulders to steady me.

Clearly, he can feel me shaking.

I've seen Brayden Wild three times in my life now, and all three times, I've ended up in his arms.

I catch my breath as I feel his chest against mine. My heart starts to beat faster, and maybe I'm mistaken, but it feels like his does too.

I swallow and pull away from him as June smirks. "I'm good," I say quickly. "Sorry about my clumsiness."

"No apology needed."

I give him a quick wave before turning to walk through the store doors. My advisor is just ahead of me at the prepared food section.

"Gerry!" I call out as I walk toward him.

"Leleila," he says politely, a boxed sandwich in his hand. "Hello. How are you today?" He speaks to me in the measured tone one would use with someone who's not quite stable.

"I'm fine," I say breathlessly. "Look, I'm sorry to have called last night, but I really would like to ask you to reconsider. I know you don't think I'm ready to try again, but I think you're wrong, and here's why." I exhale and begin the speech I'd prepared in my head on the way to the store this morning. "My data is groundbreaking. There was nothing else like it at the Psychophysiological Conference last year. You said so yourself."

"Leleila," he says again. "We've already been over this."

"But, Gerry," I plead. "Dr. Schneider. Please, will you try to talk to the panel about moving up my second try? A year is too far away."

Brayden passes by us with the ladder under one arm just as Gerry says, "Why is a year too far away? I understand it's very difficult to have to wait when you've put your whole life into this, but I can't see your heart broken twice in one year. And that's what I'm afraid will happen if you rush into this. You need to work on your data, not just regurgitate the same old stuff. And I'm happy to help, but I want you to take some time away to get a clear head."

"But..."

He sighs. "I fought for you. I really did."

"Gerry, I'm the best candidate for the psychology professor opening. Professor Andle had all but promised me the job. And I'm still supposed to go to Africa with Phillip, so I'm running out of time to find employment first."

I argue with him for the next five minutes, telling him I want to continue my research with children in Africa, and I can't do that if I don't have the credentials, but it's all in vain.

"Let's go to lunch sometime," he suggests. "And talk about your thoughts on your thesis and your life outside the lab. I'll see you soon."

I watch him walk away then I bite my lip and stare down at the boxed sandwiches in front of me. I bet they won't have boxed sandwiches in Africa. I bet they won't have much at all, especially if you have absolutely no purpose whatsoever for being there.

I hear a noise at my side, and I look over to see Brayden putting fresh salads into the shelf next to the sandwiches.

"So you want to go to Africa?" he says as he continues to stock the shelves.

I shrug. "If all works out, I will be going to Africa. Do I want to? You're actually the first person who's asked me that question."

Brayden shifts so he's facing me, his blue eyes clear and attentive. "And what's the answer?"

I swallow. I don't know what it is about this man that's always made me feel so exposed, so...raw.

"I'll be back in a bit. I have a quick errand."

"See you, Leleila." His deep voice sends shivers down my spine.

I hustle out of the store and hop into my car. I know where I'm going, but I've never actually stepped foot inside. Three blocks down, I turn left onto Front Street and see the small sign in front of the store window.

Montana Art Supplies. I throw on my signal at the last second and jerk the wheel to the right to pull into the cramped parking lot. The car behind me honks angrily, and I curse under my breath as I park in the far corner of the lot and step out.

A bell goes off when I pass through the door of the store, but nobody even glances my way. A couple of high school kids are running the registers, and the lines are pretty long. I hurry toward the paint section and grab what I'll need for June's sign and potential mural. And then, I linger in the aisle.

I had a passion for painting when I was young, and I kept at it through high school. But my parents were never fans of me focusing on art as a career. And after what happened with Noah at the party, I started to think they were right about everything. So I gradually turned away from it, and in college, I threw all of my energy into my studies.

"Can I help you?"

I jump. A young woman is standing next to me with the nametag Claire on her shirt.

"Um..." I hold up the paints I've already grabbed. "No, I'm all set. Thanks."

I leave the store quickly and look for a place to grab lunch.

When I return to Big Sky Grocer, I pull into the lot and see Brayden coming toward me.

On a horse.

He waves casually as he crosses the border between Big River Ranch and June's parking lot. His cowboy hat is low on his head, but I can still see his friendly smile.

I climb out of the car and call out a hello.

"Beautiful day, isn't it?" he says as he hops off his horse and ties him up next to the store. "I had to check on the fencing down this way, so I figured I'd give Blazer some exercise."

I step closer to Blazer and pat his chestnut fur gently. "He's beautiful."

"Thanks. I've had him for a few years now. He's a great horse."

I stare at Brayden next to Blazer with the deep blue Montana sky above and the backdrop of Big River Ranch behind us, and I've got an idea for the mural.

June doesn't say anything at first when I show her what I've done to her store sign.

"It needed something," I explain to her. "Something to attract customers other than your usual breakfast and lunch crowd. Look around right now—there's nobody here."

She finally stops staring up at the sign and brings her eyes down to meet mine. "So you called it B.S. Grocer & Ranch Supplies?"

"It's funny," I explain. "B.S. is just to get their attention. And then I painted the sky behind it with the actual words, don't worry."

"You made it artsy," she says. "With mountains and sky."

"And most importantly, you can see the sign clearly now," I say. "You need to make it clear who and what you are so potential customers will see it from the road. This can become more than a word of mouth business, June."

She takes my arm and leads me into the store and over to Brayden in Aisle 6.

"You're going to paint a mural," June says to me. She turns to Brayden. "And you're going to help her."

"What?!" I say. "I don't need hel…"

"I don't know a thing about painting," Brayden says quickly as he glances at me uncomfortably.

"Right," June says. "But you know a thing about reining in Leleila. Or you'll learn." She laughs as I glare at her. "Other than the mural, I don't want the whole place to look like an artist's easel. Make sure she doesn't touch anything else."

"June…" I try to say.

"But this one wall needs sprucing—the paint is drab and faded. Do something creative like what you did with the sign. But don't go crazy," she adds.

As she walks away, Brayden smiles at me and shrugs. "Where do we start?"

I laugh. "You can help me scrape the old paint off if you'd like."

He nods. "Get rid of the old before starting fresh. Got it."

———

Brayden

I watch the team go through their first set of reps, my mind elsewhere. Being at the store all day long with Leleila was troubling. She actually trembled in my arms when she stumbled off the ladder, and the urging I had to find out what's bothering her was almost impossible to ignore.

And when I found out she might be moving to Africa, of course I wanted to know why. But it's none of my business.

She's none of my business.

I blink as I return my attention to what's in front of me.

"What was that?" I call out to the first-team offense as the quarterback sails another ball over the receiver's head.

I hold the errant football in my hand and rifle a pass back to Wes. "Come on, man! Get your head on straight today."

Wes nods and lines up again behind center.

He barks out the play call, and this time, his pass is on the money. Gordon catches it in stride and streaks down the line before Fletcher, our star safety, tackles him at the ten.

Coach Johnson's back, and he shouts his approval before walking over to me.

"Goddamn it, Wes is off today," he says to me in a low voice.

"Yep." I cross my arms over my chest. "And I think we can all hazard a guess as to why."

Everyone in Wilcox knows about Calvin Brick and the weight he's been on his quarterback son. Father and son live in the mobile park at the edge of town; Wes's mom died years ago, and once she was gone, Calvin's drinking went from once in a while to pretty much nonstop. Our interventions and endless attempts to get him to rehab have failed, and at this point, we're all just rallying around Wes as best we can, praying he can get out of town with the football scholarship he so deserves before his father takes that away from him too.

"He needs his head in the game this week." Coach Johnson shakes his head. "There's going to be a scout in the stands."

"I know."

"Talk to him, Wild," Coach says to me with a clap on the shoulder. "The kids listen to you better than to me. You're a hero to them."

I grin. "You mean you're too damn old for them to remember you, Coach? You still hold the state record for number of sacks in a season."

He laughs and rubs his bald head. "And your total yards still stands statewide. Plus, you had to share touches with Colt. Shit, you two were competitive with one another. Dylan used to have to give out a fucking target count after games so you and Colt would stop arguing."

I remember. Playing with my cousins for three years under the bright lights is one of my greatest memories from high school.

"It's been years, but I still miss it sometimes," I admit. "The playing in front of a crowd; the adrenaline rush is fucking nuts." *But...*

Coach Johnson's watching me, and he nods before I even speak. "You belong in Montana, Brayden. Always did. You're a cowboy first, footballer second. Nothing wrong with that."

The rest of the practice goes smoothly, and when it ends, before I can beckon to him, Wes approaches me.

"I'm having an issue with the game this weekend," he admits, the calmness of his tone belying how his cleat is banging on the ground between us. "Going to Billings might be tough for me. I need to make sure I'm back home that night."

"What's up?" I walk him away from the rest of the team.

"It's my dad."

He doesn't need to say anything more.

I put my arm around Wes's shoulders and point us in the direction of the barn. "Come for a ride with me. We'll talk."

Wes shrugs out of his pads and throws on a Wilcox High sweatshirt. His blond head of hair that's the same length as mine is damp with sweat, and his dark, nearly black, eyes are filled with far more wisdom than a kid his age should have. He's been blessed with an athletic frame and the strongest arm I've seen in a young quarterback since Dylan. He has the talent and the temperament to go all the way, and I don't want anyone—especially the one guy who's supposed to be in his corner, his father—bringing him down.

We saddle up King and Blazer, and I point to the cowboy hat hanging on the post outside the stall.

"Take that for the ride if you'd like," I say as I grab my own hat and push it onto my head.

"Thanks, Coach."

We ride along my favorite trail through the forest. Wes, like most of us around here, grew up in a saddle, and he matches me as I urge Blazer into a gallop. The Montana sky is bright blue above us, and the light breeze brings with it the familiar smell of pine trees and cow manure. And then we run into another familiar scene—a few loose cows.

"You up for helping me get them back?" I call out.

He gives me the thumbs-up.

Over the next half hour, the two of us herd the three loose cows back into the adjacent field where they belong.

"I need to fix that damn fence," I say as we see the broken wire.

We hop off the horses and do a half-ass job of putting the fence back into position. I'll have to come back tomorrow and finish the job.

We ride King and Blazer into the meadow where I pull up to a walk and Wes follows suit. We tie up the horses to a nearby tree, and I gesture around me to the open expanse with the mountains in the background.

"We live in a slice of paradise, Wes," I say.

He tugs at the brim of the cowboy hat. "That we do."

"I made a choice that nothing was more important to me than having a home here in Montana," I continue as we stroll along the fence line. "But we're all built differently, and we all need different things."

"Like your cousins," he guesses.

"Like them," I agree. "Dylan wouldn't have been happy staying here forever. Neither would Colton." I stop walking and turn to face him. "And neither would you."

He swallows hard. "But my dad..."

"Needs help. We all know that. I'm working on how I can get more involved."

"Coach, it's not your responsibil..."

"And it's also not yours," I say firmly. "You can't help him if he's drowning you, Wes. All you can do is stay down there with him."

His face contorts in pain. "I know, but I can't leave him here alone on Friday. He's not always this bad, but today's the anniversary of my mom's death."

I put my hand on his shoulder. "I didn't know that. I'm sorry."

He shrugs. "I don't know what to do. This is a huge game for us, and I don't want to let down the team."

"A college scout will be at the game for sure."

Wes grimaces. "I didn't know that. I don't want to miss my shot."

"Let me see what I can do. Just promise me you'll focus on the game coming up, and I'll figure out somebody to watch your dad while we're gone."

As we're talking, I glance to my left. We're within sight of the neighbor's land, and I'm reminded of that truck peeling out of here the other day.

I turn toward the Easton's property, and Wes follows me. As we reach the fence dividing the two ranches, I glance around the area. This part of the neighboring property is around the corner from the main house, and not a soul is in sight.

But as I look at the back corner of the Easton's field, I notice a mound of dirt that looks freshly made. And in that mound, something shines in the sun. I look more closely. It looks like metal that's exposed from where the dirt didn't fully cover it.

I'm immediately suspicious.

"Stay here," I tell Wes in a low voice. "I want to check on whatever's underneath that dirt pile."

"Holy shit." He stares at me. "You mean like a..."

"Not a body." I slap his back. "You've watched too many thrillers, dude."

I hop over the fence and brush at the dirt with the toe of my boot. When I reach the metal, I realize it's a container. And then I see the symbol painted on the edge.

"Shit."

"What's wrong?" Wes calls over to me.

I point at the ground, and he peers over the fence at it.

"Oh, fuck. That looks bad, huh?"

Pretty much. Written on the top of the container, in black letters, are two words—"Hazardous Waste" along with the universal symbol for biological waste.

"Not a word about this to anyone," I mutter to Wes as we start back to the barn. "I need to get a plan in place first."

"I won't say anything," he promises.

Before I storm over to the Easton's front door half-cocked, I'm going to need some help with this. And I know who might be able to do just that—the shy, green-eyed woman from my past who says she works to save the soil.

CHAPTER SIX

After I leave Big Sky Grocer, I collapse on my couch. I spend a couple of frustrating hours looking through my dissertation notes, but the sound of Brayden's low, scraping voice won't leave my brain. Eventually, I give up and call Sophia. She's at my house in less than fifteen minutes.

"You've been avoiding me," she says as she wags her finger. Her blond hair fans around her head in a wild array of curls. "You were supposed to call me yesterday, and you blew me off. Being a receptionist bites. I live for your phone calls to drag me out of my work boredom."

I give her a hug and then lean back against the couch cushions. "I'm sorry. I planned to call, but I got caught up in a Save the Soil task, and then I..." I trail off awkwardly.

Her blue eyes narrow. "And then you what? Something tells me there's a story here. And it's better than your usual of, 'Phillip scored another paper in the latest and greatest science journal.' You've even put in your contact lenses, which means you're really serious. So what's up?"

I swat at her. "I'm wearing my contacts so I can be sure to see the dance instructor tonight."

"You're changing the subject now. Another sign of distress." Sophia pokes me in the arm. "Spill."

Part of me doesn't want to say anything, but if I can't tell my best friend, I won't be able to tell anyone, and I'm not sure I can handle that.

Sophia is the only person in the world who knows about that night back in high school. I never told Stella, and after we graduated, Stella moved away, and with her went any last trace of that night. Until yesterday when I ran into Brayden Wild for the first time in twelve years.

"A new guy is helping out at June's store," I say casually.

"Oh?" Sophia's voice rises in excitement. "Maybe I can get myself a friend with benefits."

"He's not your type," I say quickly. Too quickly.

"Wait, is he your type?" Sophia's voice lifts higher. "A man of science, not to mention a humanitarian who volunteers for any cause he can find?"

"He's not like that. He's a cowboy. And a football coach. He's um...pretty laid-back."

In truth, I don't actually know if Brayden's laid-back or not. But a part of me wants Brayden to be laid-back. Because there's a part of me that's sick and tired of trying so hard to do everything right.

"So in other words, he's the opposite of Phillip," Sophia says in a knowing tone.

"You could say that."

"Well." Sophia's tone turns teasing. "What is it about this cowboy that has you all hot and bothered? Someone to sleep with before you marry and can never have another man for the rest of your days? A final fling before the ring? Leleila Wills, is that what I'm hearing?"

"I don't want a final fling," I say firmly. "I'm not a final fling type of girl."

"No, but maybe this cowboy can help make you one." Sophia giggles. "Or at least a harmless little crush. I have to meet him.

Don't deny me, Lei. Your life is always so predictable, and you and Phillip are so boring together. Mainly because Phillip's boring, and he calls all the shots. So a potential crush before you lock it down for life? That I can get behind."

Before she can continue, I blurt out in a rush of words, "Soph, there's more to the story."

Her mouth closes immediately, and her eyes widen.

I keep going before I can stop myself. "The guy at June's store..." I suck in a breath. "He's the one. From that football party I went to in high school."

She gasps. "The one who dragged you into the room and..."

"No!" Frazzled, I wrap my arms around my middle. "No, not Noah. Sorry, I'm not being clear. Brayden—the cowboy from June's store—is the one who knocked on the door and who I threw myself against when I escaped from Noah."

A slow smile spreads across Sophia's face. "Brayden is the guy who tried to save you? The one who gave you your first real kiss?"

"Yes."

"And now he works at June's store. Interesting."

"He lives on Big River Ranch."

"So he's in Mountainview." She grabs my hands. "How was it seeing him again after all this time? Did he remember you?"

I nod and fill her in on our meeting.

"I'm going with you to dance class tonight," she says firmly. "I have to meet him."

I try to tell her *no* a dozen times, but my friend is stubborn as a mule, and by the time seven o'clock rolls around, Sophia's following me through the front doors of Big Sky Grocer.

"Are you sure he'll be here?" Sophia asks as we step inside the door. "Maybe you should have confirmed with June first."

We pass the wall Brayden helped me scrape down yesterday. I didn't have time to do anything else to it yet, so it's just a big, blank space at the moment.

"I'm pretty sure," I say, the tension already coiling in my stomach. "June said something about needing all hands on deck tonight because of some inventory count she's doing. I heard Brayden tell her he could come by after football practice. But I don't see him around, so maybe I should just go..."

I want to make sure I get to the community room in plenty of time to meet the teacher, but Sophia takes my arm and marches me down the aisle.

"I need an introduction," Sophia whispers to me. "Or at least a sighting. You promised."

"Because you insisted on driving me here," I say. "Phillip will bring me home, so please don't stick around while I'm upstairs."

"Phillip's definitely going to show?" Sophia asks me.

"He said he would." Phillip sent a text that he's running late but will "absolutely be there on time for class."

We walk into the produce section, and just as we turn the corner, I see Brayden standing by the frozen meats. He's talking to a customer, but he waves as soon as he sees me. His flannel and jeans make my mouth water, and I swallow hard as I wave back at him.

"Okay, now that you've seen him, you can go," I whisper to Sophia.

"What? No introduction?" She lowers her voice. "Oh my God! He's so hot, Leleila. Look at those biceps. And that ass. I think I may come back later and talk to him on my own..."

"What? No!"

Sophia smiles like she's won the lottery. "See? You don't want to share him. I just got the proof I was looking for."

I clench my teeth together. "Fine, a quick introduction." I grab Sophia by the arm and march her over to Brayden just as the customer he's with walks away.

"Hey, Leleila." Brayden smiles at me, and any chill I felt from being outside in the fall air disappears.

"Hey." I gesture to Sophia. "This is my friend, Sophia Loren. No relation to the actress, just a pun on words by her mother."

"Who was drunk at the time," Sophia adds with a wide smile.

Brayden breaks into a laugh. "Nice to meet you. I'm Brayden Wild."

"Wild is your last name?" Sophia asks him. "You wouldn't happen to be from Wilcox, are you?"

He nods. "I grew up there."

Sophia claps her hands. "Are you related to Dylan and Colton Wild, the football stars?"

"They're my cousins." His mouth tips up in a grin when Sophia screams and clutches my arm like we're being chased.

"Since when did you become a football fan?" I ask her.

"Last winter, that guy I was dating—Damon, remember him? We met at a Super Bowl party. Dylan was MVP of the game, and he's so damn handsome. And his equally-sexy cousin, Colton, caught the winning pass."

Brayden nods. "We're super proud of them."

"How are you cousins?" I ask. "I mean, that sounds dumb; I just meant..."

Brayden's eyes warm as he fastens his gaze on me. "It's not dumb. Our fathers are brothers—six of them in all, and five of their sons, including me, are best friends."

"Really?" I ask him. "That must have been amazing to see Dylan and Colton win the championship like that."

"It was. It's been quite a ride."

"I bet." Sophia heaves a dramatic sigh. "If the rest of your family's as hot as you and your football cousins, I'd be happy for you to introduce me."

I elbow her, willing her to stop.

"And you played football with them in high school?" I ask him.

"I was wide receiver. Now I'm an assistant coach for Wilcox High." Brayden chuckles. "Makes me feel old."

Sophia starts rambling about high school and how fun the parties were in Missoula.

"So what are you guys doing tonight?" Brayden's eyes flick to mine.

Sophia stalls. "I don't know. I was thinking of trying to

convince Lei to grab a drink, an alcoholic beverage of some kind, maybe at that new place in Missoula where they have dancing…"

I clear my throat.

"Well, maybe not," she says. "But Sunday, Lei and I will be helping out with the Food for Hunger Drive. June's store is one of the sponsors, and we can always use an extra set of hands."

Brayden's eyes brighten. "Oh, yeah?"

"Lei," June calls out as she walks toward us. "Where's next month's newsletter?"

"It's nearly done," I tell her.

"Hey, June." Sophia giggles. "I ran into a guy at Zeiss the other night. Says he knows you."

June glares at Sophia. "I don't know what you're talking about."

This would be why my sister got into an Ivy League school and I didn't. She was captain of the debate team in high school, and she has an uncanny ability to stand her ground and convince you that she's right and you're wrong.

But Sophia didn't go to an Ivy League. And she doesn't care about advanced degrees or social etiquette. She plunges onward with a smile. "Oh, sure you do. His name's Leon. Says you two got it on last week."

Brayden grins, and I'm sure I turn redder than June does. "Okay, Soph." I gesture toward the door. "Time to go."

I hustle her out the door as she's still whispering her apologies.

"You know my mouth—it's like she won't shut up even when I'm begging her to," she says, her face contrite.

"Well, go somewhere my sister won't kill you."

"Tell her I'm sorry," she says as I close the door on her and wave goodbye.

Worried that Phillip's already upstairs, I hustle toward the back of the store and take the steps two at a time until I reach the open studio-style room June uses for local classes and storage.

Looks like I'm right on time. A roomful of people turn toward me as I step into the space.

I smile as I glance around for Phillip.

Crap. He's not here.

When my phone beeps, I pull it out of my purse.

Lei, don't kill me. Dr. Lucas asked Mindy and me to stay late to go over my latest findings with him. Mindy has experience with this kind of data, and Dr. Lucas had to meet with us tonight because he leaves tomorrow for a conference, and I couldn't wait that long to show him everything in case he has concerns. I promise I'll make it up to—

I turn my phone off in frustration and toss it into my purse. Then, it occurs to me—*who's Mindy?*

Before I can make a quick exit, a bald man with thick glasses approaches. "You here for the beginner's ultimate dance class?"

"Yes, my name is Leleila. Unfortunately, my…"

"Why do you want to dance, Leleila?" The man peers at me.

"I'm getting married next month."

"Ah, wedding. Romance, love, beautiful." He sways in front of me. He's wearing bright red pants and a tight black silk shirt. "I'm Elroy, your teacher. Head over for our warm-up stretches. Is your fiancé on his way?"

"See, that's the thing. I just found out he can't make it."

Elroy frowns. "That's not good."

"Yes, I'm aware. So I'll just leave now and…"

Bang!

Elroy and I both turn around at the loud sound.

Brayden is standing next to a cardboard box over by the storage shelving. "Sorry," he says. "This box fell off the shelf."

I smile at him. "That storage area's a mess. I'll clean it up this week."

"I can help you," he offers.

Our eyes hold.

"Okay. Thanks."

Elroy steps forward abruptly and grabs Brayden by the arm.

"Is this your fiancé?" he says as he looks to me.

Brayden jerks backward like he's been burned.

"Fiancé?" he mutters so quietly I barely hear him.

"No," I say quickly. "He's not. He's my…Brayden." *Shit.*

Brayden raises an eyebrow at me.

"I mean, he's my...cowboy." *Double shit.*

Now Brayden smirks.

I take a deep breath, forcing myself to sound calm when I say, "Brayden works here. And my fiancé is...not coming, like I told you."

Elroy grips tightly onto Brayden's muscled bicep. "So dance with him instead. He'll do just fine!"

CHAPTER SEVEN

"I'm actually working. I just came up to grab a box," Brayden says immediately.

"Nonsense." Elroy frowns. "Poor Leleila has been stood up. Be her man for the night."

If only there were a way for me to magically disappear in a cloud of smoke...instead, I stand silently while Brayden freezes. I mean he *freezes*.

So Elroy takes charge. "Okay, so that's settled. Let's get stretching, shall we?"

I tell Elroy no three times. All three times, he overrides my excuses.

"I'll go talk to June and make sure she knows," he says in response to my first concern. "I've known her for years. It will be fine."

"But Phillip won't know the steps..."

"You can teach your fiancé the steps later," Elroy insists. "This way, you won't fall behind the class. This nice young man here—" He winks at Brayden, "I'm sure he'd be happy to dance with such a beautiful lady. Wouldn't you, sir?"

Brayden stuffs his hands into his jeans pockets, his gaze

anywhere but on me. For someone who normally doesn't take his eyes off me, his awkwardness is palpable.

"You really don't have to do this," I tell Brayden hurriedly. "I'll just head home and come back next week with Phillip."

But Elroy has paged June, who comes up the stairs, takes one look at the scene in front of her and, with a smile on her face, immediately tells Brayden he's off the clock.

"What?" I say to her. "That's ridiculous. He doesn't want to dance!"

"I do," Brayden says instantly.

I jerk my head to meet his deep blue gaze.

He steps closer to me. "I'll dance with you as long as it's okay with you and your fiancé that I fill in."

I stare at him, but he meets my shaking gaze steadily and without hesitation.

"Um..." I take a few steps toward the stairs. "I'll just call Phillip to let him know."

———

When Phillip answers my call, he says in a short tone, "Hi Lei, I'm really sorry about tonight, but is this urgent? I'm in the middle of my meeting."

"Not urgent," I say. "I just...one of the guys who works at June's store has offered to fill in for you as my dance partner tonight. I wanted to see if you're okay with that."

"Why wouldn't I be?" His voice is thin and impatient. "This isn't a big deal, honey. Learn the dance with him, and then you can catch me up later. Okay?"

"Okay."

"Was that all?"

I clench the phone in my hand. "Yep. That's all."

"See you at home later. Bye, hon."

The line goes dead before I can say *goodbye*.

What feels like moments later, I find myself standing face to face with a man I crushed on twelve years ago, a man who, to my innocent teenage soul, was my hero.

But now, I'm an adult.

And God, so is Brayden. The way his worn jeans ride low on his hips is driving me nuts. I swallow, willing myself to look at the teacher instead.

"All right!" Elroy claps his hands and then blows a whistle so loudly I jump.

My unplanned hop into the air brings me closer to Brayden, and he reaches over and puts his hand on my lower back.

"Ladies and lads!" Elroy shouts.

I grimace at Brayden, who pretends to kick the air.

I laugh as Elroy says, "I like to mix styles together. So if you like diversity, you've come to the right class. Tonight, we'll run through a sample of several dance styles. Next week, we'll get into specifics and start to develop a choreo combination. So get together now, and come toward the center of the room!"

He goes through a lengthy demonstration of the waltz with his assistant, Amy.

"Got it?" he asks.

Not really.

"Good!" he yells. "Let's try it on my count."

Now we need to do the thing I actually came here for —dance.

Brayden holds out his hand to me, and I stare at it dumbly.

"Leleila." His tone is gentle. "You're going to have to take my hand if we're going to follow the steps."

"Right." I smile at him. "I'm sorry."

I reach up and put my hand in his. When he puts his other hand on my waist, I feel my nipples wake up. I place my hand on his arm, enjoying the soft, warm flannel of his plaid shirt against my palm.

"You two over there!" Elroy shouts. "I know you aren't actually engaged, but for tonight, act like you are. Brayden, hold the lady close to you."

Brayden steps further into my space and tightens his hold around my back.

"Is this okay?" he asks me softly.

I nod. "Four times now," I mumble into his shoulder.

"Four times what?" he says into my ear.

"Four times I've met you, and every time, I end up in your arms." I flush because I can't hold back the vulnerable way the words come out of my mouth.

Brayden clears his throat, and my gaze roams down his chest and then keeps going. When I observe the bulge of his impressive-looking equipment behind the buttons on the fly of his jeans—no zipper, all buttons—I get so distracted I miss Elroy's cue to begin.

And of course, Elroy notices. "You!" he shouts in my direction. "Put those beautiful eyes on your partner's face and leave them there! Let's start again."

This time, out of fear of being publicly called out again, I begin when Elroy gives the go-ahead.

And we do okay. Mainly because Brayden's actually a good dancer.

"Have you done this before?" I ask at a quick break.

"My parents dance," he says. "So I've seen them do the waltz a lot, but I've never done something like this before, no."

Elroy sends us around and around the room, over and over again. Then we do a round of fox trot, followed by the salsa, which I really enjoy despite it being out of my comfort zone. All that hip movement? Not something I'm used to doing under bright lights. But Brayden and I laugh through the awkwardness, and we're getting the hang of it by the time Elroy stops the music. At the end of the hour, he claps his hands.

"All right! We've got one couple here who knows how to dance together!" Elroy shouts as he comes up behind Brayden and me and puts a hand on each of our shoulders. "Did you hear that—together! I don't care how good you all may look in the club on your own—you're here to learn how to dance with your partner. These classes are about synchrony, about chemistry with your partner!" He turns to me. "If your fiancé can't make this class, I hope you'll still come back next week."

———

It's not until we get downstairs that I realize I don't have a car, and Phillip isn't here to drive me.

"I'm sorry I can't take you," June says, her cheerful expression looking anything but. "Unfortunately, I have to stay here to oversee my staff. Why don't you have Brayden drive you home? He's all done for the night."

Brayden's cowboy hat is already on his head, and his face is in shadow. "I'd be happy to drop you at your house," he says.

"You live directly behind here," I point out. "I'm obviously out of your way."

"It's no problem," he says.

June beams, and I have the urge to throw the orange on her desk at her head.

"So it's settled then," she says in a bright tone. "See you later, guys."

I give her a look as I turn and follow Brayden out of her office and through the store.

———

Brayden

Leleila and I walk across the parking lot in silence. Her sister wasn't exactly subtle in her efforts to force us together, but I'm not complaining.

The sexual tension that's always simmering between us jacked up a thousand fold when we danced together. When we were learning the steps for the salsa, my dick felt like it was honest to God going to break through the buttons on my fly. Any denials I'd been using that Leleila was just a flash from my teenage past disappeared. I'm more attracted to her than ever.

And she's more taken than June had let on.

Engaged? Fuck. Because that means...

"So when's the wedding?" I say casually as we reach my truck, and I open the passenger door for her.

Beneath the parking lot lights, I watch as Leleila's eyes flare.

"June never mentioned I was engaged, did she?" she asks me.

"She said there was someone else in the picture, but she wasn't sure if it would last." I take a deep breath. "She said we should hang out."

"Crap," she says in an irritated tone. "She's meddling in my personal life. I'm sorry."

I wait until she's safely inside before I shut the door and then walk around to the driver's side.

We pull out of the parking lot with Leleila directing me on how to get to her house. When we pull up to a red light, I return to the unfinished subject.

"I don't think June meant to be disrespectful to anybody." My gaze travels to Leleila's left hand on her lap, a hand that seems to be missing the universal sign for someone who's betrothed. "Is your engagement ring being sized or something?"

She immediately hides her left hand underneath her right one. "Phillip doesn't believe in ostentation."

"What's that have to do with anything?" I ask her.

She meets my gaze as she hesitates and then holds up her left hand. That's when I notice the thin, frayed red string tied around her ring finger.

"No fancy diamond ring," she explains. "No ostentation. And I agree with him. We'll exchange simple wedding bands when we marry, and that's enough for me."

The light turns green, and I return my gaze to the road. We

drive in silence until she directs me to a blue house at the end of a quiet street.

"This is me here." She leans forward on her seat like she's going to charge out of the truck the second I stop moving.

Sensing her discomfort, I live park on the curb rather than pulling into her driveway. I stop just short of the front window, and before she can make a quick getaway, I shift to face her.

"Leleila."

She startles. "Hmmm?"

What comes out of my mouth next stuns even me.

"What do you say we be friends?" I ask her, my eyes searching her face. "You seem like maybe you could use a friend."

Her cheeks heat. "I have plenty of friends, like Sophia. Just because I enjoy granola and like to patronage my sister's place of business doesn't mean that I am lonely."

"I'm sorry. I didn't mean it like that."

Her shoulders relax. "No, I'm sorry I snapped. I don't have a large circle, but I never have. I'm a bit of a loner."

"I am too. My cousins are my best friends. Everyone else—it's pretty casual really." My voice dips. "I guess I just...I'd like to be friends with you. Which is unusual for me. Being just friends with a woman." *Pretty much has never happened in my entire life.*

Our eyes lock.

After several beats, when I'm certain she isn't going to answer me at all, she gives a tiny shake of her head, and her green eyes lose their brightness. "I'm not sure. My life is...very up in the air right now. I'll...get back to you on that," she adds stiffly.

Christ, I need to cut this tension.

Remembering something I do need to talk to her about, I say, "Hey, how much do you know about burying hazardous waste?"

Her hand drops off the door handle, and she turns to face me fully. Her brilliant green eyes brighten with interest. "What exactly are you talking about?"

I briefly fill her in on the container I saw at the Eastons' ranch.

"I'd have to get a soil sample," she says. "I know it's private property. And the soil can't be wet, or too dry, for that matter. Sometime soon would probably be best since it rained a few days ago. I have to tell you, though, that we'll probably have to send out to a different lab for testing. We can only do so much at our small nonprofit. Is getting a sample possible?"

"Definitely possible," I assure her. "I've got a game in Billings Friday night, but I can take you there this weekend when I know the coast is clear."

We exchange cell numbers, and I tell her I'll text her with a time.

She opens the door and slips out before I can think how to respond. "Good night, Brayden. Thanks so much for tonight."

And just like every time I'm with Leleila, she disappears so fast I barely know what hit me.

She hurries out of the truck and up the walk to her house. A house she shares with her fiancé.

I run my hand down my face. This situation is trouble. Leleila Wills makes me dance and do all sorts of things I never do. I should stay away.

And yet, I just scheduled another reason to see her. Alone. My brain tells me I'm stupid. My heart says this can't end well. And my dick? Well, he's always up for anything. Especially when it comes to a quirky introvert who makes me feel things I haven't felt in twelve years.

Leleila

I glance back, and Brayden's already pulled away from the curb. I can't help but smile at the adorable way he asked if I wanted to be friends. But the way he makes me feel like I'm crushing on him? I can't have a crush on another man. What does that say about me? I'm engaged. Phillip and I have our entire futures planned out, and I can't change course. You have to stay the course. That's what Dad always says.

I definitely need to take a break from Brayden Wild. I'll help him with the soil issue if he calls, but other than that? I need some time.

I send June a quick text that I won't be in to work until next week and head inside the house.

CHAPTER EIGHT

I spend the next two days alone at home. Phillip's at the university all day and a good portion of the evenings, and by day three of my "time away from Big Sky Grocer, AKA Brayden Wild," I'm bored and irritable.

June was right. The one day I spent working at her store was the only day in the past month I didn't obsess over my data and my thesis.

Plus, I'm out of granola, my only staple, and I've hardly seen Phillip at all. When he has been home, all we've done is talk about his research and stare into the microscope. No cuddling, no intimacy.

I really need my granola fix.

I reach for the phone and ask June to bring me by four spoonfuls of granola after she closes.

"Why?" she asks. "Can't you just come get it?"

"I want to show you the newsletter," I lie. "It's easier if I can do it here on the desktop rather than transfer everything to the laptop. That way I can bring you the final edits, and you won't need a new version."

She sighs. "Fine. I'll come by when I close, after ten."

"Make sure it's the nine-grain, please!" I call into the phone. "No flavors!"

———

It's nearly ten-thirty when June knocks on the window to get my attention. I'm lying on our living room couch, wrapped in an afghan, and she waves at me through the glass next to the front door.

"Hey," I say as I let her in. "Thanks for coming over."

"Where's Phillip?" She cranes her neck to peek into the kitchen.

"Working. He wants to finish his research before our honeymoon."

"Is it a honeymoon or a science expedition?" She peers at me through her glasses. I'm so used to her contact lenses I forget she's near-sighted sometimes.

"Please not now, June." I walk back to the couch and take a seat. "You've made your opinion about Phillip clear. And I appreciate your concern. This just isn't your business."

She takes a seat next to me and places a paper bag on the coffee table. "Here's your granola."

"Thanks."

"Are you sleeping down here?" She gestures to the pillow propped up at the end of the couch.

"Just until Phillip gets home," I say. "I've been helping him watch the specimens through the scope the last few nights."

"But you two do still sleep together, right?" she asks me pointedly.

I ignore her obvious insinuation, but she presses me again. "Do you?"

"Why are you so nosy about my sex life?" I say. "There are lots of ways to express love, you know. It doesn't have to involve sex."

"No," she says. "It doesn't. But when you're about to marry

somebody, I would expect you would want to show your love that way as well. At least sometimes."

I fish in my pocket for an elastic and pull my hair back. "If you must know," I say. "Phillip and I have sex as often as possible. We're like any modern-day couple; sometimes life gets in the way."

I peek into the bag of granola.

"June!" I shout, even though she's sitting right next to me.

"What?" She peers into the granola bag too.

"This is that awful fruity kind! It's swarming with apple chunks, and it's too sweet!"

She shrugs. "Sorry. That's what you get for avoiding the store because a hot guy works there."

"He's not that hot," I say in a way that doesn't even convince me.

June bursts out laughing, her green eyes flashing with amusement. "He's not? What do you consider hot then? Besides a burning stove?"

Silence while June cocks her head and studies me. "Lei," she finally says. "Don't let the hot guy run you off."

I nearly break and tell her the truth about my past with Brayden. Not because I think that would get her to back off, but because maybe then she'd understand why my connection with him scares me so damn much.

Before I can decide, June says, "He's away all day Friday if you want to come in to work. He's got a game in Billings, so they're leaving in the morning and won't be back until the middle of the night."

"Wow." I picture Brayden coaching football, and the image is so hot I nearly fan myself. "Sure, I'll come in."

"Great." She walks over to the desk where my computer sits. "Is this your portfolio?"

I forgot I'd pulled it out of my closet the other day. "Yeah."

"Do you mind if I look through it?" she asks me. "It's been so long since I've seen it."

"Um..." I finally give a half-shrug. "Sure. Go ahead."

She flips through the pages in silence before looking up. "You're an amazing artist, Lei. You know that, right?"

I shake my head. "Thanks, June. It was a long time ago."

"And you can still paint circles around most of us. Your freaking storefront sign is attracting customers."

I look away from her. "Thanks. It's been fun to paint again. But you know, it's not a career."

"It could be."

"No," I say. "My future is in my PhD. Painting was always a hobby."

She drops the subject and begins to look at the newsletter file sitting open on the screen. "Maybe one day you should try the sweet, Lei," she says over her shoulder. "You might find you like it."

———

Brayden

I haven't seen Leleila since I drove her home after dance class. A part of me is relieved. I shouldn't have pushed her on the "let's be friends" idea. That wasn't my smartest move. But I do need her help. It's supposed to rain this Sunday, so there's no time to delay. But I don't want to bug her when she's clearly busy.

"Hey, little brother."

I lift my head just enough to see Luke approaching. His cowboy hat covers his dark head of hair that's always a little too long, like mine. We may have matching eye color, similar builds, and be competitive as hell, but our temperaments are pretty different. He's the life of the party and seems to know everyone in the county. He never played football; instead, he competed in rodeos across the state and beyond. Being brutally thrown off a bronc ended his competitive career although he still claims he's going to make a comeback.

I raise my hand in a wave and then return to the issue at hand —fence mending.

"Need a hand?" He steps up to the fence before I can answer and holds it steady while I bang the last post into the ground.

"Thanks." Wiping the sweat off my brow, I grab my tools and toss them into the back of my truck. "How are things at Wild Ranch?"

"Things are good." Luke leans up against the side of my truck and gives me a hard look. "Got your message. What'd you want to talk about?"

"I've got a kid on the team—his dad's got an addiction issue."

"Wes Thompson." Luke lifts an eyebrow. "The whole town of Wilcox knows about it, Bray. You don't have to beat around the fucking bush."

Ignoring his sarcasm, I plunge ahead. "Wes is worried for his dad this weekend. It's the anniversary of his mother's death, and his dad's taking it hard."

"That's tough." That shadow I know too well passes behind Luke's eyes. "But what does that have to do with me?"

"I want your permission to contact Hal."

"No way in hell." Luke slaps the side of the truck hard. "How would you ever explain it to Wes?"

"I told him I would figure something out. I'll tell him I had contacts."

"Like your brother's former sober companion, the guy who made sure he wouldn't pop the painkillers he'd gotten addicted to after a bronc nearly killed him?" Luke's tone is hard as stone, and I have a flash of memory of our brutal fights as kids.

Luke fights hard. He plays hard. And he never had a drinking problem. But any mention of an addict, and he's right back to his life after the accident when he couldn't get through a minute without a painkiller. He kicked the habit with a lot of help and an intervention. And we managed to keep the issue private, no small feat in a small town. He wants to make sure it stays that way.

"Look, I understand why you're worried. I just…"

"No." He glares at me.

I blow out a breath. "Fine. Thanks for coming by. I'll figure something else out. A college scout is coming to the game on Friday, and Wes just…"

Luke's watching my face. "Wes what?"

I hold out my arms. "He's fucking got it, Luke. Everything he needs."

"Are you serious?" His expression changes from anger to enthusiasm. "You think this kid can make the pros?"

"A hundred percent, yes. I wouldn't put so much effort into getting him to keep going if I thought he should pursue a different path."

"You so rarely think one of your kids should dream that big."

"Because the chances are one in a million."

"So you think Wes is one in a million material."

"Yes."

We face each other in a staredown. Finally, Luke bangs the truck again. "Christ. Fine, I'll help you out."

I exhale in relief. "I owe you."

"You always owe me," he jokes. "But I'm not giving you Hal's info."

"So then what…"

"I'll babysit the dad on Friday."

"What?"

"That's my offer. Send me his address, and I'll make sure to take care of him for the day and night until you get home at two a.m."

"You're not a professional at this kind of thing," I say with concern.

"Maybe not, but no layperson is going to be better equipped to understand what this guy's going through than a former addict. And alcohol never did it for me, you know that. I could sit at a bar all night long and nurse one beer. I can work with him. Deal?"

He holds out his hand. Not sure I have any other option right now, I take the deal.

CHAPTER NINE

Leleila

I wake up Saturday morning feeling cranky. Just what I want to do—stand outside on the middle of Main Street and collect donations. I love to help Mountainview's homeless, but I prefer to do it less publicly. But Phillip and June love these Food Drives—Phillip because he can chat up the locals for his research, and June so she can advertise her store.

I reach for my glasses on the nightstand and climb out of bed. I pad downstairs in my t-shirt and pajama pants and go find Phillip, who's staring into his microscope in the living room.

"Good morning," I say.

He looks up at me with his left eye, keeping his right one expertly trained on the lens. After years of practice, I've gotten used to us having quite intimate conversations this way. We discussed our first time having sex like this, and had our first make-up after our first fight, among other things.

"Hi, baby." Phillip pats the couch next to him. "Have a seat."

I sit down and lean my head on his shoulder. "What do you say we stay in this morning? Maybe drop off some cans of food later at the shelter? We could even spend some time talking to the people while they eat?" I kiss his neck. "And for now, we could get back into bed together."

Phillip smiles. "That sounds nice. I know we haven't had much time lately. The thing is, I promised Arthur I'd help him with the bins. Not many of the volunteers are available this weekend, so I don't want to leave him hanging. You don't mind running the table for a little while, right?"

I exhale. "Sure."

"Great."

I change the subject. "So dance class was fun the other night."

"Oh, yeah?" Phillip still has his eye pressed into the lens.

"Yeah. Brayden, the guy who works at June's store, was kind enough to fill in for you, but I missed you there."

"I know." Phillip pats my shoulder. "The thing is, baby…"

Here it comes.

His one eye that's trained on me blinks at whatever expression I'm making.

"Let's get a snack and chat for a few minutes," he says, leaning back from the microscope and standing up. "You must be hungry."

We walk into the kitchen, and I make myself a bowl of granola.

Phillip leans over and kisses my cheek. "Hey, did you see the new steakhouse that opened on Main Street?"

"Yes!" I say. "It looks really nice, and I heard they use pastured beef. Maybe one night we can go try it…"

"They don't offer veggie burgers." Phillip shakes his head as he reaches into the cabinet for a glass. "I stopped by to ask. The guy got annoyed with my questions."

He fills his glass with water from the filtered tap and takes a seat on one of the bar stools at the kitchen counter.

I turn away from him and open the refrigerator door to grab the hummus and then take a box of gluten-free crackers out of the cabinet. I shake some crackers into a bowl and place the dish and hummus on the counter in front of him.

Phillip reaches for a cracker and dips it into the hummus. "Lei." Phillip's tone is unusually gentle. "If you want to take the dance lessons, that's great, and we can still do a dance together at our wedding if it means that much to you. I just don't think I can put in the practice this month. You can teach me the steps a few days before."

I purse my lips. "But the lessons are about spending time with each other. That's part of the fun of it, learning to dance together. Besides, I can't go take the class on my own. Everyone has a partner."

Phillip snaps his fingers excitedly. "What about that guy who filled in for me last week?"

I try to sound calm. "What about him?"

"Well, I figure he must be trustworthy if your sister's impressed. Just ask him to be your partner for the rest of the classes."

My pulse starts hammering in my neck. "I don't really even know Brayden," I say quietly.

"So get to know him enough that you feel comfortable." Another huge bite of cracker and hummus.

I stare at him. "You want me to get to know Brayden?"

"Of course. You're in training. It's not like you're going on a date or something." He chuckles. "Besides, I know you—you're like me. This guy could never satisfy you; you'd be bored in days."

I tap my metal spoon against my now-empty cereal bowl.

"Do it, Lei. Take the class." Long silence again to swallow. "We'll dance together after we marry. Besides, we don't have anything new to learn about each other; we've already lived together for years. This isn't our parents' era, baby."

"Right."

"In terms of today, if you can man the table for a while, I'll take over for you as soon as I can," he promises.

That's about as good an offer as I'm going to get. I take it and go upstairs to shower. Our house phone rings, and I yell down to Phillip that I've got it.

"You're still going, right?" Sophia's voice comes through so loudly and with such enthusiasm I have to hold the receiver away from my ear.

"Going where?"

Judging by her happy tone, she can't possibly mean the food drive. Sophia hates these things; she only does them because I drag her.

"Food for Hunger? Gazebo? Have you forgotten?" She sounds breathless.

"Yes, I'm going. I have no choice. You can skip it and just pick me up there around eleven if you prefer, and we can get coffee. I'm sure I'll be more than ready to leave by then."

"I've got two umbrellas next to me in case it rains," she says. "And my best raincoat. You wear yours, too, Lei. As well as something slutty and easy to take off underneath."

"What?!" I close the bedroom door and then sit down on the bed. "Sophia, I'm not..."

"Not dressing up for Brayden?" Sophia's tone is impatient now. "Remember him? He's coming today." She laughs. "Hopefully in more ways than one. And before you get mad, I'm only teasing you about the coming part. Kind of. You know June and I just want what's best for you. We want you to be happy, Lei. And this feels like your last month of freedom. You know?"

I lie back on my pillows, trying to ignore the feeling of suffocation I get at her words. "Sophia, he probably won't even show up. I doubt Brayden's big on food drives."

"Nooooo." She says it slowly and draws the word out as if she's talking to someone who's not very smart. "Brayden's big on you, Leleila. And you'll be there. Trust me, so will he. Plus, he's got the perfect excuse—June tries to get as many staff as she can to help out. And you're her sister, plus you're working at the store too. So even though you're technically forbidden to him, you're actually not. And that little interplay right there? Priceless. I'm hot just thinking about it."

I swallow and sit up quickly. "I'm getting off the phone. This is a ridiculous conversation."

"Just remember to wear something slutty!" I go to hang up the phone, but I can still hear her. "Or go topless underneath your raincoat—that's even better!"

I slam down the receiver. My face is burning hot as I stand up to go shower.

While the warm water washes over my body, I chide myself for worrying about Phillip and me. Phillip cares about me, and he loves me dearly.

The thing is, he hasn't been looking at me very much lately, and until Brayden re-entered my life, I think I'd tuned out Phillip's lack of attention. Somewhere along the way, I stopped noticing that Phillip's focus was on his work far more than on his relationship. Our routine of living nearly separate lives has become just that— our new normal.

Feeling another man's eyes on me has done more than awaken my sleeping libido; it's alerted me to issues in my relationship that I've been sweeping under the carpet and refusing to look at.

As I rinse the shampoo out of my hair, I try to remember when it started. Was it once Phillip got tenured? Maybe. That moment was so exciting at the time, and I remember making love that night, and thinking how proud of him I was, and how lucky that I found him before somebody else did. Because once he was tenured, all these female scientists came calling under the façade of seeking professional advice. And Phillip loved every second of their attention.

It bothered me, but then Phillip proposed. When he held out his hand and asked me to take it forever, I felt cared for and special. But after I said yes, I had a nagging feeling inside, a whisper of what felt like entrapment. I thought it was because I always thought of marriage as old-fashioned and antiquated, and I never wanted to feel owned. But Phillip agrees with all of that. I think.

I take the soap off the dish and run it down my body. When I reach my breasts, I start to think about Brayden again, and I can't stop. I run that soap over and over myself until I'm fully lathered up, and yet I don't want to rinse off and get out of the shower.

But I do.

I put in my contact lenses, which always takes me at least two tries, and take my time getting dressed.

Just as I reach the bedroom, my phone buzzes.

My heart lurches when I look down and see Brayden's name flash across my screen.

I flick the screen to read his text.

Just found out this weekend could work if you're free at all to grab that sample.

I write him back. *I should be able to find some time, yes. I'll get back to you on it.*

————

I sit gratefully underneath the umbrella Sophia somehow tied to the back of my chair with one of her many scarves. It's not raining yet, but it could start any second, and I don't relish the idea of being wet and cold.

June scampers past us with three boxes piled high in her arms. "I've got help coming!" she says. "I heard the county women's shelter is sending a few volunteers over. So we're going to need a lot of food."

I shift my gaze to the sky, at the gray thick canvas broken only by pockets of darker clouds. "The colors are amazing."

"What colors?" Sophia says. "It's all gray!"

"But it's different shades of gray. At least four."

I've still got my face pointed to the sky when Phillip comes over. "You guys need any help setting up?" he says.

I force my gaze down to his face. I want to tell him about the shades of gray, but he looks too stressed out to care. "Nope. We've got it covered, honey. See Sophia's nifty contraption?" I point at the umbrellas over our heads.

"Very smart." Phillip nods at her, impressed. "I don't like those umbrella patterns, though, Soph."

I glance back at the umbrella protecting me. It's painted a pretty shade of purple with interlocking pink flowers.

"Oh, Phillip, ease up." Sophia laughs. "You hate anything beautiful, don't you?"

He turns red. "That's not true. I don't like pastels is all."

I wave him goodbye as Sophia taps my arm.

"Is your mom sad you won't need a wedding dress?" she asks me.

"Why would she be sad? It's not her wedding."

"I don't know. My mom's a drunk. But isn't wedding dress shopping like this big mother-daughter thing to do together? Like an event?"

I shrug. "My mom agrees that it's a silly tradition. She says there are people starving in third world countries. Why would you spend your money on a dress you'll wear once?"

Sophia stares at me. "Wow. No wonder you're so serious. You probably picked it up in the womb and just popped out that way."

I admire Sophia's ability to be uncensored and fearless. The one time I acted like that, I got attacked.

But ever since I failed my dissertation, I've felt less and less certain about playing it safe.

I break down and tell Sophia about the dance class. And of course, she loves Phillip's suggestion.

"Wow," she says, her smile a mile wide. "I wish I could pat Phillip on the back. Your own fiancé is telling you to ask the hot guy at June's store to dance with you? So freaking do it, Lei. Once you and Phillip marry, your chance to dance is over. Or to make sweaty, hot love."

I let out a squeak.

"What?" Sophia studies my face. "You know I'm right. Your fiancé is the most serious man in existence. He doesn't have time to dance, or play, or engage in mind-blowing sex."

My face heats.

"Does that push a button?" she asks me. "Good. Because I don't want to see my best friend saying, 'I wish I'd just had fun when I could.' You're going to be a professor's wife, Leleila. You'll be expected to host dinner parties, attend conferences on his arm, and all this other crap I know you secretly hate doing but won't admit to out loud. So accept this God-given—or Phillip-given—reprieve. Take some dance lessons, and let your hair down for the next month. Flirt with Brayden, or just friend him. But at least have some fun with a guy who sounds like he knows what the word means."

When a blue pick-up truck pulls up, I immediately straighten in my chair.

Sophia pokes me. "Is that him?"

I don't have to answer her because Brayden has hopped out of the driver's side and is heading toward the gazebo. Wearing a deep green flannel shirt and dark jeans, he's carrying a large box in his arms.

Sophia waves as he reaches us.

"Hey," he calls out, his eyes on me.

"Brayden, take my seat," she encourages him. "A guy just showed up that I used to date." She nudges me. "Wish me luck, Lei. If I don't come back, I'll call you later."

She jumps up and waves goodbye.

"Thanks, Sophia." Brayden smiles and puts down his box before he sits next to me. "Hey, Leleila."

"Hi. How was the game?"

"Great. We won by three touchdowns." His blond hair peeks out from underneath his cowboy hat, and his piercing blue eyes focus on me like nobody else is around. His blue eyes have a hint of gray in them—that must be part of the reason they look so unusual. His mouth turns up in a half-smile, and he looks genuinely happy to see me.

"Congratulations." I decide to tell him the truth. "So in answer to your question the other night, here's the thing: I don't think we can be friends once I'm married because my fiancé's career is all-encompassing, and I'm expected to play a big role in that. He's a professor at the university, and as his wife..." I trail off.

Brayden nods. "I understand. You'll have a lot of expectations to live up to."

Yes. My hands clench into fists. "But leading up to our wedding, which is in October, Phillip is super busy. So busy that he's decided he can't take the dance class with me." I lift my chin and look Brayden right in the eyes. "He suggested I ask you to be my partner for the class."

Brayden's eyes widen. "Whoa."

My cheeks blaze. "I can introduce you to him. He's right over there." I point to Phillip by the food bins. "He knows you work at June's store, and he trusts her judgment. And I've always wanted to learn to dance. It's been a bit of a dream of mine to have a fun first dance at my wedding. Phillip doesn't want to let me down."

"What's he so busy with that he can't be your partner?" Brayden says. "Dancing's very erotic. I would think he'd jump at the chance."

My stomach does cartwheels. "Our honeymoon is tied in with his research on ecosystems, so he has a lot to get done beforehand. We're going to the Galapagos," I add politely. "Anyway, he doesn't have the time."

Brayden's gaze seers into mine. "How do you feel about his request that you dance with someone else?"

I stare at him. He's the first person to ask me that, to actually care how I feel about my fiancé telling me he would prefer I dance with someone other than him.

"I'm not...sure," I admit. "I just wanted you to know that we can hang out and dance if you'd like, and Phillip won't care. In fact, he'll probably be relieved of some of his guilt."

Brayden's eyes fill with concern. "I'm sorry, Leleila."

Okay, this is not how I thought this exchange was going to play out. I didn't expect pity.

Brayden tugs at the brim of his hat. "Does he, um, know we met back in high school?"

"No. I never told him," I say in a bare whisper.

Brayden leans closer to me and lowers his voice even though no one's within hearing distance of us. "You never told him about what happened to you?"

"*Almost* happened," I say quickly. "I defended myself."

"I know." His tone is gentle. "I just meant...that must have been pretty terrifying. I thought maybe you would have shared the story with the man you're going to marry."

Yes, that would make sense. But I've never wanted to relive the memory of that night. I told Sophia the one time she and I got drunk off tequila shots together, and I was horrified when she brought it up to me the next morning.

"Let's just say I haven't really wanted to discuss that night again." I swallow hard.

"Leleila. I'm not turning you down." His gaze flicks over to mine, and I swear I catch something else in his eyes, something close to heat, before he shutters his reaction. "I'd like to hang out."

"Lei!" Sophia calls out as she bounces back over to us. "Guess who's got herself a date for tonight?"

I smile. "That's awesome."

Brayden stands up and grabs his box off the ground. "I'd better drop this donation off."

I smile and wave as he heads for Phillip's table where all the bulk food is kept.

"It's almost like the universe shouldn't put those two together," Sophia whispers to me. "Phillip and Brayden are like night and day, or oil and vinegar. I've never seen two people less alike."

"They don't really have much in common," I agree.

Just then, June wanders over to them, and I watch as she introduces Brayden to Phillip. As the three of them stand together and continue chatting, I wonder what they're so deep in conversation about. When they all turn slightly and Phillip points directly at me, I start to have a clue.

———

Brayden

Leleila's fiancé extends his hand.

"Phillip Rowe. Thanks for helping out my fiancé the other evening."

I want to ask him how the hell his work is so important that he couldn't be there for Leleila, but I force myself to simply nod.

Leleila's fiancé is taller than me by a couple inches, but he's rail thin. He's in good shape, the way someone who bikes or runs would be, but he doesn't look like he's ever lifted a weight or been involved in a contact sport. He's got lines of tension around his mouth and eyes like he works way too hard.

"I have a favor to ask of you," he says.

"Okay," I say noncommittally.

When he explains that he's going to be too tied up to attend dance lessons with Leleila, and could I fill in for the next three weeks, my answer is instant.

"I can't. Sorry."

June gives me a hard look. "Why not?"

I gesture to the box of canned food I placed on the table a few feet away. "You mind helping me unpack that?" I say to her pointedly.

She takes the hint and leaves Phillip and me alone.

Phillip eyes me carefully. "What'll it take for you to say yes? I can pay you double what June does for that hour of your time."

I stare at him like he's nuts. "This isn't about money."

"I get it. It's time you don't have. Time is money. I guess Leleila will have to skip the dancing then." He sighs, and the frown on his face...he actually looks genuinely upset. "I just hate to disappoint her. I haven't seen her this excited about something in ages. She's going through a tough time right now."

I tug at my hat. "So if I don't do it, she won't be able to take the class?"

"I just have no time. But maybe I can find someone else to dance with her." Phillip scans the area like he can pick up a guy right this minute.

A pain hits me in the gut. I don't want to stop and analyze what it means. "Fine, if it's just three weeks, I can fill in," I find myself saying.

His eyes flash with relief. "That's great. And it's definitely only three weeks. We're getting married right after that, and once that happens, Leleila won't have time to do anything frivolous. She'll be too busy being my assistant. Now that she's not going to be a professor, at least for the time being, I've decided to hire her as my assistant as a wedding gift. She doesn't know yet, so don't say anything."

I wouldn't dream of it.

He doesn't have time? What kind of an idiot a-hole is this guy? Leleila Wills is the most unique, beautiful, intriguing woman I've ever met, and her damn fiancé treats her like she's expendable.

From the little I know of her, Leleila is smart, and she's strong, but this "find yourself a stand-in dance partner bullshit" clearly has her feeling vulnerable. And the idea of any man hurting her slays me.

For some reason I can't explain away, I feel an urging to look after her. The way she reacted when we ran into each other again —it was like we were still on the same damn wavelength or something. Her green eyes glittered with the same intense interest they had the first time we met, and the curiosity staring out of the emerald depths nearly knocked me over. I felt her unspoken message immediately—she still felt a connection to me, but she didn't understand why.

So I'll be her friend. The loneliness in her eyes is haunting, almost like she's never really felt close to anyone. I ball my hands into fists at the thought of her dick of a fiancé demanding she find a new dance partner. I can't imagine how much that must have hurt.

But he's clearly not going to help her out with the class, and she seems pretty damn determined to learn to dance.

So I'll be her partner.

Because if she can't dance with her fiancé, no way is she going to dance with any other man but me.

I nod at Phillip as June rejoins us. "The women's shelter just called, and they want produce in addition to canned food," she says. "I wish they'd mentioned that yesterday."

"I've got plenty of extra produce at the ranch," I offer.

Leleila

Phillip hustles over to me as Brayden heads for his truck.

"Lei," Phillip says in a rush of breath. "The women's shelter volunteers are on route, and Brayden said he has extra produce at his farm stand. You mind coming to help us pack it up?"

"Um." The three of us together? That's going to be awkward as hell. "Sure."

I follow him to the curb, but before we can turn toward our car, Phillip's phone beeps.

"Oh, crap," he says as he reads the screen. "Mindy's coming by."

"Mindy?" The woman he mentioned the other night?

"She's a researcher, and she's new here," he explains to my obviously worried expression. "She just moved to Montana two months ago, so I invited her to the Food Drive. She wants to help."

"Oh. Well, that's kind of you."

"Except now I can't leave..." Phillip looks over at Brayden just stepping up into his truck. "Can you go with Brayden and pick up the produce then bring it back here?"

"Me?"

"I have to wait here for Mindy." He's already urging me toward Brayden's truck and waving to him at the same time. "I'll see you soon."

CHAPTER TEN

As I reach the truck, Brayden leans over from the driver's seat and opens the passenger side for me. I step up onto the cab and climb in, taking care to buckle my seat belt.

I peek over at Brayden and realize he's waiting for me to get settled before taking his foot off the brake.

"You all set?" Every single time he puts his eyes on me, he gives me all of his attention, and I'm not used to that. To be honest, when Phillip gives me one eye, even with the other concentrating on his research specimens, I feel lucky.

"I think so." I turn my gaze to the road as we start driving down Main Street. "So, what did you bring to the food drive to donate?"

"How about myself?"

I freeze. "What?"

"I'll be your friend. And I'll be your dance partner."

As we reach a red light, he turns to me, his expression serious.

I stare at him. Part of me wants to turn away because the feelings coiling inside me feel dangerous. But the other part of me wants to get lost in Brayden's sapphire eyes for as long as I can.

"I thought you said no to the dance lessons," I say too sharply.

He shrugs and shifts his gaze back to the road as the light turns green. "Changed my mind."

"How come?" I don't know why I care or why I'm pushing him on something that's clearly uncomfortable for both of us.

"Because Phillip said this means a lot to you. And I don't want you to have to look around for some random guy who can't be trusted, who doesn't deserve to be within a hundred miles of you."

I bite my lip. "But you're a guy."

"Yep. The right guy for the job."

"How come?" I say again.

We've pulled into Big River, and Brayden slows the truck to a crawl as we reach the farm stand.

He turns off the truck and leans toward me until his eyes are burning into my hot skin. "Because I would never take advantage of it."

I lick my lips, and Brayden's gaze travels to my mouth and stays there. Then, he abruptly jerks back and resumes a blank expression on his face.

"Okay." My voice comes out hoarse. "You've got the job. You're my dance partner for the rest of the month."

Brayden's nod is quick and definitive like we've sealed the deal. "Cool."

My phone buzzes in my pocket as we're walking to the farm stand.

"Hi, Phillip, we just got here," I say as I pick up.

"Scratch the produce," he says to me. "The volunteers got into a fender bender on their way here. They're not coming after all."

"Okay, we'll head back," I say.

"The whole operation's shutting down early due to rain in the forecast, so take your time if you want to grab a coffee or something," he says. "Mindy and I are going to the university for a quick slide analysis."

"Wait. You're..."

"Let's plan to meet back at the Food Drive in an hour or so, and I'll drive us home."

I exhale. I want to ask Phillip more about this Mindy person, but Brayden's standing about a foot away, waiting. So I end the call and fill Brayden in on the change of plans. Then, I have an idea.

"I don't suppose this would be a good time to get that soil sample, would it?" I ask him.

"Perfect," he says. "The owners are away all weekend."

We make a stop at Save the Soil for me to grab my equipment, and twenty minutes later, I'm tacking up a mare named Dolly and preparing to climb into the saddle.

"You sure you know how to ride?" Brayden asks me when I miss the stirrup and nearly wipe out on my first try.

My face is on fire, but I go for honesty. "I definitely know how to ride, yes. It's just been a very long time. My grandfather had a ranch, and June and I rode all the time growing up. But after he passed away, we stopped. My parents aren't into recreational activities."

Brayden leads his powerful gelding, Blazer, into the paddock and returns to my side.

"Here, I'll give you a leg up," he says.

I try not to react when he takes my foot in his hand and hoists me upward onto the horse.

Once I'm in the saddle, though, I relax. Brayden hands me the bag of supplies I need for the sampling, and I place it in my lap.

I pat Dolly's neck while Brayden mounts Blazer. And then, we start riding at an easy pace past the barn and down a marked trail until we reach a beautiful meadow lined on both sides with tall trees. The sky is still gray, and the rain looks imminent. Still, I can't remember the last time I felt this peaceful.

"This is awesome," I say genuinely. "I really missed riding. And just being outdoors for fun."

Brayden smiles. "You live in Montana, and you're surrounded by ranches. You could ride every day of the week if you wanted to."

"I know. But for the last five years, I've been cooped up in a classroom."

"Was it worth it?" he asks me as he slows down, and I follow his lead.

"Not so far," I admit. "I thought it would be, but then again, I didn't expect to fail."

"You have a second chance, right?" He asks in a concerned tone.

"Yes, but not for a while." *Too long of a while.* "I'll be married before I can present my thesis again."

"Maybe one life change at a time is enough," he says.

"Maybe."

Brayden turns his head toward me. "Your honeymoon destination sounds amazing. I'd love to see the wildlife there. And I bet the water will be really nice for swimming."

"The Galapagos are perfect for scientists." I shrug. "Phillip wants to make the world a better place."

"I thought it was your honeymoon," he says.

"So?"

"So doesn't this guy want to spend all his time with you?" he says. "You know, just being happy he's found the woman he wants to spend the rest of his life with?"

My cheeks are now an inferno of embarrassment, and I slow the horse to a walk and turn my face toward Brayden's. His blue eyes get bluer until they're all I see.

Looking into his bright eyes and handsome face, I feel my body involuntarily shifting closer to him like he has the ability to turn me on without trying at all.

"We're here."

Brayden pulls up on Blazer, and I blink out of my reverie and do the same.

"We'll have to walk this last part," he says. "You okay?"

"Sure," I say as I dismount, and we tie both horses to a nearby tree.

We walk for a short mile before he stops. "It's right here on the other side of the wire fence."

"I should probably grab a sample on your side of the fence first, for comparison's sake."

"Good idea."

I take a jar out of my bag and go about collecting a core soil sample. Then I label the jar and close up the lid.

When I'm done, Brayden leads me to the corner of the field and bends the wire down so we can climb over it. When he points at the ground, I say, "All I see is the cattle pasture. Is it under here?"

"Exactly." Brayden kneels down, and I squat next to him. He pulls a small collapsible shovel out of his pocket and digs just underneath the surface, then he taps the area with the shovel until I hear metal.

"It's a container," he says. "It's massive."

I look at his face in the darkening light, and I know we don't have much time before it rains. "I'll have to work quickly," I say. "The sample can't be tested if it's waterlogged."

He shovels until the container is clearly exposed.

"Look at the label," he says.

"Hazardous materials," I read aloud.

"I don't think it's here legally," he says, stating the obvious.

"You mean they buried it here rather than pay to dispose of it properly," I say.

"Exactly," he says. "Is this something you can test at Save the Soil?"

I shake my head. "We tend to stay away from toxic dumps. But this doesn't look good at all. The reservoir's right behind here, isn't it?"

Brayden looks toward the hill. "Shit. I didn't think about the runoff going that far; some of the town's water supply comes from that reservoir."

Pulling a second glass jar out of my bag, I take Brayden's shovel and dig deep enough and close enough to the container until I think it's a pure soil sample. Then, I take a second core sample and put it into another glass jar just to be sure. I seal them both up, and together Brayden and I cover up the hole we made.

I stand up straight, and we cross over the fence back into Big River Ranch. "I can take a quick look at the soil through Phillip's scope. Then I'll talk to someone at Save the Soil and see what can be done about testing it."

Brayden rubs his jaw. "I'd rather you not say where it's from straight away. Chuck Easton's not in the best health right now."

"I understand," I say. "But this could be a serious public health concern. Do you think the owners are in on it at all?"

Brayden shrugs. "I don't think so, but that's why I want the results back before I ask him." He stops in the middle of the path and turns to me. "I shouldn't have gotten you mixed up in this. I'm sorry."

"I'm not sorry," I say. "You did the right thing. Is it okay if I mention it to Phillip? He may have some ideas on how best to test the sample."

"As long as he's willing to wait for the results before he acts," Brayden says.

"My parents are away, or I could ask them," I say.

"Did your parents travel a lot for work when you were young?"

"They did. They were trying to save the world." I stare up at the dark clouds filling the sky. "Still are."

"What about just being parents instead of heroes?" Brayden asks.

My jaw drops as I make eye contact with him. "Nobody's ever said that. Everyone always admires them for their courage and says how lucky June and I are to have such great role models."

"I'm not saying they aren't good role models. I'm just saying— where were they when you needed them?"

Usually on a fishing boat somewhere, or camping in a third world country where they were completely unreachable, or standing behind a podium with several hundred people watching them from their seats below, learning from and admiring their field research.

"We had a really great nanny," I mumble as I clench my fists.

Brayden starts to laugh.

"What?" I say. "We did! Her name's Annette, and we're still in touch with her."

But Brayden's still laughing. And it's contagious. I start to laugh too, despite myself. I laugh until I cry. And then that turns into a couple of real tears, something I rarely do and never in front of others.

Brayden runs his hand down my arm. "Hey. You're okay." His voice is soothing and strong. It's safe. "Did they ever take you with them?"

"Once." I wipe away the lone tear that made its way down my cheek. "It was a two-week trip to Belize, and June and I had school break at the same time. We were so excited to get to go, until the first adventure, where we had to wade across a low-lying river. The waters were very calm, but then the guide told us to walk quickly because there were alligators, and we were terrified." I shudder even now. "I was convinced I'd be the one to feel those huge teeth around my legs. We made it safely across, but then June spilled a little water out of Dad's jar specimen he'd collected. He said she contaminated it." I let out a deep breath. "They decided it was better we stay home after that."

Brayden watches me, looking like he wants to say something more. But then we head for the horses and mount them in silence.

———

Luckily, the soil samples are securely wrapped up and tucked away, inside the glass jars I placed in my waterproof bag, because the skies open up on our ride back to the barn.

It pours—I mean it *pours*—for our entire return trip.

My hair is plastered to my neck, and as we ride into the barn, my jeans are so wet against my legs that I get stuck sliding off Dolly.

Brayden and I take off the horses' saddles and bridles, and then we make sure to brush them down and dry their coats as much as possible. After leaving them in the dry barn with fresh water and food, he and I head for the front of the barn.

"I'll go get the truck and come get you," he says.

But I laugh. "I'm already soaked. I'm fine to go to the truck with you."

He takes my hand in his, and I'm so startled at the show of affection I just stare up at him. "I don't want you to slip," he says, his expression unreadable. "Hold onto me along the trail, okay?"

I swallow and wrap my fingers around his strong, rough hand as he starts walking through the trees and toward the main driveway. It's chilly, and I'm freezing. I fight the strong desire I have to snuggle in next to Brayden's side while we walk.

As soon as we get inside his truck, Brayden cranks the heat while I call Phillip to make sure he's on his way to the town square.

Phillip doesn't answer my phone call. Instead, he texts me to say that he and Mindy are at the university and may be there for another couple of hours. They're "stuck" with a slide that can't be redone, or they'll "lose everything."

I make a noise of frustration.

"Everything okay?" Brayden asks me.

"Fine," I say with a quick smile. "I'm going to call Sophia to come pick me up. Turns out Phillip's busy."

Trying to ignoring Brayden's clear frown, I hit Sophia's number. It goes straight to voicemail.

I text her. *Can you come get me at Brayden's?*

In a couple of hours, okay? I'm having the best time with Slammer.

Undeterred, I call June. Nothing. I text her. My sister is notoriously bad at answering texts—it could literally be a week. I don't bother to try again.

Out of options, I grip my phone and shut my eyes as the worst part of this situation hits me—my only set of house keys are in my purse, which is in Phillip's locked car, which is with him at school. I could go try to track him down, but I don't know what lab he and Mindy are using, and he has always hated when I interrupt him at work. So, I can't get into my house, and I'm as wet as a drowning rat.

What the hell am I going to do?

I raise my gaze to meet Brayden's. "My house keys are with Phillip, locked in his car. We don't keep spares anywhere because Phillip's paranoid about break-ins. Long story short—I'm kind of stuck."

"I have an idea," he says.

CHAPTER ELEVEN

When we pull up to a single-story cottage with a small barn next to it, I whip my head around to face Brayden.

"Where are we?" I say.

"This is the guesthouse," Brayden says. "I live here."

I widen my eyes.

"Leleila, relax." He touches my arm like he knows what I'm thinking. "I'm not taking you home to have my nefarious way with you. It just made sense to bring you here so you could dry off your clothes and warm up. If we went to a coffee shop, you would sit there shivering the entire time."

I let out the breath I've been holding. "You're right."

The cottage is simple but homey with gray siding and a white door.

Brayden turns off the truck and takes the keys out of the ignition. "I'll come help you out," he offers as I open my door.

"No worries. I'm fine," I say as I step down.

We follow the cobble-stoned walkway as it curves and winds to the front door of the cottage. Brayden leads me inside where we walk through the cozy-feeling living room and out to a screened-in back porch.

"This is so cool," I say. "It's like being outside while you're still inside."

"I love to watch the rain from this porch." He gestures to the blue couch facing the windows. "Have a seat if you'd like."

I sit down and try not to shiver overtly. I really am freezing.

Brayden notices, and he goes over to close the partially-open windows. "This will make it warmer, and I can start the fire, too."

I glance over at the wood-burning stove in the corner. "That's awesome."

"It's all filled and ready to burn," he says over his shoulder as he finishes closing the windows and then starts the stove.

I stare at his ass the entire time, wondering if staring is as bad as touching. Everyone's allowed to fantasize, even married people, right? But I'm not married yet. I remember Mom telling me she had two suitors besides Dad for a time, and they were all courting her at once. Of course, Mom wasn't living with one of them.

Brayden turns around, but I'm still focused on his pants area, so I find myself staring at the buttons on his jeans. I go hot and bring my eyes up to his face.

The corner of his mouth lifts. "You want to throw your clothes in the dryer? You shouldn't stay soaking wet."

I stare at him awkwardly, not sure what he expects me to do while my clothes are nicely drying—sit around naked perhaps?

"I'll grab a pair of my sweatpants and a sweatshirt and you can change in the bathroom," he explains.

I think about this for a minute before finally deciding it's the most practical thing to do. I usually pride myself on being practical, but I don't feel very good at it right now.

"Sure." I shake my head to clear the cobwebs as I stand up to follow him out of the room. "That's a good idea."

———

I stand in front of Brayden's front-loading dryer and watch my clothes spin round and round inside. Wearing his clothes like this,

I can feel him on me as if we'd just slept together even though, of course, we didn't. His sweatshirt smells so good, manly and with a hint of detergent. Brayden sits with his legs hanging off the edge of his folding table and helps break the awkwardness by telling me more about himself.

He says he's always loved football, but he loves ranch life even more. His four cousins are his best friends.

"Plus Jenson," he adds. "He's Colt's best friend since they were kids and all of ours as well. The six of us are pretty inseparable even though we aren't living in the same place. And now, four of them are either married or will be getting married; they're not all officially engaged, but they might as well be."

"Wow. That must have changed things," I say.

"It did. But only in good ways."

The longer Brayden talks, the more he fascinates me, from his relaxed attitude to the way he doesn't seem to overthink anything.

He spent his whole life up in Wilcox, the tiny town a few miles to the north, and he played wide receiver all four years on the high school football team.

"You said you played with Dylan and Colton?" I ask him.

"Yep. After we graduated, I stayed in Wilcox and got my teaching degree. I taught physical education at the high school for a while, and then I got an assistant coaching job for the football team."

"That's amazing," I say. "Wilcox has one of the top teams in the state."

He nods. "I love working with the kids."

"What do you like most?"

His blue eyes soften. "I like how each kid is different. Not a one is the same, and you can't coach them the same, or use the same techniques, because what will work for one of the boys will absolutely fail with another one. I just want them to succeed after high school, and not just on the football field. I want them to follow their passion. It may not be football, and my goal is for them to trust their gut. Nothing worse than getting stuck on a career path that's not right for you. It doesn't work, and it's bound to make you miserable."

I suck in my breath. His words are hitting a little too close to home.

"So you stock groceries on the side in order to be able to buy a ranch?"

He chuckles. "Sounds crazy when you put it like that."

I cringe. "Shit. I didn't mean for it to. I think it's amazing, actually, that you're working so hard to pursue a dream."

Brayden reaches out and gently tugs on a strand of my hair. "I'm still at the beginning of the journey, but that's okay. I'm not in a hurry as long as I'm headed in the right direction. I'm trying to follow my heart, you know?"

I nod, my eyes locked with his, and I can't tear my gaze away. "Following my heart has never been my strong suit," I murmur.

"No?" His tone is laced with meaning.

"No," I say in a hoarse whisper.

He watches me as I fidget with the drawstrings hanging from the hood of his sweatshirt I'm wearing.

"These are the best kind of dryers," I say finally. "They evenly dry clothing and use less energy as well."

I look back at my clothes nervously. They seem secure behind all that glass and metal, just spinning around and around and actually getting somewhere at the end of it all.

"Let's go sit down." Brayden jumps off the table and touches my back lightly.

———

While the flames flicker inside the stove, Brayden and I drink hot chocolate on his enclosed porch. Phillip and I never eat sweets, and I'm getting a sugar high. I start giggling and look outside at the rain still pelting down.

"You're my lucky break, Brayden Wild." Apparently sugar makes me say things that would normally never come out of my mouth. "Taking me out of the storm and onto the warmth of your porch. Thank you."

Brayden grins. "I'm lucky your sister runs Big Sky Grocer and that you really like granola, or I might not have run into you again. It's been a long time, Leleila."

"It has." My voice cracks, and I turn toward the window as a large gust of wind shakes the trees outside, and a cascade of orange and yellow leaves falls to the ground.

"Why do the leaves change in autumn?" Brayden says hastily, and I know he's trying to change the subject to something more neutral.

"Not enough light or warmth in winter for photosynthesis," I say automatically. "The trees rest and shut down their ability to make food, so the green chlorophyll disappears from the leaves. They end up orange and red and yellow. Small amounts of these colors are always in the leaves, but you just can't see them because of the chlorophyll."

His eyes search mine. "You're smart. I guess I meant more like —why do they have to fall?"

I think about it as the leaves swirl around in the wind. "I don't know," I say finally. "I guess sometimes things have to end in order for life to continue. So the leaves die, but the tree lives on for another season. Trees are amazing."

We lapse into a comfortable silence, sitting side by side with our hands wrapped around our mugs of hot chocolate. I point excitedly out the window when two deer stop underneath the largest tree in Brayden's backyard. The brown coat of the deer is an even deeper shade from the rain on their backs, and I can see their dark eyes from here.

Brayden smiles at my enthusiasm. "They stop by sometimes. I get a lot of wildlife here, and I'm away from the cattle fields, so there's a lot more open space."

I'd love to sit here all day and paint. I've always loved nature. Mom and Dad got me involved in environmental biology, but I can't remember the last time I just sat and actually enjoyed the environment.

But that's what I do with Brayden today. For the next hour and a half, we sit and do a lot of nothing. We watch the deer before they run off into the woods. We try to count the leaves falling but give up quickly. And we laugh a lot. We laugh about the strange noises coming out of his wood stove and about our dance teacher's admonishment to practice dancing.

"I'll be lucky if I remember any of the steps," I say. "I'm getting married twenty-four days from now, and I don't know if a choreographed dance is possible. Besides the fact that I have to teach it to Phillip."

"Twenty-four days to learn a dance? That's definitely possible."

"You're right," I say, feeling optimistic. "For some species, that's a lifetime. For others, it's several lifetimes."

"You're still smart." The cool blue of his eyes turns hot as he meets my gaze with his own. "People probably tell you that all the time."

"Not really," I say honestly. "I'm surrounded by geniuses."

———

When neither Phillip nor Sophia have texted me after cup two of our hot chocolates, Brayden lies down on his rug in front of the wood stove. "It's relaxing. And you can hear the rain in a really cool way from here," he says.

I get down on my back next to him on his dark green shag rug and feel the warmth of the fire at my feet. "Now what?"

"Just close your eyes." His low voice is soothing. "The rain sounds like it's all around you instead of just over your head."

I close my eyes and try to relax. I'm jazzed from the chocolate and from the company so close to me right now, but I do hear the rain. It *is* cool.

"That's neat," I say. "Almost like being in a waterfall without getting wet."

"Yeah, it does sound like that. I could lie here all afternoon."

"Do you?" I ask him curiously as I open my eyes.

"Sometimes," he says. "I work a lot, so not as much as I'd like. But at night, I like to just hang out."

"Do you read?"

"Sometimes. I do a lot of film study during football season."

I gesture at a crack in his ceiling. "That looks like the Big Dipper. The big crack and then those dots around it."

"I see it." He points above his head. "That looks like an elephant."

I laugh. "There are no elephants in the sky at night."

"This isn't a night sky, Leleila." His tone is amused. "It's a white ceiling. We can make whatever we want to on it."

I point out a swirl of paint on the ceiling that looks like a puffy cloud, and Brayden finds another swirl that he claims looks like Rain Man.

"Rain Man? That's a character!"

"Well, it looks like Dustin Hoffman, then. Look more closely and tell me you don't agree."

"Fine. I actually see what you mean." I smile. "But you're still crazy for seeing it in the first place."

"Creative. I'm creative."

I laugh before closing my eyes again and listening to the rain and remembering the deer. I wonder if animals in the wild do this, just lie together and feel the rain.

"Are you hungry?" Brayden asks me. "I could make us some dinner if you'd like."

His thoughtful invitation brings me back to reality, and I sit up slowly. "Actually, I think I should wait for Phillip."

As if on cue, my phone rings, and I stand up as I answer.

But when I grab it, it's Sophia. "Hey, Soph."

"Lei, I'm at my apartment if you want to come by. Or should I pick you up?"

"Um..."

Brayden reaches for his car keys on the coffee table, and we make eye contact. He holds up his keys, signaling that he can drive me.

As he goes to retrieve my clothes from the dryer, I say to Sophia, "I'll be right there, Soph. Thanks."

————

After I change back into my top and jeans, Brayden locks his front door, and we walk in silence to his truck. As I step up into the cab and close the door behind me, I debate how to articulate what I want to say to him. But I've never been good at this sort of thing.

So as soon as Brayden sits down in the driver's seat, I burst out with, "I kept your hat."

He jerks his head in my direction. "What?"

"Your cowboy hat that you gave me all those years ago? I still have it," I say as I buckle my seat belt.

He stares at me in silence. His blue eyes flash with an unnamed emotion, and when he opens his mouth to speak, nothing comes out.

Oh, God.

The ship of mortification has left the dock. In fact, it's sailing gloriously toward me. Oh, and look…it's now docked at my feet.

I avert my gaze and start to fidget with the seat belt. "Anyway," I say quickly. "It's not a big deal…"

A warm hand lands on my fumbling fingers, and I look up.

"I'm sorry." His expression has changed to warm. "That is just, literally, probably the last thing I expected you to say to me."

"Oh." I swallow. "I just wanted to thank you. For being there for me that night and for giving me your hat. I never got a chance to truly thank you for what you did for me."

His voice is gruffer than usual when he says, "I'm happy if holding onto the hat helped you in some small way."

"It reminded me every day that most people are good," I say softly. "You didn't save me physically that night, Brayden. But you saved me in just as important a way—you gave me strength in salvation."

"Leleila." His gaze feels like fire on my skin.

I bite my lip, and he gives my hand a quick squeeze and then abruptly shifts to face the steering wheel.

"I better get you to Sophia's," he says in apparent explanation.

But the spark between us will not die. The electricity heats up the car during the entire ride even though we only speak occasionally. And guilt tugs at my chest. I try to calm myself with the truth —in a few weeks, any time spent hanging out with Brayden will be over for good. And if I weren't already having so much fun with him, it probably wouldn't be so painful to imagine it ending.

CHAPTER TWELVE

Brayden

I'm falling for her. For the brilliant, green-eyed, shy on the surface but sassy on the inside woman who got inside my heart with one curious glance, and no matter what I do, I can't shake her out.

But I have to.

Leleila's engaged, for fuck's sake. I've never once been drawn to a woman who was taken. Not one fucking time. So why is this happening now?

And Christ, why'd she have to go ahead and tell me she kept my cowboy hat? The whole time I drive her to Sophia's, I'm picturing her wearing my hat. And yeah, sometimes she's naked. With me.

Riding me.

Bent over in front of me.

Fuck, fuck, fuck.

I pull into Sophia's driveway, and Leleila nearly leaps out of the truck. We say goodbye politely and in measured tones, completely faking the fact that this truck is about a thousand degrees right now. Because of us.

Once she's finally gone, I exhale and head for home. I force the dirty images of Leleila out of my mind by focusing on what plays we should run in practice Monday. Next Friday is a big game, and it's at home. So no worries about Wes and his father, although to Luke's credit, everything was in good shape when we got home late last night. Luke was at Wes's house. Wes's dad was sitting up next to him watching an Old Western movie. Sober.

No idea what the fuck my brother did to conjure up that magic, but I took it. We said goodbye to Wes, and we left.

So yeah, I have enough going on with football and the ranch. So much that I could easily tell Leleila I can't dance with her. I *should* tell her that. With the way my truck nearly combusted just now, I should definitely back out.

But I don't break promises. And Leleila clearly needs a friend. So somehow, I'm going to have to ignore my heart and stay on the proper side of the line. I'll be her friend. Just her friend and nothing more.

Thoughts of kissing her dominated my brain when we were chatting on the couch. Dirtier thoughts of taking her against the washing machine raced through my head while I tried to keep up a casual conversation about my career plans. The way Leleila looked wearing my clothes had me so turned on I could barely focus on anything else. Everything was too big on her, but it didn't matter because she wore my sweatshirt and pants like she owned them. And she relaxed for the first time since I've known her. She seemed...at peace, almost. It was a turn-on. I run my hand down my face. And now it's time for me to turn off.

As I reach the ranch, I pull down the driveway until I reach the guesthouse. I step out of my truck, close the door, and jog up the steps to the front door.

Before I can put my key in the lock, the door opens wide.

"Hey!" My cousin, Cam, has me in a headlock before I can answer him.

He releases me immediately.

"What the hell are you doing here?" I ask him. "You look like crap."

Cam chuckles and runs his hand through his dark hair, which is standing up every which way. His always-there facial hair is thicker than usual, and his dark eyes are bloodshot.

"I found your spare house key under the same broken stone where it's always been. We took a cab here."

I punch his arm. "I meant, what are you doing in Montana? You live in Minnesota."

"Had some time off and decided to come see you for a few days. Ayden, Bella, and Jasalie are out on your porch."

"No shit. They flew in from L.A.?"

Cam nods. "Just for the night. Totally spontaneous, but Jasalie wants to check out the wedding venue that Dylan located online, and he and Colt can't take time off from practice. So Ayd and Bella came with her. Let's go out and party tonight, and we can go see the venue tomorrow."

I drag my hand over the back of my neck. "I've had a long day. I'm kind of beat."

Cam's eyes narrow. "From doing what? Or who? Because the only way you'd blow us off is if there's a woman involved. And I haven't heard anything about a woman. So who is she?"

Before I have to answer him, my other three surprise house-guests come down the hall.

"What's up?" Ayden gives me a hug and immediately narrows his blue eyes, much the same way Cam was just doing. "You look weird, Bray. Everything okay?"

"It's a woman," Cam says confidently.

I don't even get an opening to deny it before Bella throws her arms around my neck.

"Oooh, who is she?" she squeals. "I've never met one of your girlfriends before!"

"That's because Bray keeps everything on the fucking down-low," Cam says with a smirk at me. "Good thing we walked in on him tonight. He says he had a long day."

Jasalie shoots me an apologetic look. "I'm so sorry we didn't call you ahead of time," she says, pulling her long blond hair up into a ponytail. "It was completely last-minute."

"It's no big deal," I assure her. "I know your husband doesn't work on a normal person's timetable."

She laughs, amusement dancing in her eyes. "No, Dylan thinks everyone can just jump on a plane at a moment's notice to go check out a wedding venue a thousand miles away. If he didn't have a game to prepare for, he'd be here too."

Dylan and Jasalie got married this past summer. They eloped to a private island and didn't tell any of us until they returned with rings on their fingers. But they're having a public wedding ceremony and reception this fall in Montana, and we're all in the wedding party. The renewal will be on a Monday, the day after Dylan and Colton have a big home game in L.A.

"Dylan wants to make sure this venue is perfect," Jasalie says. "So here we all are."

Ayden's gaze shifts to Cam. "Although I didn't expect you here, Wild. What made you decide to fly out?"

Cam shrugs noncommittally and doesn't answer.

Ayden and I look at each other.

Something's clearly up with Cam, but we know better than to push him. His father's done enough of that for a lifetime.

Ayden puts his arm around Bella and kisses her temple. "Bella's working on a demo already."

She blushes and buries her head in Ayden's shoulder. Her blond hair covers her face, and I laugh.

"You've got to get over that, Bella. People are going to find out you sing soon enough."

"I know," she answers me, her voice muffled by Ayden's shirt. "I just want everything to go right this time."

"It will," Ayden promises her, his tone certain.

With my hand halfway to tossing my sweatshirt onto the nearby table, I halt. The way Ayden's supporting Bella, looking out for her, hits me in the gut.

Because for the first time, I recognize that reaction, that need to protect someone else.

When I turn back around, all four of them are staring at me.

But I do what I'm good at. I keep my feelings to myself.

"Changed my mind," I say to Cam. "Let's go out."

———

Leleila

When Phillip finally calls to tell me that he can't leave the lab for another two hours, I nearly lose it.

"Could you do the rest of the experiment at home?" I hate that I sound like I'm whining. "I really would like to get into our house before midnight."

"Wish I could, Lei," he says. "But the lab's got the equipment—with the industrial scope, the lighting is so much better. You know that. If you need to go home that badly, you can come by the lab if Sophia doesn't mind driving you..."

Because Phillip always talks three volumes higher than needed on the phone, and Sophia is sitting literally right next to me on her couch, she hears everything.

"Leleila can wait another two hours!" Sophia says loudly. "We'll go have some fun."

"That's a great idea," Phillip says through the phone. "Maybe you and Soph can go out. I know you don't like socializing, honey, but try to enjoy yourself. I haven't seen you smiling much lately."

I nod even though he can't see me.

"I promise to send you a text the minute I'm leaving. But stay out as late as you want, okay?"

"Okay." I hang up and turn to Sophia. "I guess we're going out."

"Yay!" She breaks into a big smile. "Let's get you dressed."

———

An hour later, Sophia is still smiling as she hustles me into a little black dress that she's been *dying* to lend me.

"That dress just looks so damn hot on you, Lei," she says as we look together into her full-length mirror hanging inside her walk-in closet.

I refuse the light coat she's offered me. "I'm fine. It's not that cold out, and it's stopped raining. But I feel weird dressing up for no reason."

"And that's why you never dress up," she contends. "You and Phillip don't go out on dates unless you're attending one of his boring work functions."

"That's true. I don't know when we stopped doing stuff just for the fun of it. I miss that, you know?"

She gives me a hug. "That's what tonight is about, Lei. We're going to have fun."

"What bar are we going to again?" I ask her as we head for her front door.

"The Cowboy Saloon on the edge of town. Near the Mexican restaurant we've gone to loads of times before."

"Oh, right. I know where you mean." I glance at her mini-skirt and fitted pink top. Then I take a closer look at her heavily made-up face. "You're wearing a lot of makeup. Who else is meeting us there?"

She hits me playfully on the arm. "Don't be silly, Lei. Why do you say that?"

"Because you look like either a hooker or a Broadway star." I touch my finger to the excessive amount of rouge on her cheeks. "You're so gorgeous without all of this. You only wear this much makeup when you have a date with some guy you already know isn't nearly good enough for you."

Sophia sticks her tongue out at me.

We step outside the house, and I lock it behind me before following Sophia down the path to her car.

"Seriously, who's meeting us there?" I ask again as I get into the passenger side and shut the door behind me. "That guy from the food drive?"

"Yep. Glenn." Sophia starts the car and backs out quickly, far more quickly than I do on this steep driveway. "You remember Glenn." She puts on her turn signal and takes the first left. "I slept with him a few times about a year ago."

I strain to think back. "I don't know. I'm not sure I do remember someone named Glenn..."

"His nickname is Slammer. That's his last name."

"His last name is Slammer?" I say. "That's horrible."

"Well, he's great in bed. And I'm lonely."

I put my hand on her arm. "I know what today is, Soph."

She glances at me out of the corner of her eye. "Lei! You promised you would never mention what today means. We have a pact!"

"I know." I pretend to seal my lips with my finger and thumb. "And I won't say anything else. But you know I'm here for you."

"I do. But I really like Glenn."

I give her a look.

"Okay, fine. I'm not sure I can trust him at all. But I'm willing to find out. What could go wrong?"

———

The tingles start on the back of my neck as soon as we walk into the saloon. I glance around, feeling like I'm being watched.

When my gaze locks with a pair of sapphire-blue eyes, I halt, causing Sophia to slam into me from behind.

"Sorry," I murmur, my eyes not leaving Brayden's.

"What is it?" she asks me as she scans the bar. "Ohhhh. Your secret crush is in the building. Welllll. Tonight just got a hell of a lot more interesting. I may not have invited Slammer if I'd known about this little development."

She raises her hand and waves enthusiastically at Brayden, who gestures us over to the corner where he's standing with two beautiful blond women and two handsome dark-haired guys. One has facial hair, and the other is clean-shaven, but they're both equally attractive and well-built.

"Who are those other guys?" Sophia whispers to me.

"No idea," I say as I drag my feet getting over to him. "Not sociable" is a kind way of describing my level of comfort in a group gathering. And not having a warning that I was about to meet Brayden, as well as four other people who look far more together than I feel inside, is making my palms sweat.

But luckily, Sophia's the opposite of me. She charges forward, introducing herself and me before Brayden even has a chance to open his mouth.

Brayden shifts his gaze to me, and my pulse immediately picks up. His hair's damp, like he just got out of the shower. His cool blue shirt matches his eyes, and the top two buttons are undone, and the sleeves are rolled up, revealing light blond hairs on his arms. God, he looks better every time I see him.

"Have you all met June? She's Leleila's sister." Sophia asks his friends.

The guy with the facial hair shakes his head. "We don't live in the area, and we all just flew in today. We haven't been to Brayden's new job yet." He shoots Brayden a meaningful look. "I can't wait, though. Seems like lots of new shit is happening in his life lately."

Brayden clears his throat and introduces his four friends as Cam, Ayden, Bella, and Jasalie. I should have realized the two guys were his cousins, but I'm far too busy trying to think of what to say.

"Where—" The word comes out raspy, and I clear my throat and try again. "Where do you all live?"

Ayden and Bella explain how they just moved from Maine to L.A. where Jasalie also lives, and Cam says he lives in Minnesota but grew up in Louisiana.

"And Leleila, you two met through your sister?" Cam gestures between me and Brayden, whose focus is squarely on me.

"Um." I fidget with my purse strap. "We re-met each other. I kind of accidentally dumped granola on his head."

Ayden and Cam laugh, and Ayden's ocean blue eyes flash with something as he gives me a closer look.

"What happened then?" he asks me. His question sounds innocent, but Brayden smacks him on the shoulder. Ayden turns to Brayden. "Hey! I'm curious."

"Right." Brayden steps closer to me, and the way he protectively leans in, it's almost like we're...together.

Both his cousins react. Cam's mouth twists into a mischievous grin, and Ayden's gaze flicks between Brayden and me. Bella and Jasalie smile at me warmly like I've somehow joined their unofficial club.

And I...withdraw. I take two very clear, purposeful steps away from Brayden and cross my arms over my chest. Cam frowns at my retreat, and Ayden cocks his head, almost like he's confused.

Desperate for a save, I look wildly to Sophia. As always, she uses her inappropriate no-filter mouth to rescue me.

"You're so hot. You look like a professional model," Sophia says abruptly to Jasalie, who flushes pink. "Seriously. You said you live in L.A., right?"

"I do," she says. "But I don't model. I've always loathed the idea, actually."

"Jasalie and our cousin, Dylan, just got married," Brayden says to Sophia. "They're having a renewal ceremony here in a few weeks."

Sophia shrieks and clutches at Jasalie's arm. Jasalie's eyes widen in alarm, and I try to pull Sophia back. But she's too enthralled to let go.

"You're Dylan Wild's *wife?*"

Jasalie nods, and Bella breaks into a soft laugh. "Yes, every woman," she says to Jasalie. "Every woman has a thing for your husband. Get used to it."

Sophia drops her death grip on Jasalie's arm. "I'm so sorry," she says contritely. "I didn't mean to be so rude. Dylan Wild is just... well, he's freaking beautiful."

We all laugh, and Jasalie smiles. "He is. Even more on the inside, though."

"And that's why we love her," Cam says, wrapping his arm around her shoulders. "She was never a screaming fangirl."

Sophia beams at Jasalie. "You and Dylan give me hope," she says. She glances over her shoulder. "Awesome. Slammer's here!"

She rushes off, and I catch eyes with Brayden, who says quietly, "My cousins flew into town unexpectedly."

"That's nice," I murmur.

"Hey, Bray," Cam calls over to him. "Your bro just walked in."

Brayden glances behind me. "That's Luke."

I turn to see a guy who looks an awful lot like Brayden but with dark hair instead of blond. He takes off his cowboy hat as he comes closer, and I note the same piercing blue eyes and muscular build. But his expression is harder than Brayden's even though he's grinning. He bears a jagged scar on his right cheek, but that doesn't take away from his attractiveness; instead, it almost adds to his rugged sex appeal. He oozes hot cowboy, and he knows it. He smirks at me as he joins our group and nods hello to Brayden.

"Long time," he says as he gives Cam and Ayden hugs. He turns to Bella. "Holy fuck—I haven't seen you in ages. You look beautiful."

"Ayden and Bella are engaged," Brayden says to him.

"What—you think I'm hitting on her?" Luke laughs. "She's like a little sister."

Bella kisses Luke on the cheek. "And this is Dylan's wife, Jasalie," she says as Jasalie and Luke shake hands.

Brayden introduces me as the sister of the owner at Big Sky Grocer. Luke cocks his head and gives me an obvious once-over.

"You two go back?" he says immediately as he jerks his thumb at Brayden.

"Um..." I stammer. "Sort of."

"Sort of, huh?" He winks at me. "That's what I thought."

"It's not like that," Brayden says in a hard tone. "Shut the fuck up, Luke."

Luke puts his hands up in a surrender gesture. "Hey, I meant nothing by it. You two just look like you aren't only connected through your employer's sister. You're far too cozy for that."

Cam grins. "My thoughts exactly."

Sophia returns with Slammer, whose hand is already on her ass.

She laughs at something he says in her ear, and then she catches eyes with Luke.

Who's unabashedly staring at her.

"And who are you?" he asks her, his blue eyes lazily scanning her from head to toe.

Sophia loves attention of any kind, and she turns on the charm. "I'm Leleila's best friend. Sophia Loren."

"Like the actress?" Luke says right away.

She smiles. "Nope. My mom's a drunk who probably never should have procreated, and she named me that accidentally."

Sophia may not have caught the way Luke flinches at her story, but I did. He covers by saying hey to Slammer, and then a woman proceeds to scream his name and throw herself at him.

His easy-going attitude returns, and he gives the red-headed woman a squeeze while he flirts with her. Sophia rolls her eyes and returns to flirting with Slammer. But Luke's attention keeps flicking back to Sophia, who's acting oblivious.

"Hey, Sophia Loren," he calls over as the redhead huffs and walks away.

Sophia twists around in Slammer's arms. "What?"

A smile plays around his lips. "How come you're in a bar if your mom's an alcoholic?"

"Christ, Luke." Brayden glares at him. "Try the polite route once in a while. It won't kill you."

Sophia's face turns red.

I don't think I've ever seen her embarrassed.

She steps away from Slammer and walks right up to Luke. Then she keeps walking until he backs up a step. His eyes are burning into hers, and she jabs her index finger at his chest.

"You. Don't talk about my mother again. Ever." Another finger jab. "Only I can talk about my own mother, not some cocky-ass cowboy who looks like he had to quit the rodeo a little early. Are we clear, Mr. Wild?"

Luke clears his throat as he and Sophia continue to engage in some sort of long-ass staring contest.

He breaks first. "We're clear, Ms. Loren."

She steps back from him. "Good." Then, she whips around, her hair flying off her back, and returns to Slammer's side.

I take a seat at the bar, sensing this is going to be a long night.

———

A couple hours later, I'm sitting on the same bar stool with Brayden and Sophia on either side of me. I'm on my second beer and have a little buzz going, and I haven't seen anything but Sophia's back for the last hour. She's been wrapped up in a tongue-wrestling match with Glenn Slammer.

Luke has disappeared somewhere, and Brayden and I are chatting with the others. Everyone's really friendly, and I can't remember the last time I enjoyed hanging out at a bar. The few times Sophia has dragged me to one, I've counted down the minutes until we could leave. My party side began and ended with one bad night all those years ago. Even through four years of college, I never enjoyed socializing.

But tonight, I'm having fun.

When Cam, Ayden, and Brayden get into a long conversation about football and the Cougars' chances to repeat as champions, Jasalie and Bella huddle around my stool. They're both genuinely nice, and Jasalie tells me about her upcoming wedding renewal. I've been to the venue she's looking at tomorrow, and it's beautiful.

"I'm not getting married in anything other than the city courthouse," I say with a laugh. "But one of my sister's employees got married at The Montana Club, and it's very nice. You'll love it."

Jasalie and Bella both furrow their brows.

"What?" I ask them in confusion.

"When you said you're getting married in a courthouse," Jasalie says, "you sounded so positive. Almost like you're already..."

"I'm engaged," I say, holding up my left hand. "I'm getting married in a month."

Bella peers down at the red string tied around my ring finger. "I had no idea," she says softly, her eyes confused as she glances at Brayden's back, which has straightened. "We thought that maybe..."

"That you were with Brayden," Jasalie finishes for her. "Or at least, that you were available to maybe be with Brayden. But," she adds brightly, "you're obviously not. Congratulations on your engagement."

Her sentiment is meant as sincere, but I hear the hollowness behind her words. It almost sounds like she's disappointed.

"Brayden knows," I say hastily. "My relationship is no secret."

Next to me, Brayden's shoulders tense.

Bella scrunches up her nose. "So you and Brayden are just friends?"

"Yes." I open my mouth to tell her about our arrangement as dance partners when Brayden jerks around to face us.

"Leleila." His tone is neutral. "Did you get your keys back yet?"

I shake my head, but like magic, my phone buzzes. I glance down and read Phillip's text that he'll be home in an hour and will text me when he's leaving campus.

I hold up my phone. "In about an hour."

Brayden glances behind me at Sophia. "I can drive you if Sophia wants to stay."

He sounds like he wants to get rid of me. I can't blame him, but my chest aches nonetheless.

I thank him for the offer, and he excuses himself for the restroom.

As soon as he's gone and Bella starts chatting with Ayden and Cam, Jasalie says to me, "Leleila, since you live so close by, I hope you'll be able to come to my and Dylan's wedding renewal in a few weeks."

Her gray eyes are wise like she's seen more than her share of pain. Swimming in the stormy depths, I catch a hint of sympathy as if she knows what it feels like to be trapped like a caged bird.

"Oh, that's such a nice invitation," I say. "I don't know if I can, but I really appreciate the offer."

"Think about it, okay?" She pauses and then says hurriedly, "I was engaged once, before Dylan."

I stare at her. "You were?"

She nods. "Not for long, but it was one of those moments where, as soon as I said yes, I wished I'd said no." Her expression is neutral, but her eyes flash with understanding when she adds in a tone so quiet there's no way anyone else could hear her, "We're always entitled to change our minds. And the thing I've learned is, when it's really right, we don't want to. All we want is to say yes forever."

Forever. Her word hits a nerve, and I excuse myself and go in search of the Ladies Room.

I've turned the corner to the hallway that leads to the bathrooms when a man texting on his phone steps out of the nearby alcove.

And my world stops.

I thought he'd left Montana.

I know he'd left Montana.

Noah Rice is walking toward me. The very same Noah Rice who assaulted me twelve years ago.

CHAPTER THIRTEEN

His attention is on his phone, and he stops walking momentarily to lean against the wall. But I know I need to move quickly if I don't want to be seen.

Still, my feet are locked to the floor.

I'm screwed.

But then...

An angel, in the form of Brayden Wild, steps out of the Men's Room across from me. Our eyes catch.

Terrified he's going to say my name, I act on instinct. I cross over to him and, using his body as a shield, I throw my arms around his neck and bury my face in his chest. His flannel shirt smells so good—like detergent and pasture and him.

His arms go around me immediately, and he presses me against the wall. From Noah's angle, it would be impossible to see my face.

"Hey! Noah!" A raspy voice comes from behind me. "You ready to get out of here? This place blows like always."

"Yeah, let's go into Missoula," Noah says in response. "Glad I'm only here for the weekend. I forgot how fucking boring it is here."

Hearing their voices get closer, I keep my face pressed against Brayden's solid chest, and he rubs my back with one hand while keeping the other on my hair.

I stay motionless until the sound of the footsteps disappears, and then I let out a ragged breath.

"They're gone," Brayden says in my ear.

I pick my head up and stare up into the cool blue depths of his eyes.

His arms are still wrapped around my back, and I step back cautiously.

"I'm so sorry," I say to him as I smooth down my hair. "I just... that was..."

"I know who it was." Brayden scowls. "Let me get you out of here. You can text Sophia once we're in the truck."

All I can do is nod.

Brayden's warm hand touches the small of my back as he guides me through the hallway. "We'll go through the back, and I'll text Cam to let him know. I'm parked on a side street."

A shiver runs through me. "Okay."

———

"Phillip's still not home," is all I can think of to say once Brayden and I are in his truck and he's finished texting Cam. "So I can't get into my house yet."

"It's okay," he says softly. "Are you hungry?"

"Starved," I admit. "Sophia was more worried about dressing me up than eating before we went out. Thus my outfit. I'm pretty sure I'm way overdressed for a bar."

"You look gorgeous," he says casually as he puts his hands on the wheel.

I press my hands onto my lap to stop them from doing something crazy like touching him. "Thank you." I send off a quick text to Sophia to let her know I'm leaving and will talk to her tomorrow.

"How about we stop at Clyde's, the new steakhouse on Main Street?" Brayden asks me. "Do you eat meat?"

"Yes." And while I feel a bit guilty eating somewhere that

Phillip was so disapproving of, I know it's a good decision. There's no way Noah and his friend will go out for dinner right now. They're too busy trying to find the best place to get drunk. "That sounds great."

We take seats across from one another at a private booth in the back. No other customers are seated in our section, and I feel the relief of it being just Brayden and me. The dark wood paneling of the walls is filled with large photographs of Montana. Two beautiful pictures of Glacier National Park and Flathead Lake are closest to our booth.

"I'd love to paint one of those scenes," I say spontaneously.

Brayden looks at the photographs and then returns his gaze to me. "I saw what you did with the sign outside June's store. Looks like a professional artist did it."

I flush with heat. "Thank you. I used to dream of painting for a living, but then..." I wave my hand in the air. "Life got busy with more important things."

Half-wishing I hadn't blurted that out, I open my menu. Rib-eyed steak and potato. That sounds so good. And it's a special tonight, which means it's within my price range.

The waiter comes over, and Brayden and I each order a steak special for dinner. I'm relieved that I can feel my slight buzz wearing off already even though I haven't eaten yet. Just leaving the bar seems to have sobered me up. And I've always loved steak. Phillip only eats red meat on occasion; I've learned to seriously curb my carnivore tendencies since we moved in together.

"I've been wanting to try this place," I say to Brayden. "Thanks for suggesting it."

"Sure. I saw it as soon as it opened, but I never had an occasion to eat here."

I take a sip of my water.

"Leleila," Brayden says in a careful tone. "We need to talk."

I keep hold of the water glass in my hand, staring down at the clear liquid. "That's the first time I've seen him since I was sixteen," I say quietly. "I'm sorry you were there."

"I'm not," he says. "But I hate seeing you upset. I want to help."

"I know he can't hurt me," I say. "I just don't want to dredge up old memories. He got kicked out of school shortly after the party and left town to go to a private school somewhere in Colorado. Then he played football for a big college in the south and even made the pros." I raise my gaze to meet his. "After it happened, but before he got kicked out, I went to the school counselor and told her I was going to report him."

"Let me guess." Brayden's blue eyes darken angrily. "She advised you not to. Said his football career would be over, and what happened wasn't really that bad."

I inhale. "That's scary how close to the mark you are. She said nearly those exact same words. She added that *my* reputation would be ruined; that it didn't matter what he did or did not do; no one would believe me. And without any evidence..."

Brayden reaches over and drops his warm, heavy hand over mine. Tears clog my throat, and I fight them back.

"I was a kid," I say with a shrug that I hope deflects from how affected I am. "I believed her. I like to think that as an adult, I wouldn't listen to her. But the fact is that in court, my story probably wouldn't hold up. I had no witnesses to what went on inside that bedroom."

"I saw..." Brayden starts to say.

But I shake my head. "You saw a guy knocked on the floor. Sure, I had a cut on my cheek, but he could have claimed self-defense. He could have claimed anything at all, and without an eyewitness, it would have been my word against his. Maybe if I'd gone to the police straightaway, but even then..." I pause. "Noah has a lot of connections in this town. To the PD, to the mayor, you name it. His family's been around for generations."

Brayden rubs my hand. "I'm sorry you had to see him tonight."

"I was lucky," I say honestly. "I escaped, and he disappeared from my life. Him being expelled from school for dealing drugs felt like nothing short of a miracle. He's one of those guys who always seemed like he could get away with anything."

Something flickers behind Brayden's eyes.

I open my mouth to ask him what he's thinking, but before I can, the server comes by with our meals.

And we both settle in to eat.

Eating is a nice respite from the heavy conversation, and the steak is delicious. The tension from running into Noah starts to subside, and I smile at Brayden.

"So what happened with your plans?" he asks me in a curious tone. "The PhD and all?"

I tell him about my data, about how Gerry said my heart wasn't in it, how I thought it was perfectly clear, and how Phillip swore up and down that I'd pass for sure.

"It sounds dumb when I talk about it out loud like this," I say. "It's not life and death, and I'm beyond lucky to have had the opportunity at all. It's just a diploma, but for some reason, it felt like my whole future rested on it, like Phillip and I wouldn't..." I trail off before I finish the sentence with, *"like Phillip and I wouldn't make it if I failed."*

Brayden clears his throat and shifts direction. "So you had big plans once you got your degree? You're gonna save the world, too —make your parents proud?"

I take a bite of steak and look away from him as I chew it. "I used to think so. But right now, I'd be happy just having a clear plan of what to do next."

"Maybe you're too focused on the PhD," Brayden suggests as he finishes his meal. "You should do something you enjoy for a bit and see what happens."

"You enjoy working on the ranch? And coaching football?"

"I don't want to do anything else," he says. "What about you? You have a talent for painting for sure."

I tell him acrylics and oils were always my favorites. "But

when I went to Montana Art Supplies and purchased supplies for Big Sky Grocer, I thought maybe I'd get some paints for myself so I could work at home. It was so overwhelming I just walked out."

"I'll go with you if you want," he offers.

"You know about paints?" I say with a smile.

"Not a thing," he says. "But you obviously do. Maybe you just need a friend there."

My throat constricts, and I fight the emotion back. Because Brayden is a friend. More of a friend than I'm used to and more than I ever imagined I could find in a man. I don't know why God would put someone like Brayden into my path just to have it all end in a few short weeks.

"Yeah?" he says, raising his hand for the check. "We'll stop there now."

I glance at my phone. Phillip still hasn't texted. "I don't have much time."

"This will just take a few extra minutes," Brayden says. "Then I'll drop you home."

Brayden has his credit card out and has handed it to the server before I can blink.

"Thank you for the dinner," I say sincerely. "I'll treat next time."

He smiles at me, and it lights up his whole face. "You feeling better?"

I nod. "Definitely. I think I just needed to unwind before I go home. In general, I'm not a social person; I hardly ever go out to a party or a bar."

"Even when you were younger?"

"Not really. I tended to avoid high school parties after..." I cut off. "And college was more of the same."

My face heats as I remember my college roommate freshman year. Marnie went out five nights a week and called me uptight and boring behind my back. I told myself I had a boyfriend, that I didn't need to socialize like all those girls who just went out to get drunk and try to hook up, but her words hurt me nonetheless. Phillip was off at Princeton, and I was alone in Colorado.

"Were you with someone in college?" Brayden asks.

I notice he doesn't ask me if I was with Phillip— just if I was with someone.

"Yes."

June was constantly surprised that Phillip and I stayed together through those four years apart. Every Christmas break when I came home, she would greet me with, "Did you guys break up yet?"

Then Phillip returned to Mountainview, and I did too, and while he was spending all those years obtaining his PhD, I was working toward mine as well. He finished early, and I was by his side, holding his hand through the all-nighters, editing his thesis and sitting in the front row as he delivered it. We knew getting married before he finished school made no sense, but then we delayed a bit longer until he was granted tenure and we had the security. Breaking up was never on the table, not in our conversations and not in my head. Whether or not it was in my heart, I can only guess.

I shrug. "I know the percentage for couples staying together through four years of college when they're at different schools is probably nil, but I'm kind of weird, I guess."

"Maybe you just like beating the odds," Brayden suggests.

Maybe. Or maybe I just didn't know any better.

———

The art store parking lot is nearly empty when Brayden pulls his truck into a spot.

"Maybe they're closed," I say. "I don't want to go to the front door and have them just wave me away. That's always awkward."

"This type of place usually stays open pretty late," Brayden says as we step out of the truck.

Sure enough, the store's open. We walk inside, and I practically drag Brayden down the aisles, waving away a male employee who calls out to ask if we need help.

We reach the paint supplies aisle, and I reach out impulsively and touch his arm. "Thank you for coming here with me."

He puts his hand on my hair gently. For a moment, he almost looks like he's going to kiss my head. But he doesn't. Instead, he turns quickly toward the shelves of paints and brushes and asks me what I'm thinking of starting with.

We've just left the store with a bag of paints, brushes, and some canvases when Phillip texts that he's home.

And I feel ready to face him.

I'm going to tell him what happened to me twelve years ago. Instinctively, I know it's partially why I've had such issues in the bedroom, and maybe by sharing my story, it will help us to figure out a solution.

As we head across the parking lot for Brayden's truck, I say, "Your cousins are really nice. And Jasalie and Bella too. Jasalie even invited me to her wedding renewal."

Brayden slows up, nearly coming to a stop. "She what?"

"It surprised me too." I let out a quick laugh. "She's really welcoming."

"She can be." His lip twitches. "If she doesn't like you, look out. She's very loyal, and she keeps a small circle of people around her."

"Nothing wrong with that."

"Not at all. I love her. She and Dylan are really perfect for each other. We were all worried he'd never find someone who didn't give a shit about his fame or his money, and then he met Jasalie."

"It sounds like a fairytale romance."

"It was in a way." Brayden's gaze turns serious as he looks at me. "If you want to go to her and Dylan's wedding, you're absolutely welcome. Don't feel awkward because of me. I didn't mean to make it feel weird."

"I know. But I hardly know her." Plus, I'm pretty sure Jasalie was trying to play hopeful matchmaker between Brayden and me.

He starts walking faster again, and when we reach his truck, he unlocks it and holds the door while I climb in. Our eyes catch and hold as I'm fixing my dress so I don't flash him, and a spark of current zips between us.

Brayden freezes with his hand on the door, and time stops as we stare at each other in the silent, otherwise-empty parking lot.

This is a moment I would have killed for were I single. This is one of those first "I think I really do like you as much as I hoped I would and actually much more" moments, and yet I can't go home and dance around my room about it.

Brayden and I are so different. But he looks perfect to me. And he makes me feel like I could be perfect for him too.

I reach for my seat belt, and the moment snaps. Brayden backs up and shuts my door and then walks around to the driver's side.

He starts the truck and pulls out of the lot before he speaks again.

"I didn't tell them you were engaged because I didn't tell them about you at all," he says to me.

Ouch. "That's okay. I understand."

"That sounded shitty." He runs his hand through his hair, looking agitated. "What I meant was I'm typically a very private person. To be honest, you're the first woman in my life that any of them have met. Well, since high school when I was around Dyl and Colt every day."

My lips part. "Wow."

A quick nod is his only response.

"I'm sorry if running into me tonight made things awkward then," I say. "It seemed like you kind of wanted to rush me out of there at the end."

"I did." His jaw tightens. "I heard you talking to Bella and Jasalie about your fiancé, and I knew they'd never let up on the gas. And once my cousins overheard? Those two are unstoppable when it comes to digging for any clues. They would have wanted to know everything, and I didn't want to put you through that. Our history of how we met—yours and mine—is...unusual, and it's none of their business."

"I get it." This conversation has taken a completely awkward turn, and the chemistry between us is simmering at a level far beyond simple attraction. Brayden's gaze is hot as he glances over at me while he's driving, and I have to squeeze my thighs together to maintain any sort of composure.

We reach my house, and I step out quickly and wave goodbye. As Phillip lets me inside the house, I look back once. Brayden's truck is just disappearing around the corner.

CHAPTER FOURTEEN

"Lei!" Phillip kisses my cheek as I step inside the foyer. "How was your night?"

"It was okay," I look up into his eyes. "Listen, I need to talk to you."

"Hi, Leleila."

I jump at the female voice and turn to see a pretty woman with a face that's so familiar I do a double-take. It takes me a minute to realize why: she looks exactly like Phillip but in female form. It's actually shocking.

"Mindy, this is my fiancée, Leleila." Phillip smiles broadly. "Leleila, this is Dr. Mindy Cox."

She's wearing a wrap-around black skirt that falls to the floor and a thick white Irish sweater with a dark turtleneck underneath. Her hair is worn down and falls to about her shoulders. It's thin, straight hair, like Phillip's, and the same color brown. Her eyes are what strike me the most. They're not only the same color as Phillip's. They're set back in her face the same way, and they have that same lifeless look his often have, especially after he's been working a lot. Her eyes look so tired and have such dark circles underneath them I almost ask her if she's okay.

She shakes my hand and smiles. I smile back, but my chest tightens as we stand across from each other.

"What's going on?" I say politely.

"Mindy needs help with her research," Phillip explains. "I drove her here from the university so she could take a look at my specimen."

I don't want to touch that sentence.

Phillip's still smiling. I can't remember the last time he was this genuinely enthusiastic about something.

He heads for his microscope. "Mindy, come sit here." He pats the seat next to him on the couch, the exact spot where I usually sit with him when he works. "It will just take a moment to get my specimen set up."

Oh my God. It's like porn for scientists. I go into the kitchen and make myself a cup of chamomile tea. I feel rude not offering a cup to Mindy or Phillip, so I go back out to the living room.

"Does anyone want some tea?"

Mindy shakes her head no, but Phillip's so wrapped up in his specimen he doesn't even hear me come into the room. And when he does finally notice me, he barely reacts before going back to the microscope.

"Sorry, honey," he says with his left eye trained on the lens. "This specimen's fresh, so it's best if we work with it now."

"Don't let me interrupt you." I return to the kitchen and take a seat on one of the bar stools at the counter. I stare out the dark window aimlessly for what seems like forever although, in reality, it's probably only about fifteen minutes.

Then I hear talking. Enthusiastic, animated talking that I tune out as fast as I can. I do not want to hear any more talk about specimens.

"Lei! Are you in there?"

I get off the stool and walk into the living room. "I'm right here."

"Great." Phillip looks at Mindy, and they smile widely at each other.

When he turns back to me, it almost feels like he has to force his head to rotate in my direction because he doesn't want to stop looking at Mindy. I can see it clearly in his expression—he doesn't want to stop staring into her eyes.

"Mindy and I were going to go grab a drink before we call it a night," Phillip says to me.

"I love that vegan restaurant that serves Kombucha tea." Mindy turns to me politely. "Would you like to join us?"

I close my eyes. Maybe when I re-open them, Phillip and Mindy will have disappeared to their kombucha restaurant, and I'll be left here alone. But when I open my eyes, they're both still here, waiting for my answer.

"I'm not thirsty," I say lamely. "Why don't you two go? Phillip, I'll see you when you get back."

As soon as they walk out the door, all the tension that had been festering inside the house goes with them.

I decide to air-dry the soil samples I gathered this afternoon so I can get a quick look at them under Phillip's scope once they're ready.

I call Sophia, hoping to catch her before she goes to bed. No answer. She probably spent the night with Slammer, and I'll hear from her tomorrow with details I don't want to know.

I feel so down I sit at the computer and email my parents. I don't know what possesses me to do it; the chances of them writing back are next to nil. But I miss my mother right now, and I'd love to know when they're coming home.

As soon as I hit send, I feel so restless I think I may go out of my mind. I walk around the house in a circle for over five minutes, finally flopping down on the living room floor in exhaustion. I lie on my back and realize, from this angle, I can see the stars through the window. I relax into the carpet, grabbing my afghan off the sofa to put over me.

I remember lying on Brayden's rug with him the other day and how easy it felt to be with him. I close my eyes and breathe, giving myself permission to be still in a way I never have.

Something about tonight has me all sorts of wired, and I'm desperate for a way to relax. I slip my hand inside my pants, and I don't hold back from making myself feel good. I can't stop the unbidden fantasies that come to mind as I'm touching myself—images of a blond, gruff cowboy with his head between my legs. The sensations hitting me are so intense I moan out loud. And when I reach that place I haven't been in a long time with Phillip, I'm surprised to feel tears stain my cheeks.

I rarely touch myself. And when I do, I never achieve orgasm. But thinking about Brayden Wild just got me off, my orgasm rocking my body with a power I've never felt before. Guilt overwhelms me, and I sit up, fix my jeans, and try to smooth my hair back into a ponytail.

I go upstairs to wash the tears off my face. I'm not sure where all the emotion is coming from. Maybe it's relief because I never knew I could do this by myself. I never knew I could do what *I* wanted, something just for me, for no other reason than that I deserve to be happy.

When Phillip's still not home after I've taken a shower, I give up on talking to him tonight. I climb into bed alone and turn off the light.

———

Brayden

I drive back to the ranch, but I don't go directly to my house after dropping Leleila off. I can't. I'm so fucking wired from spending time with her—I feel like my dick is going to explode.

And my heart. Because the vulnerable way Leleila threw herself at me when she saw that excuse for a human being in the bar—it was all I could do not to put my mouth on hers until she calmed down.

Knowing that wasn't an option, I went for the second best thing I could think of; I held her. Taking her to dinner and getting a chance to know her, to talk, was the highlight of my night. Leleila's funny and quirky and down-to-earth. She's also ridiculously smart, which just might be the only thing she and her fiancé have in common.

I drive along the dirt path through the back of the property and pass by the edge of an open field. Stars litter the sky, and as I watch, a shooting star crosses above me. I keep driving, though, because the kind of dreams I'm wishing for right now involve a woman who's not available. And that's not the kind of guy I am. I want Leleila to get married to the man she loves and to live a happy life. She deserves that. If I can help her get there by being her friend, I'm happy to do it. And if it hurts? That's something I'll have to figure out how to work through.

Everything will be fine. Leleila and her fiancé will get married. I'll buy the ranch. And we'll go our separate ways.

Trying to ignore the ache in my chest, I turn for home.

By the time I step inside the guesthouse, Ayden and Bella are asleep in my room, Jasalie's in the spare room, and Cam's sacked out on the couch. Not wanting to talk about Leleila, I sneak past him and go out to the porch to try to get some sleep.

As soon as Leleila walked into the saloon, I knew Cam and Ayden were going to see right through me.

That's why I've always kept my personal life private. I love my cousins, but having five nosy guys is as bad as five curious women. Maybe worse because my cousins aren't polite or civil about wanting to be in on a secret; they just keep pushing until they know everything.

———

Sure enough, while the five of us are touring Jasalie and Dylan's wedding venue the next day, Cam and Ayden corner me when the three of us are outside taking a break from hearing about flower arrangements and meal options. The mountains are all around us, and the air is still and quiet. It's peaceful, and the sun is shining. But I know what's coming, and Cam doesn't disappoint.

"So. Leleila's a nice name." Cam's tone is light, but I know he's just getting started.

I point at him. "Don't."

"She's got a nice ass, too."

I'm on him so fast he doesn't have time to fight back. I pin one arm behind his back and wrestle him face first onto the grass. Not enough to shut him up, though.

"And a nice rack," he says in a tone meant to drive me over the edge.

I dig my knee into his thigh until he curses. I'd keep going, but Ayden's involved now; two strong arms wrap around my middle, forcing me to release my youngest cousin, who I want to put through the damn picture window not ten feet away from us.

"Cam, back the fuck up," Ayden says. "Forcing Brayden to talk about a woman never works."

Cam flips over onto his back. His face is red, but his devilish grin is still in place. "You can't keep her from us forever," he says. "What's the big deal, anyway? You obviously like her."

I don't say anything; instead, I pick up a stray rock and chuck it toward the open field to our left. It doesn't come close to hitting the mountains, but it sails.

Ayden whistles. "You can still throw. You'd think you'd played quarterback and not receiver."

Some of the unbearable tension I've been feeling since last night leaves my shoulders, and I let out a deep exhale.

Ayden takes a seat next to Cam on the ground, and I sink down to a squat in front of them.

"She's fucking taken." My voice is so quiet I'd have thought they didn't hear me except for Cam's low whistle. "Bella and Jasalie didn't say anything?"

"Bella said something, but honestly, I had a little too much to drink, and I was so jetlagged I didn't really understand what she was saying," Ayden says.

"Well, she's got someone else."

"But she's not married." Ayden sounds certain. "I didn't see a wedding band, and she acts…"

"Lonely," Cam finishes.

"That's because she is," I say roughly.

I take a breath and tell them about our arrangement.

"You agreed to help her prepare for her first dance with her husband?" Ayden says incredulously.

"Her fiancé sounds like a selfish bastard," Cam says.

I frown. "That's what I'm afraid of."

Cam stares at me hard. "You fucking like her."

"I would never hit on someone who's taken."

"Not saying you would, but you want her all the same. And you can't have her. You can't use your Brayden Wild moves to woo her, either." He says it jokingly, but the heaviness behind his words is weighty.

Ayden's eyes flash with sympathy. "Sucks, man."

I exhale. They're right. I'm fucking screwed.

CHAPTER FIFTEEN

Leleila

Phillip and I spend all of Sunday in our pajamas, going over his research. My courage from last night has disappeared, and I don't tell him about Noah. I also don't ask him about his new friendship with Mindy. His bike race is Tuesday, and he's anxious about everything. He keeps asking me if I think he has enough convincing evidence to support his claims regarding poisons in the ecosystem and how they negatively affect life on the planet, including humans.

"Yes," I say with a confidence I don't quite feel. "I definitely think you have enough evidence."

"Don't be influenced by your emotions," he says to me, his eyes bloodshot from the hours of reading and re-reading. "Just because you want me to be right doesn't mean I am."

I stop in the middle of my train of thought and stare at him. I don't know that I've ever thought about it in those terms before.

"What you need to do is get your emotions out of the way," Phillip continues. "Pretend I'm a stranger and you're hearing these results for the first time. Would you believe it? Or would you think it was forced?"

I reach over and touch his cheek, which is chapped from his bike rides.

Looking for a way to get his mind off his own worries, I tell him about the container at the ranch. "It's right by the reservoir," I say. "I mean the land backs to it. It could be a really big deal."

"You alerted the ranch owners?" he asks me.

"First, I'm sending a sample out to be analyzed."

"Leave it alone, Lei," he says. "Don't get involved where you don't belong."

"It's not that simple," I say. "The owners of the ranch are going through a tough time, and Brayden doesn't want to alarm them unduly..."

"So you're doing it all yourself?" Phillip frowns. "Honey, you're being naïve. I'm sure it's nothing, anyway. Just because a container says something doesn't mean it's truly dangerous."

"I just have a bad feeling in my gut."

"It should never come down to your gut," Phillip says. "Not as a scientist. Because then you'll be influenced by your emotions, and science must come from the brain."

"Speaking of me and science," I say. "I ran into Gerry at the store."

I tell Phillip what he said. "Every day that goes by, I just feel like my goal is slipping away from me," I admit.

Phillip rubs my arm. "I could try to talk to him if you want. Maybe he'll cave and agree to let you re-try your dissertation before we get married."

"That would be amazing," I say. "Thank you, honey. You've always been there for me."

I lean over and hug him. He gives me a light squeeze before turning his eye back to the lens.

———

By the day of Phillip's bike race, the soil samples are dried and ready, and I decide to see if anything shows up on a slide before taking them to Save the Soil.

Phillip leaves early for class, and I promise him I'll be waiting at the rest stop outside June's store when he bikes by later this afternoon. Once he's gone, I check the soil samples I took with Brayden. They're sufficiently dried, so I fish around on Phillip's shelf for a clean slide that's large enough.

I know I won't be able to decipher much with my limited knowledge, and I know a microscopic exam is more outdated than the methods now in use, but I want to see if anything looks different between the two samples before I involve Save the Soil.

The soil fills each slide easily, and I put my eye to the lens.

The first sample, the one taken from Big River, looks the way I would expect. But the second one doesn't.

It looks ... off. But I'm not an ecologist, and I have no clue what I'm actually looking at. I just know it doesn't look right, not from all the samples I've had to look at for both my parents and for Phillip through the years. I know enough to spot an abnormality. So I place the slide into a plastic bag, making sure to keep it flat and immobile, and then I gather up the two core samples.

I jump in my car and drive to Save the Soil.

"I need you to send this out for analysis," I say to Patsy, handing her the slide and jar of soil. "I'll fill out a form, but this soil needs to be analyzed for toxins and contaminants ASAP. And let me know when the results are in—I want a rush order on them, please."

When I walk into Big Sky Grocer, I immediately look around for Brayden. I haven't seen him since he drove me home. I don't see him anywhere, and I try to push down the feeling of disappointment in my gut.

"I'm going to start painting the mural today," I say to June.

"Great. But before you do that, I have a favor."

She sets me up at the cash registers. "It's not hard," she insists. "I just have no one to cash right now—Kim called in sick, and I have a vendor meeting in two minutes. Just scan and total. The codes for bagels and fruits are here." She shows me the list taped next to the register. "And the morning crowd will pick up any minute now, so get ready."

Talk about being thrown right in. The line is around the corner and down the aisle within a half hour. Gerry comes by and asks if we can meet for lunch later in the week. Something about the way he asks makes my stomach twist with nerves, but I don't have time to ask him what's going on. So I say yes gratefully and am momentarily buoyed, only to inwardly cringe when Dr. Matt Lucas comes through the line.

"So this is what you've been doing since you took a break from school," he jokes.

"Just helping out my sister," I say with a fake smile.

Brayden happens to be stocking magazines by the register, and I catch him giving Dr. Lucas a hard stare, a stare that grows more pronounced when Matt adds, "Remind me never to fail my dissertation, huh? It's a hard fall."

I grit my teeth and don't answer him, but the receipt paper in the register manages to pick this time to snag. The entire line gets held up, and I can't unsnag it.

Brayden jumps over the counter, so I get a great view of his ass while he's unwinding the paper, and that almost makes up for what Matt Lucas is loudly going on about for the whole store to hear.

"Seriously, Leleila, you holding up okay?" he presses me. "You really should take my wife's "Spousal Support for Professors" class. It would give you something to focus on."

I try to interrupt with a quick, "I'm fine, really," but Dr. Lucas won't stop. "I feel like I'd have nothing without my research. But I admire your fortitude. Honestly, I don't know how you're getting up in the morning."

"Leleila's doing great," Brayden says abruptly as he jumps off the counter and Matt's receipt finally prints. "She doesn't need any letters after her name to tell her that."

Matt Lucas turns red and leaves quickly.

I swallow and turn to Brayden. "Thanks," I say quickly.

His gaze slides over me like he's checking for injuries.

"I'm fine," I assure him. "And while I appreciate your support, that guy you embarrassed is Phillip's boss."

"Well, he should have more respect for you," he says, his jaw tight as he turns back to his work.

I agree with him. But Matt Lucas is typical of a lot of Phillip's colleagues—too smart for his own good.

I finish cashing in relative peace, and then I spend the rest of the morning at the big white wall at the front of the store. With the image of Brayden on his horse in my mind, I begin to sketch.

A long while later, I step back to see what I've done.

A cowboy on what will be a chestnut-colored horse stands proudly in the foreground with large pastureland behind him. Snow-capped mountain peaks, lush green grass, and Montana's signature big sky surround the scene. The mural typifies Mountainview, and my hope is it will showcase the store's aisles filled with local produce, meats, and cowboy tack and gear. I'm so immersed in my work I don't stop to think about the fact that anyone and everyone will have their eyes on it. It's been years since I painted, and I don't really know what possessed me to do something so crazy as to paint a mural in the middle of a public space.

"Don't worry," I say to myself. "You can cover it completely with a solid color if it looks like crap when you're done."

I pick up a paintbrush and start to bring the sketch to life.

I'm immersed in my work when my phone buzzes, alerting me to Phillip's bike race. He should be coming around the corner in the next half hour, and I need to make sure I'm ready.

I drop all the brushes into a bucket to soak, clean up the drop cloth, and go find June.

When I find her standing with Brayden by the front door, my heart rate picks up.

My physiological reaction has nothing to do with the hot, sexy cowboy next to her. Not at all.

"I'm off to the pit stop," I say to her as I jerk my chin toward the outdoors. "Phillip should be here soon, and you know how much support he needs at these races. I'm the only one he's trained."

Brayden cocks an eyebrow. "He trained you?"

I sigh. "If you glance out the window when the riders come by, you'll see what I mean."

"Actually, Brayden," June says sweetly, and I could kill her. "I'm going to need help outside. I've got the bottled drinks and waters lined up at the table on the sidewalk as well as some on-the-go energy snacks. Would you mind staying out there when they come by?"

"Sure. I'm leaving for practice in an hour, but I'll work until then."

"Perfect."

As soon as Brayden leaves, June smirks at me. "This is going to be a fun bike race."

"Why?" I say suspiciously. "Who have you been talking to?"

"Mom."

"What do you mean?"

I smile when I hear that Mom and Dad are back in the country.

"I emailed them and never heard back," I say. "When did they get in?"

"Late last night. Apparently, Phillip called and invited them." June shrugs. "You know how he likes to show off to Dad, especially when he's eyeballs deep in research for a new paper he hopes to publish."

"But he won't even get to talk to Dad. Remember these races?"

"Oh, I think I do," June says. "I have nightmares about them still sometimes. Phillip's sweaty body hunched over his teeny-weeny bike and all of us standing there cheering him on while he demands you deliver him water and petroleum jelly for his chafing. Ugh."

She shudders at the memory, and I have to dig my heels into the ground to not join her. These bike races are so unpleasant.

She gives me a shove toward the door. "You should get out

there and stake your spot. And keep your cell with you so you can phone me in for a listen if things get really interesting."

———

.

As I make my way to the corner where the pit stop is located, I do a double-take.

I'm not the only one here from the Phillip Rowe Fan Club.

Mindy's in my spot. I say "my spot" because she's standing with her right foot directly next to the curb, in such a way that nobody can get next to her on that side and push her out. Phillip taught me to stand that way. Several people are lined up behind her, but nobody's getting in front of that girl. She knows her place, and she's not giving it up for anything.

I don't want to make small talk with her, but she nods at me immediately.

"Hello, Mindy." I nod back. "How are you?"

"Hello, Leleila." She nods again, and a flush slowly fills her cheeks, almost like she's guilty about something.

Probably the fact that she's got an obvious massive crush on my fiancé.

I introduce her to Brayden just as Sophia screams out, "Hi," while she and Slammer cross the street toward me.

"You skipped work for this?" I say to her when they reach me.

Sophia laughs. "Honey, I always find an excuse to skip work. You know that. Plus, my boss is away for the day. Nobody will even notice I'm gone. Slammer and I were going to get dessert tonight. You and Brayden should come with."

Brayden's blue eyes sparkle with mischief. "Where to, Sophia?"

She nods at him approvingly. "I have a surprise, something I know Lei will like."

Somehow I doubt that. "We have dance class tonight," I say with relief. "And I have Save the Soil after that."

"So we'll go hear you speak and then all go out. Right, Slam?"

The bulky guy with the blond crew cut and brown eyes nods amiably. "Sure thing."

Sophia turns to Brayden. "Leleila's speeches are pretty boring, but she looks hot giving them."

"Thank you for the support, Soph," I say sarcastically.

Sophia slings an arm around me. "You're a hot nerd. Nothing wrong with that."

"Where do you speak?" Brayden asks me, his gaze running over my face in a way that makes me sweat.

I tilt my head toward the building behind us. "In the suite right next to Big Sky Grocer. It's got a small auditorium, and people pile in there."

Sophia eyes Mindy. "Who's that?" she whispers too loudly.

"This is Phillip's colleague, Mindy Cox," I say politely.

As Sophia chats up Mindy, I feel like I'm going to throw up. Brayden glances over at me as he stands next to the refreshments table.

"Uncomfortable?" The corner of his mouth quirks up. "You seem tenser than usual."

I can't help smiling. Brayden's dirty blond hair is messily styled, and his dark shirt fits him perfectly. I've seen his jeans before, but even they look brand-new today, like they popped out of the washing machine full of answers, such as how to make all the uncertainty in my life fade away instantaneously.

Then my parents call out to me from the other corner. I wave at Mom and Dad as they hastily cross the street. Mom's got her sun hat on, the same one she wore in the Amazon.

"It's fall, Mom," I tease as soon as she and Dad reach us.

"What do you mean?" she asks me as she gives me a long hug.

"Fall." I touch her hat. "This is for hot jungles, not autumn days."

"She wanted to keep the sun out of her eyes," Dad explains. "Very practical."

This smile I've perfected in the last five minutes is a lifesaver. I can be as uncomfortable as I want, and nobody's actually certain what's going on because I just keep smiling. Brayden seems pretty certain, however. He's looking at me like I've gone a little loopy, and he seems like he wants to be anywhere but here right now. That would make two of us.

Sophia says hello to my parents and introduces them to Slammer. "And this is Brayden Wild," she says with a glance at me. "Brayden lives at Big River Ranch, but he does some work for Big Sky Grocer. Bet you didn't know that, did you?"

"No, we didn't." Mom shakes Brayden's outstretched hand and smiles at him. She's always been a sucker for men; June and I used to joke that if it had a penis, it worked for Mom.

Dad asks Brayden how long he's been working at the store just as Mindy clears her throat loudly.

"Oh, I'm sorry." I gesture to Mindy. "This is Dr. Mindy Cox, a friend of Phillip's."

"Oh, yes." Mom shakes her hand. "Phillip mentioned you would be joining us here. Welcome to Montana."

He *mentioned* her to them? Why?

"Yes, welcome," Dad says. "And you're also a scientist, I hear. What field?"

"Ecology, same focus as Phillip," Mindy says. "Although he's far more brilliant than I am in the subject. But we've already had the most wonderful time talking about the biochemistry of the alpine tundra and the forest ecosystems."

From my right, Brayden touches my shoulder ever so briefly, and as Mindy keeps trying to impress Dad, Mom glances at me with a pointed look. Her message is clear—she wants to know who this Mindy is and why she's at his race.

I shrug at her and try to divert her interest by focusing on their trip to New Zealand. "You both look good. Not too jetlagged."

"No." Dad runs his hand through his graying hair. "We're doing all right. We're a little on the reverse schedule, but that will clear up quickly."

"Right. Because you were over a half day ahead out there."

"Do you know hurricanes rotate in the opposite direction there?"

Dad always comes back from every trip with an assortment of fun facts. Sometimes, I say I don't need to go anywhere because there'd be nothing left to discover.

"Really?" I say. "That's neat."

Then Mom shows us all the mini hair wrap she had done in southern New Zealand. "Just one section of my hair, like a tiny braid," she explains.

"That's cool, Mom," I say. "It looks very trendy."

Brayden asks my parents how they enjoyed New Zealand.

"Oh, it was just gorgeous there. And our boat ride was wonderful." Just as Mom begins to gush about the boat and the calm seas they experienced, Mindy starts screaming.

"Here they come!" she shouts. "The racers are coming!"

Holy crap. You'd think this was the Tour de France. Even Dad gives me a quizzical look, but I just keep smiling. Mindy is Phillip's new friend, not mine.

Phillip's not in the first group of riders, but he comes screeching around the bend right behind them.

"Phillip!" Mindy waves wildly at him. "Over here!"

My father's "do I need to look out for my daughter" radar is on track as Dad tosses another concerned look in my direction. This time, I pretend not to notice, and I step forward to Phillip. He veers over to us and hops off the seat of his bike, remaining straddled over the middle bar. Sweat is everywhere— on his face, his shirt, I can even see it glistening on his handlebars.

"Lei!" Phillip shouts. "Do you have that second stopwatch? This one broke about ten miles back."

I rustle through my purse and give him what he's asking for. Mindy's eyes narrow, and she looks so jealous I think she's going to explode.

Sophia appears at my side. "How's it going, Phillip? You seem worked up."

"This is only a fifty miler," he says to her. "I don't have time to stop. I should be biking right now."

Mom and Dad say hello to him, and he turns politely to thank them for coming. Then he asks me for the petroleum jelly, which I hand to him wordlessly. He puts a little in his hand and returns the tube to me.

"Keep on spinning those wheels," Sophia advises him.

I take the new stopwatch out of Phillip's hand and snap it onto the front of his bike the way he taught me, and he hands me his broken one. Mindy leans in between us to tell him she'll meet him at the next station.

Phillip's already got one foot in a pedal. "You don't need to," he tells her as he smiles widely at her. "Ask Lei. It's quite difficult to make it through the crowds on time even if you did park close by." He forces his eyes away from Mindy's and back to mine. "I'll see you at home tonight? You have dance class, right?"

I nod and wish him luck and a safe ride. His wheels spin around and around as he cycles off. Soon they're spinning so fast it's all a blur, and then he's gone.

As soon as his bike disappears from view, Mindy throws her bag over her shoulder and hurries down the sidewalk, pushing people aside as fast as she can. She insists she's mapped out a shortcut where she can get to the next rest area on foot faster than he can bike past it. I don't have a clue what she's talking about, so I just nod and wave her on.

Mom and Dad have been watching this whole drama unfold with great interest. They heard my conversation with Phillip. They observed Mindy observe me with Phillip. And they listened to Mindy and Phillip's exchange. But it's when Brayden touches my back and carefully hands me the pink ruffled tie that fell out of my hair while I was clipping Phillip's stopwatch onto his bike that my parents really perk up.

Mom's eyes widen, and she turns fully so she can check Brayden out. Head to foot, my mother scans him. Apparently, she likes what she sees. "Leleila, since you and Brayden know each other," Mom says. "How would you both like to come over for tea?"

"Thanks, but we can't," I say quickly. "We have dance class."

"Dance class?" Mom says.

"I started learning for—" I don't know how to explain. "Phillip told me I had to get a new partner," I end up saying. "He couldn't dance with me. He was too busy."

Mom's jaw drops open, and Dad shifts so he can look more closely at Brayden.

"Phillip and Leleila asked if I could be her stand-in partner for the class," Brayden says hurriedly. "And I said sure." He smiles over at me. "We really enjoyed the first class. I didn't realize I liked dancing before this."

Mom and Dad turn their heads to me in unison.

"I actually really liked it," I say. "It was a lot more fun than I thought."

"For me, too," Brayden says. "It felt very natural."

"But you know. We're just beginners."

"The foundation is the key," Dad says. "If you've got that, the rest will be smooth sailing. Sure, you'll hit some gusts of winds, some squalls, but if you're rock solid on the foundation"—he raps his knuckles firmly on the telephone pole conveniently placed next to him—"then you've got it. You can write that ticket now."

My gaze shifts to Brayden, and I smile.

Mom and Dad say goodbye after that and head for home, and Sophia starts giggling as soon as they're out of earshot. "Look who's on her way back and at lightning speed."

Mindy's running toward us. I sigh.

"Wonder what the hurry's about," Brayden says.

Turns out we don't have too long to find out because Mindy reaches us within seconds and heads straight for me. She's so out of breath she can hardly get her words out, and as soon as she does, I wish she hadn't.

"Leleila," Mindy says. "Phillip had to stop again. He needs

petroleum jelly, and he says you always carry it in your purse for him. He's chafed," she adds in a low voice.

I glance at Brayden. Sophia and Slammer are grinning.

Without a word, I hand Mindy the petroleum jelly from my purse. "I just gave him some, and he doesn't usually need more this fast," I say. "But here you go."

"Thanks." She runs off to get the petroleum jelly to Phillip to help prevent any further chafing of his crotch.

Sophia collapses in laughter as soon as she's gone. "Phillip's identical twin with long hair," she whispers to me. "Does it look like there's something between them?"

"I don't know," I say, feeling sad. "Mindy looked like she was loving being here."

Sophia turns to face me. "And you looked the opposite— like you wanted to be anywhere but here."

I study her sharply. She's right, of course. I didn't want to be at the race, but I've never enjoyed being at those races. Being Phillip's cheerleader is clearly something Mindy enjoys more than I do, and there's never been room in his life for any other role.

CHAPTER SIXTEEN

Phillip comes home for dinner, and we spend most of the time talking about his upcoming conference. I remind him I have dance class and then Save the Soil, and he nods distractedly. He says he has to go back to the university for the evening, so after he leaves, I take my time getting ready for tonight. I take the advice I gave Brayden and dress casually in blue jeans and a long-sleeved green top that has a cute decorative tie in the back. The shirt matches my eyes, and when I look in the mirror, I'm surprised how alive my expression is. I normally look almost bored when I see myself in the mirror, but tonight something's different in my face, and it's a good thing.

———

Brayden insisted he would pick me up when he was done with practice so we could go to dance class together.

I'm already standing outside on our front steps when he pulls up in his truck and honks. I jump from the noise and then walk down the driveway, self-consciously pulling my hair down around my neck.

"Hi, Leleila," he says. "I didn't see you standing there; sorry to honk and scare you like that."

"That's okay," I say, smiling at him. "I was ready, so I just figured I'd wait for you outside."

We chat during the drive to the store, and when we step out and walk into the store, I inhale.

Because the way those black jeans hug his ass should be criminal.

I follow him up the stairs to class, and within ten minutes, we're standing across from one another. As usual for Brayden and me, it's awkward as hell. Because the tension...I swear I can see the air thickening around us.

"You ready?" Brayden locks eyes with me as Elroy shouts for us to start the waltz.

"Yep." I stand before him awkwardly before placing my hand in his.

As we begin to dance, Brayden asks me about my upcoming speech.

"There are always empty seats—Save the Soil isn't some big event, believe me. I met Sophia at one of the meetings."

"Really?" Brayden says. "She doesn't seem like she's that big on being in an audience."

"She's not. She was there trying to pick up a guy."

"Well, that makes more sense," he says as we both laugh.

The class goes quickly, too quickly. Before I know it, I'm stepping out of Brayden's arms and have restored the requisite distance between us for two people who aren't together.

Fantasy hour is over.

And I don't want to analyze the pang I have in my chest as I wave goodbye to him and head next door to get ready for my talk.

———

As soon as I reach the conference room, I hurry backstage. Sophia pops behind the curtain a few minutes later to tell me it's a full house tonight.

"Really?" I say to her. "Why so crowded?"

"Don't know. Slammer said he'd tell some buddies, but..." She trails off as she peeks out the curtain. "Oh my God, he's here!"

She jumps up and down.

Does she mean Brayden?

"Who's here?" I say, trying to sound casual.

"Slammer." Sophia leans through the curtain and waves wildly.

I exhale. I need to calm down.

But by the time I step onto the stage, my palms are sweaty. I smile at the audience and pick up the pointer while I wait for Cliff to give me my cue through the earpiece.

But I can't hear him. The earpiece must have gone dead. I look back but I don't see him anywhere.

"Should I speak now?" I mouth to Dolores at the side door.

She shrugs her shoulders and cranes her neck to look for Cliff.

The audience is starting to shift around, and I can feel their eyes on me as I continue to stand silently on stage.

"Speak now?" I mouth again to Dolores as we make eye contact.

She puts her hand to her ear like she can't understand what I'm saying.

Well, if the earpiece isn't working, then my microphone probably isn't, either. I take a few steps toward Dolores and say loudly, "Should I speak now?"

My question comes clearly through the microphone attached to my shirt collar, and the audience laughs loudly. At that exact moment, Cliff's voice crackles into my earpiece. "Sorry, Lei, just got everything up and running. We're all set. You can speak now."

My face is on fire as I turn back to the podium and say hello to the audience. Then I begin. "Here's our first slide, which is a wonderful portrayal of toxic soil..."

The audience gives a small, polite laugh, and I turn to look at the screen. A cow is staring me in the face. I flush with heat and look down at my notes, which are apparently out of order.

I flip through the iPad anxiously, praying for a page that says *Slide One* on it. After one painfully silent minute with the only sound me tapping keys, I find the correct slide. *Cow,* it says at the top. No shit.

I pick up the pointer and start again. "Starting over, if you take a look at the cow on slide one, you will see an animal that relies heavily on soil being turned over and pesticides being used at a minimum. Soil is the mainstay of our environment, the foundation for the growth of vegetables, fruits and grains, as well as a necessary ingredient for many animals to remain healthy."

By the time I hit the fifteenth slide, I'm in a groove. I even crack a small joke, and it's as the audience is chuckling that I glance out and see Brayden. He's sitting near the back on the outside aisle. His eyes zero in on mine like lasers, and I lose my breath temporarily. How silly I must look standing up here talking about dirt. I will myself to keep it together and move on to slide sixteen.

———

Brayden

Leleila's voice always sounds sexy, but it takes on an authoritative tone as she delivers her speech, and it's driving me fucking wild. The way her jeans hug her curves—those hips that look like they were made for my hands to hold, those breasts that are trying to peek through the thin fabric of her blouse, and that sweet ass I can't stop staring at whenever she turns to point at a slide.

I like Leleila as a friend and as a person. But the more time we spend together, the less I can deny the truth: like my cousins said, I also want her.

Once everyone cleared out of my house and I was alone, she was even harder for me to stop thinking about. I got off to her in the shower this morning, and after watching her like this on stage, no doubt I'll be doing the same thing tonight. I'm addicted to her curves that I can never touch, to her lips that I can never taste, and to every other part of her that's forbidden to me.

So what the hell am I going to do about a crush that makes me feel like a teenager? I have no fucking clue.

Even if I were to quit working at her sister's store and try the walk-away route, I know I wouldn't be able to stay away. Because she's my friend now. I care for her more than I've ever cared for a woman. And she needs me right now. I wish she'd always need me, but I'm not naïve. Once she marries, our friendship will essentially end.

So I'm going to be everything she needs for as long as she wants me in her life.

———

Leleila

After I'm done speaking, I stand at the edge of the stage with the sign-up sheet next to me. Dolores corrals people into line as one by one they come up to glance at the literature on sale and sign up for our free e-newsletter.

As Dolores takes payment from attendees who want to become annual members, I catch a glimpse of Brayden chatting with Sophia and Slammer. Sophia throws her head back and laughs, obviously enjoying being able to flirt with two men at once.

"Leleila?" Patsy appears at my elbow. "If you need to leave, I can take over from here."

I thank her and grab my purse from the back of the stage. As I walk toward Sophia, I pray someone will look up and notice me before I have to awkwardly insert myself into their conversation.

Of all the options, it's Slammer who calls out to me. "Hey! Leleila's here!" He throws his arm around my back as soon as I reach them.

"Hi...Slammer," I get out.

I turn and say hi to Brayden, hoping no one will mention my talk and how much I screwed up.

"Let's get out of here." Sophia grabs Slammer's hand and pushes me so that I end up ahead of them and next to Brayden. "Save the Soil creeps me out when I'm around it too long."

———

We end up at CeeGee Cakes. I love the cupcakes at CeeGee's, and Sophia and I come here at least once a month for a treat.

The four of us take our time picking out what flavors we want to try. I wind up with a lemon strawberry mix, and Brayden goes with the all chocolate one. Sophia and Slammer can't stop making out with each other in line, so I eventually order for the both of them.

"Yum," Sophia says as she takes a big bite of hers on the way to a table. "Key lime with raspberry filling. Good choice, Lei."

I would like to paint a still of these cupcakes. The key lime one is the most beautiful shade of green, and the raspberry is in at least three different tints of red.

We take seats at the back, and within seconds, Sophia and Slammer are mouth to mouth again.

I roll my eyes at Brayden, who reaches over and, taking hold of the back of my chair, gently turns me so I'm facing him instead of Sophia's back.

"Good idea," I say.

We chat for a few minutes about the bike race. "My parents showing up was a surprise," I say. "My mom promised she'd be back before..." I don't want to bring up my wedding. "Before too long."

"Your parents seem cool," he says.

I nod quickly. Explaining Nina and Fred Wills to anyone is difficult to do.

"So you speak for your parents and you write for your sister," Brayden says. "What do you do for you?"

"I'm a cheerleader, I suppose. For pretty much everyone."

"Your speech was great, by the way."

I raise my eyebrows in surprise. "It was horrible." I laugh. "Probably my worst ever."

"I thought it was great," he insists. "I can't imagine public speaking like that."

"Speaking of Save the Soil," I say to him in a low voice. "I took a quick look at the sample under a lens. It looks off."

Brayden's eyes narrow. "How off?"

"Enough that I asked someone to send it out for analysis."

"Shit." He runs a hand through his hair. "That's not good."

"No. But the analysis will go into a lot more detail. I'll let you know as soon as I find out the results."

Brayden offers me a bite of his cupcake, and the chocolate blends nicely with the strawberry taste I already have in my mouth. I wonder if CeeGee Cakes could make a dessert for my wedding reception. I know Phillip won't like the idea.

But I'm in too good of a mood to care.

I walk up to the counter. "Could I schedule a tasting for my fiancé and me?"

"Of course. And we make cupcake-tiered cakes if you'd like that," she says.

"That sounds amazing."

"How's the night after tomorrow?"

"I'll take it."

I return to the table as Sophia peels her face away from Slammer's long enough to ask Brayden when his team's next home game is.

"This weekend we have one in Wilcox," he says. "But our big home game of the season is the next weekend against the Tigers, our long-time rival. The coaches have a bonfire party after for all the 'adults'—" He chuckles. "And our friends. This year, I'm throwing it at Big River Ranch."

"Can we come?" Sophia asks.

I frown at her. "Soph. It's for his friends."

"Which you are," Brayden says firmly, his eyes on me. "You're all welcome."

That's two weeks before my wedding.

And Sophia knows it. "That timing sounds perfect, Brayden." She elbows me. "Lei and I would love to come."

"No, we wouldn't," I say firmly. "I don't go to parties. Or football games."

"I promise I'll keep you safe," he says.

His tone is casual, but his eyes lock onto mine. He's saying that because he knows. He knows I'm scared shitless from twelve years ago. And he wants me to heal.

Part of the wall around my heart cracks open at the pureness of his offer. Part of me lets him in even more.

Sophia reaches over and squeezes my hand underneath the table. "Thank you, Brayden. It sounds like a lot of fun."

"We can sit on the back of my truck together," he says. "I won't let anyone bother you."

Oh, God. This sounds like the kind of thing where rational thinking goes straight out the window. "I thought it was a bonfire party," I say.

"Tailgating, bonfire, dancing—all of that. It's just the kind of party I grew up with."

I don't want to know what kind of growing up he's referring to, so I don't say anything.

I'm getting a sugar high. I start giggling. "My kind of parties were AP all-nighters."

"So you always liked to study?" he asks me as Sophia and Slammer start kissing again.

"Yeah." I flick my hand in frustration. "I don't know if I liked it, to be honest. Academics were what was expected, and getting good grades was supposed to set me up for the future. Doesn't seem to be getting me very far right now. But I'm meeting with my advisor this week, so hopefully he'll have good news."

CHAPTER SEVENTEEN

I don't get a chance to talk to Phillip until the next night when I stay up and wait for him to get home. I'm determined to reconnect with him and hopefully break through the distance that's between us.

But he's bleary-eyed from his work, and he's in a dark mood.

"Honey?" I say from where I'm sitting on the couch. "I have an idea that may cheer you up."

He looks at me expectantly.

"Wedding cupcakes." I smile. "Instead of a cake, we order custom cupcakes. Just enough for each guest to have one. Or maybe two. We won't have any waste. CeeGee Cakes uses recyclable wrappers, and their frosting is natural with no artificial dyes. They also have gluten-free and sugar-free alternatives for you."

"I don't think so, Lei."

"I set up a tasting for us night after next," I say, putting my arms around his waist. "Your colleagues come over tomorrow evening, but early next week, you have nothing on your calendar, not until you leave for the conference. What do you say? It's free; no strings attached. If we don't like the cupcakes, we don't use the company."

He rubs his eyes wearily. "Sounds fine. If it means that much to you, sure. Just text me the time, okay?"

If it's not within his subject area, Phillip doesn't usually have much to say. Versatility is not his strength. He's a good man, and I know he'd sooner die than hurt me on purpose.

He just doesn't consider being married to his work as a sting.

He says he's going upstairs, and I don't know why, but I go for the one thing I know will get his attention.

"Do you, um...ever wish you'd ended up with a science professor?" I say abruptly. "You know, a colleague. Because even if I pass my dissertation, I'll never be a professor like Mindy Cox."

His back stiffens and he pauses a few feet up the stairs. "I don't know what you mean, Lei." He turns around, and his eyes find mine. "What are you saying?"

I shrug. "I know you have that fantasy..."

"Leleila." He sighs and comes over to the couch and sits down. "I told you pretending wouldn't be the same as the real thing. It's fine. It really is."

I narrow my eyes. "It's just...I know you told me that sex with an academic is on your bucket list, and now that I failed my thesis, it makes me wonder if you're..."

"If I'm what?" His tired eyes flash with panic that he tries to cover. "Finish your sentence, Lei."

I keep my gaze on his. "It makes me wonder, if I don't actually become a professor, you'll feel like you're settling."

There. I've said it.

"You're going to pass that dissertation and get hired at the university," he says firmly as he takes my hand in his. "I know you are. And in the meanwhile...I was waiting to tell you this, but..."

"But what?" I say, a sense of doom filling my chest.

"You can work for me." He beams. "As my assistant at the college. You can start as soon as we're married."

I tighten my fingers around his subconsciously. "I'll be your assistant?"

He furrows his brow in that way he gets when he's truly confused. "Don't you want to get back to work?"

"Yes. I do." I pull my hand away and sigh. "But not as your assistant. Honey, I think we both know that won't end well."

His mouth turns down into nearly a scowl. "I don't know how to get you to realize that I don't need you to be a professor to make me happy. I just want you to be by my side."

I fiddle with the string on my ring finger. It's getting awfully frayed, and I'm not sure it's going to make it to the wedding after all. "Phillip, sometimes I wonder if this—us—isn't working as well as it used to. I feel like we're growing apart, and I even wonder if maybe you have a specific woman in mind for your professor fantasy, and maybe you have for a while."

Phillip rubs his temple. "Lei. Don't. There is no specific woman."

I fiddle some more with the string. Now I'm pulling so tightly that my finger is turning white from lack of blood flow. "I've suggested we try professor role-play in bed. Why won't you consider it?"

"Because. You're not..." He trails off.

"I'm not a hot professor who you can have illicit sex with in your office or at a conference. Right?" My voice sounds surprisingly calm to my own ears, considering my insides are shaking. I take off my glasses and keep talking. "You were waiting—hoping—for the day when I'd pass my dissertation and maybe then, even though we both know you don't consider psychology to be on the same level as biology and ecology—you thought maybe then we could do all those dirty things you dream about."

Phillip pats my knee. "You're the woman I want to marry. That's why you have the ring around your finger, Lei." He points to the string I'm busy tugging at. "It's not about getting a degree. You're stressed out, honey," he says, and I don't miss how he, as usual, manages to turn the focus onto me like I'm the problem. "This wedding isn't supposed to be a source of anxiety. That's why we're making it as low-key as possible. Until our wedding, will you promise to have as much fun as possible? Go out, have a few drinks, and hang out with some friends. Okay?"

My response comes out in a pained, yet clear, tone. "Sure."

CHAPTER EIGHTEEN

The following evening, I sit by myself on our couch and look up at Phillip and Matt Lucas schmoozing together by the fireplace. Two glasses of sherry in and Phillip's eyes have that glassy look they get when I know he's going to pass out as soon as his head hits the pillow. I look down at my ring finger, and I'm still looking at it when Elsa Lucas takes a seat next to me, uninvited. I turn to smile at her, wondering what Matt's perfect scholarly wife is doing sitting next to little old me, but I don't have to wait long to find out.

"Leleila," she begins. "Don't you look lovely tonight."

"Thank you," I say stiffly, knowing that line has to be just her lead-in to something more sinister.

Her badly-colored hair doesn't hide the fact that she's twenty years older than me, and I know she's had to attend these parties for far longer than I can imagine doing myself, so I try to cut her some slack.

"You know," she says. "Now that your marital status is about to change, Phillip's going to need you more than ever in order to stay on track."

When I don't answer her, she keeps going. "I teach a class at my home that's vital for someone like you," she says. "Someone who's a bit resistant to accepting all the pressures that come with becoming a professor's wife. This department is the most prestigious one at the university. Your fiancé will need a lot of support the further along his career he gets."

I clench my jaw and make a non-verbal sound that she must take as consent because she smiles at me.

"I host a quarterly dinner party," she says. "Hors d'oeuvres, organic wine, and a full-course meal, of course. I bake my desserts, but you could always do store-bought as long as it's decent."

"I'm not sure that Phillip wants to host a party every quarter..." I begin.

"What Phillip wants and what Phillip needs are two different things," Elsa says in a sharp tone. "How do you think Matt's paper got accepted to the Journal so quickly last year? We invited the best over—remember the party you and Phillip attended at our home?"

Yes, and I remember wanting to run screaming from it. Everyone standing around in suits and holding napkins filled with crab cakes. Nobody dared to sit down for two hours. Phillip stood by the fireplace with Annabeth Franklin for ninety minutes while she rambled on about her latest research. I texted Sophia from the bathroom twice.

I look away from Elsa and nod quickly.

"It went perfectly," she says. "A lovely gathering. You should plan the same, Leleila. It will help take the pressure off Phillip's shoulders."

"With all due respect, Elsa," I say politely. "Phillip is brilliant. He doesn't need to host social gatherings to continue his career success. I mean he's already an author on a number of papers."

"But not on a book," Elsa says. "He would just kill to get a book out there, I imagine. Am I right?"

I frown and don't answer her. I know Phillip wants a published book, but I figured that was a few years away.

"You and I both know every research scientist wants to publish as much as possible, as frequently as possible," Elsa continues.

"Phillip is no different. And he needs your help. The spouse is invaluable, my dear. And since you don't have a doctorate yourself, there's really no excuse…"

She trails off purposely here and leaves for the bathroom, taking with her any trace of happiness I still had with me tonight.

"Who wants more wine?" I say as I bounce up from the couch.

I discover we don't have that third bottle of wine I was sure we had.

Seeing as I'm the only one here who's sober, I tell Phillip I'll be back in thirty, and I jump in the car.

When I reach June's store, I exhale.

June's working the register again, and I surprise her when I jog over to the counter, hair flying out behind me because I never took the time to pull it back.

"You look eager," she says. "But he's not here. I like your outfit, though."

I glance down at my long, white skirt and ribbed blue top. "Thanks. This is my professor party attire, I guess. And I'm not here to see anybody."

"Uh-huh. Sure you're not."

I stick my tongue out at her. "I'm grabbing more wine. Apparently Phillip's department is filled with lushes."

"Not a shock. They're probably so bored with themselves they need to drink to numb their brains." She narrows her eyes and cocks her head as she appraises me. "What's going on?"

I take her by the arm and hustle her into her office where I shut and lock the door behind us.

"I have a question. I know you don't like the women flirting with Phillip, but you hated him long before that. How come? You two seem so alike—both brilliant, anal-retentive, successful."

June grumbles something I can't hear and takes a seat on her desk. I stand before her, not sure why I'm here or what I'm looking for from my younger sister, but wanting to feel better than I'm feeling right now.

"Somehow I don't think you're only here about Phillip," she says. "What's happening with Brayden?"

"Nothing." I look away from her. "But he's super nice. We have fun together."

"You guys are friends?" she asks me.

"He's like the best guy friend I've ever had." I sigh. "It's just..."

"You're engaged." She puts her elbows on her knees and rests her chin in her hands.

"Brayden and I are just friends. Nothing's happened."

June narrows her eyes at me. "Why do I have the feeling you're not telling me everything?"

I stand up and glance out the office windows to make sure nobody's right outside. Then I sit back down. "June...something happened to me when we were in high school."

Her eyes flash with anger. "Who hurt you?"

"I fought him off." My voice sounds far away to my own ears. "He didn't...even though he tried..." I can't continue due to the sudden lump in my throat.

"Lei." June reaches out her hand, and I take it. "I can't believe you never told me before."

I nod, accepting the tissue she hands me. "I'm okay. But when I escaped, I opened the door and there was...Brayden Wild."

Her eyes go huge. "Brayden? Our Brayden?"

I smile at her affection for him. "Yes. We met twelve years ago. Just that once."

She sits back in her chair. "So he knows what happened to you."

"Yes."

"This is a lot to take in," she admits. "Did you start dating Phillip right after?"

"Pretty much," I say. "He was stable. He was consistent and safe, and he never made me go to parties or push me out of my comfort zone."

Her face relaxes. "I get it."

"Phillip was my partner. He was there for me when Mom and

Dad were always traveling. He was all I had for years." I fidget with my hands in my lap.

June says nothing. She just sits and looks at me.

I play with the zipper on my purse. "But he's been acting... distant. It's been going on for a while, but I was in denial until recently. I'm afraid we're growing so far apart that we won't be able to stitch things back together in time."

"Do you want to stitch things back together with Phillip?"

I chew on my lip. "I'm not sure."

"I know I give you a lot of flack over it, but I'm not the best person to talk to about this." June shrugs. "I haven't been in a serious relationship since I broke up with Sammy senior year of high school."

"I admire that you don't need a relationship to define you."

"No, I just need random sex once a month," she jokes.

I smile. "You sound like Sophia. You guys are too hard on your-selves." I stand up. "I'll see you tomorrow."

"Lei."

I turn back to her.

"I'm sorry that happened to you." Her face is drawn. "I wish I could have been there for you. But I'm glad somebody was."

"Thanks, June. I'll meet you out front."

I head down Aisle 8 and grab two bottles of Phillip's favorite red wine.

When I reach the register, June's there too, and she starts to ring me up. "Do you have Brayden's number on your phone?" she says in far too casual a tone.

"Yes," I say suspiciously.

"Good. I need you to call him for me."

"Call him yourself."

"I can't call him. I'm very busy cashing."

I shoot her a death stare. "June, come on. I have to get home." *Even though I know what these parties are like. They won't even notice I'm gone.* "What do you need to talk to him about?"

She reaches underneath the counter and hands me a large cloth bag.

"This is all the unsold produce from Big River Ranch for today. Brayden usually takes a portion home with him to feed his livestock or to compost anything that's spoiled. He had to hurry out today for practice, and he got caught up helping one of the players afterward, so he never stopped back. I hate for him to not have it for the feeding tomorrow morning, so I texted him earlier and said I'd bring it by shortly. Then, Kim left without telling me. If I wait until we close, he'll be stuck staying up later than I'm sure he'd like. "

I blow out a breath and grab the bag from her. "You so owe me for this," I say. "And you call him first to make sure he's actually still up."

————

When I pull into Brayden's driveway, a strange sensation washes over me.

I feel at peace, more so than I do when I pull into my own driveway sometimes.

Brayden opens his front door as soon as I step out of the car. I wave, fully aware of him watching me walk toward him. He's standing there in a fitted red t-shirt, worn blue jeans, and bare feet, and I have to catch my breath as I reach him. I hand him the bag of produce, and he invites me inside.

As I step forward, I almost think he's going to hug me, but instead he puts his hand briefly on my lower back and guides me toward the living room.

"So what are you up to?" I ask him.

The lights are dimmed, and the curtains are drawn. The television's on, and a dinner plate with chicken and pasta sits on the arm of the couch. The whole room feels very cozy.

Brayden chuckles. "Watching two things. One's very manly and would get a stamp of approval from the outside world, and the other's more...culinary."

I take a seat on the couch. "What are they?"

"I've got a Wilcox football game on film that the head coach sent me to determine a few play formations for this week's game," he says. "And I've also got on a cooking show because I'm thinking about stealing one of the recipes for dinner sometime."

"That's awesome."

I lean back against the cushions and look up at the ceiling.

"I see a pine tree," I say.

Brayden settles on his back with his head at the other end of the couch. Our legs cross the same stretch of cushion, but they're not touching. Not quite.

"I see it," he says. "It looks like a pine tree on steroids, though."

I kick his leg with my foot. "No, it doesn't!"

"It's huge," he says.

"You've been watching too much football. You've got steroids on the brain."

"Speaking of football..." He hesitates, and I sense he's worried about something important.

"Yeah?" I say.

"I've got a kid on my team—he's a great kid and really has a shot to go all the way to the top."

"But..." I prompt him.

"But his dad's a drunk."

My eyes fly to his. "I'm sorry. That's tough."

"Yeah. And I'm trying to help him out as best I can, but I can't always get someone to watch his father during games."

"For my practicum, I worked at an assisted living facility in Mountainview," I say. "The program accepts people suffering from addictions. They also deal with mental illnesses of all kinds."

"Is it a private facility?"

"It is. And I know that makes it out of range financially for a lot of people."

"Pretty much anything that's not free will be out of range for this guy," Brayden murmurs.

"The thing is," I say. "Maybe we can get creative somehow."

"What do you mean?" His blue eyes zero in on mine.

"Well, for example, if one of your cousins runs any kind of a charity, they could potentially sponsor him through a scholarship or some type of aid."

"Are you serious? The facility accepts patients that way?"

"Absolutely. They take several people a year who qualify through scholarships. I don't know if that's feasible, of course, but it's one idea. And if that doesn't work, I'm sure we can figure out another solution."

Brayden moves his foot so that it's touching my thigh. "Thank you. I would never have thought of that."

Where he's touching me is burning up, and my nipples tighten. This is not good. Not good at all.

"How late can you stay?" he asks me in a soft tone.

I glance at the time on my phone. I can't believe I'm having so much fun with this man that I nearly forgot about my fiancé and his wine.

"I should have left ten minutes ago."

Brayden nods, and his sapphire eyes lose their sparkle. I want to say more, but I don't know how.

He sits up and gestures to the red string around my finger. "How long has this been on?"

I inhale. "Six months. You know... it's one of those knots that stick."

He nods. "Must be some strong string."

"I don't know where he got it, but the red is supposed to be for love."

Brayden's lips part as his eyes fix on mine, and my heart beats faster.

I fight the urge to lean forward and throw my body passionately against his. God, that sounds like such a ridiculous soap opera moment.

I've always admired those soap opera characters in a way. They really seem to live life to the fullest, not caring if they make fools of themselves or whether or not they're going to piss somebody off. They just do what they do in the moment and live with the consequences. I'm not certain I'm courageous enough to live with the consequences of what I've set into motion, and I don't know that I have the necessary tools to come out of it gracefully. I don't want to lose Brayden at the end of the month, but I don't see any other way around it, because once a gold band replaces this piece of red string, everything will change.

It's hard to believe that in a little over two weeks, Phillip and I will be married and on our way to the Galapagos. He and I have never felt farther apart, and my gut twinges uncomfortably.

It's almost like Phillip thinks we'll just show up at the court-house and exchange vows ASAP so he can get back to his research.

"Are you okay?"

"Uh-huh." I flash a quick smile before blurting out, "Phillip and I had a talk. I was concerned that he's unhappy in our relationship. He didn't say as much, but the implication was there."

Brayden's expression is blank. "Did you tell him how that made you feel?"

I feel my face go hot. "Sort of. I asked him what he likes."

Maybe I'm imagining it, but the pulse on Brayden's neck seems to pick up, and his breathing quickens. "What do you mean?"

"He has a bucket list to sleep with a professor. And because I failed my thesis, well…"

A strangled sound escapes Brayden's throat, but his expression remains blank.

I hit the heel of my hand against my forehead. "TMI. So sorry."

A long silence ensues. Brayden leans his head back and gazes up at the ceiling for over a minute as if there's an answer up there for him. When he finally makes eye contact with me again, his lip quirks up. "You know you look like you're holding your breath?"

I let out a heavy exhale. "Sorry."

"Please don't be sorry. I like spending time with you."

And I like spending time with you.

"And Leleila." Brayden locks eyes with me as I stand to leave. "You deserve to be treated like the incredible, brilliant, beautiful, funny woman you are. No matter who you're with, I don't want you to ever forget that."

My throat constricts, and I can't answer him.

"One other thing? I don't think anybody else can understand or analyze this." He doesn't expound on what he means by "this," but I assume it's us—him and me. "And to be perfectly honest, I really don't care what anybody else thinks about it. When you really look closely at this world, there are a lot of things that don't make sense, but that doesn't always matter, you know?"

I nod. Yes, this friendship I'm in with Brayden while being engaged doesn't make much sense. But our friendship works, and that's the most complicated part of all.

———

Brayden

My house feels empty as soon as Leleila leaves. I didn't realize it was missing anything until she came by. The silence left by her absence is nearly painful.

A sense of frustration comes over me as I clean the dishes from dinner. I haven't been looking for a relationship. Quite the opposite—I've been enjoying being single and coming home alone. Until Leleila walked into Big Sky Grocer, and now I feel pathetically lonely when she's not around. Outside of my cousins' significant others, she's the first woman I've really been friends with—just friends with—ever. And the fact that I also want to take her clothes off and make love to her? That just makes me want her more.

I like hanging out with her. I like hearing about her life and telling her about mine. She and I are opposites, and yet somehow, we fit.

My phone rings, and I groan when I see who it is. Dylan Wild is the number one quarterback in the league for a reason—he fights for what he wants until he gets it. And I have no doubt that right now, he's going to want to know who Leleila is. He hasn't called since Jasalie was here visiting, and by now, I'm sure she's told him the story.

I swipe the screen. "Hey, Dyl."

"Bray. What's up?"

"Nothing. Congrats on Sunday's win. You guys looked awesome out there."

"Thanks. Hey, can you do me a favor for the wedding reception?"

I chuckle. "A wedding favor. Jasalie's really got you good, doesn't she?"

He laughs. "She does. And I love her, but I have no clue what she's talking about half the time, between the flower arrangements and the food...anyway, don't kill me, but..."

I groan. "What does Jasalie need done in person?"

"She's changed her mind on the wedding cake flavors."

"Dude..."

"I know. I would ask Colt's mom or mine to do it, but my mom is away with my dad on business, and you know how Colt's mom is diabetic and never eats sugar. You want me to call your mom instead?"

"No," I say quickly. "That'll just get her revved up about why none of her own sons are married yet."

Dylan chuckles. "I figured as much. I'll text you the address and the time—the lady at the shop said she'd fit you in next week."

"That's fine. And I've got a favor of my own, actually."

"Shoot."

"You know Wes Brick, the quarterback for Wilcox?"

"Of course. He's a great kid. Huge fucking arm."

"No doubt. The thing is his dad—"

"Calvin," Dylan says right away. "He's had problems for years."

"I know. Things aren't improving, though. If anything, they're worse."

Dylan lets out a frustrated huff. "I'm sorry to hear that. How can I help?"

That's the thing about Dylan. His first, second, and last question is always, "How can I help?" Doesn't matter how big he's gotten or how wealthy—he's never forgotten where he came from and how blessed he is.

I tell him what Leleila suggested about offering a scholarship through his charity.

"I'll make a call and see what I can do," Dylan promises. "It's a great idea, Bray."

"It is, but it wasn't mine," I say. "A friend suggested it."

Pause, and I know it's coming. Sure enough—

"So, who's this engaged woman you're into?"

"Fuck, Dylan."

"Is she the friend who came up with the plan to help Wes?"

I blow out a breath. "Leave it, okay? I've already told Cam and Ayd to back the fuck off."

"I heard." His tone is amused. "Heard you practically took Cam out. I don't doubt he deserved it, of course. The little cousin doesn't know when to shut his mouth."

"That's an understatement." I take a beat. "Look, I'll fill you in when you come into town. That's the best I can give you right now."

"Okay. But on that note, I'm setting you and Cam up at the reception."

My heart slams against my chest. "No."

He chuckles. "Why not? Is this woman going to be there? Jasalie told me she said no to her invitation. Although I have to say my wife doesn't like many people on sight, so if she invited her to our wedding renewal, she must really be something."

"She is." I grip the phone tightly. "But she's not coming. And I'm not being set up. I'll fucking kill you if you try."

He laughs again, and I think I get him to agree with me before we hang up.

But do I trust him? Absolutely not. Dylan's been on a kick to get Cam and me into relationships ever since he married, and I know he won't give up.

Which means I need to outmaneuver him. And there's only one way to do that: if I have a date, Dylan can't set me up. Problem solved.

But I don't want to go with anyone but Leleila Wills. And she's not an option.

I pull at my hair with both hands. I'm insane. I've totally fucking lost it. I'm hung up on an engaged woman to the point that I'm refusing an offer to be set up with a woman I could actually have sex with?

Yep. That's exactly what's going on. Because I don't want to have sex with anyone if I'm not having sex with Leleila. Which, again, proves how completely screwed I am. In a few short weeks, she'll be a married woman, to another man, and I won't be hanging out with her anymore. The idea of no more time with Leleila is like a sucker punch to the gut, and I push the thought out of my head and go take a shower.

CHAPTER NINETEEN

Leleila

"Awesome." Sophia claps her hands when she shows up at my house the next night. "A wedding cake. Finally something about these upcoming nuptials of yours that's not drab."

"I don't think Phillip's going to like a wedding cake much. Even if it's made of gluten-free cupcakes."

"Of course, Phillip's not going to like it much. So what? Do something outside Phillip's box for once in your life. Start with your wedding planning, because if you wait until after you're married, there'll be nothing of you left."

Phillip said he'll be coming straight from the university, so Sophia drives us to the bakery.

"So. Phillip's going away tomorrow night?" she asks as she drives.

I know the darkness she's headed toward. "Don't go there. It's morally wrong."

"What are morals anyway?" Sophia says as I pick up my purse.

I hate when she waxes on. It's the worst, because half the time, she's got a point, and it's always the opposite kind of point from what I was raised with. So she always ends up confusing me.

"Soph..."

"Morals are simply rules made in the sand by human beings," Sophia continues. "They're codes. And everybody has their own. Slammer, for example, has very few moral codes. That bastard hasn't called me back in two days," she grumbles. "But that's another story. Now Phillip—he's surprising the fuck out of me. The man has screwed-up fantasies *and* a bucket list? That is not the Phillip Rowe I know. This Phillip is certainly a hell of a lot more interesting. Still selfish to the core but with a level of intrigue to him now. Not that you deserve to have to deal with his bullshit, and I don't approve of his new 'I'm too busy for anyone because I have research' attitude. So, on that note." She points at me. "What are your plans while Phillip's away? Because you at least need to spend time doing things for you, Lei, such as painting."

We park in the bakery lot, and I say, "I painted all afternoon." I pull up the picture I took on my phone and show her.

Sophia whistles. "A couple horseback riding. That's beautiful. Were you inspired from your ride with Brayden?"

A blond woman behind the counter interrupts before I have to answer. "Are you girls here for the wedding cake tasting?"

"Yes," Sophia says. "This is Leleila, the bride-to-be..." She puts her arm around me. "And I'm Sophia, the best friend. The groom is late but should be here shortly."

"Wonderful. I'm Winny." She pats at her blond hair with bright orange streaks running through it. "Another party will be doing a tasting tonight also. No one else is here yet, though, so just take a seat at that table in the far back, and I'll be right over."

Sophia insists on me sitting in the outer chair... "So the first thing Phillip will see when he walks in are your legs. That *is* why you're wearing the skirt, right? So he'll notice you."

I try to deny her statement but take the seat she points out. She sits across from me as Winny approaches us with a two-tiered glass plate in her hands. Gorgeous bite-sized cake morsels, in various colors and styles, are scattered on both tiers.

Sophia claps her hands. "This is the perfect dinner, Winny," she jokes.

Winny puts the plate in the center of the table. "I know. Dessert instead of dinner. Why do you think I wound up in a bakery?"

She puts one napkin in front of me and one in front of Sophia. "Okay, girls, try this top one here." She gives us each a piece of vanilla cake with buttercream icing.

I bite into mine. "It's so good," I say just as the bell rings at the door.

The back of my neck tingles.

"No way," Sophia says, her mouth dropping open. "I think you'll want to see who this is, Lei."

I turn my head, and the cake in my hand drops onto the plate.

Even from across the room, those blue eyes are blazing into me. "Brayden?" I say.

He shoves his hands in his pants pockets and nods. "Hey."

"The other party is here!" Winnie hustles over to greet him.

"Other party?" Sophia mutters to me. "He's getting married?"

Brayden flicks his gaze to me. "I'm here for my cousin. For Jasalie, really."

I smile at his obvious discomfort as he rocks back on his heels. "You look like you're really looking forward to this."

He flashes me a grin. "Yeah. I'm not a wedding planner kind of guy. Yet here I am."

Winnie whips her gaze back and forth between the two of us. "If you all know each other, would you like to sit together for the tasting? Ms. Gordon has already given me her style and decorating specs, so all you're here for is the tasting, Mr. Wild."

Brayden hesitates, his eyes on me, and I bite my lip. But Sophia waves him over. "Come take a seat!"

Brayden takes off his coat and puts it on the back of the chair next to me. Sophia kicks me under the table and smiles widely, and I know she's loving the fact that he's here.

Could this be any more awkward? And where is Phillip?

Like his ear is burning, my phone beeps with a text.

You're going to have to do the tasting without me. Dr. Lucas asked me

to stay to run through some analysis with him. I promise I'll make it up
to you.

I turn off my phone angrily. Phillip can make all the promises
he wants, but the thing is, there's always going to be another paper.
And his workaholic nature is never going to end.

When I look up, all three people in the room are watching me.

"Everything okay?" Brayden murmurs, concern etched on his
face.

Willing myself to pull my shit together, I give him a bright,
completely false smile as I nod.

And he knows I'm full of shit.

He reaches for my hand, like he's not even thinking about it,
and covers it with his own.

Sophia gasps.

Brayden's cheeks redden. He never shows embarrassment like
that, and I stare at him in surprise as he immediately removes his
hand and pats my arm awkwardly like his movements were all
planned.

Winny grabs three pieces of chocolate cake covered with red
icing. "Cherry flavored," she explains about the red frosting.
"Maybe Ms. Gordon will like this flavor."

For the next hour, the three of us eat cake. And it's fun.
Sophia's silliness breaks the tension in the room, and Brayden
FaceTimes Jasalie to give her his opinion. Jasalie's thrilled when
she sees Sophia and me.

"Let the ladies help you choose, Brayden!" she says to him.
"And Dylan said he's going to set you up? What's that about?"

Brayden tugs at his hair. "Jasalie, your husband doesn't know
when to mind his own business."

She laughs. "And Leleila, I still hope you'll come to the wedding
also!"

"Um..." I pause, and Brayden jumps in.

"If she can make it, I'm sure she will."

I glance over at Sophia, and she puts her hands over her face
and giggles.

Brayden says goodbye to Jasalie and then leans closer to me so he can disconnect the call. Maybe it's my imagination, but it feels like he lingers for a moment longer than necessary. I can smell his cologne, and him, and my pulse starts galloping.

And then, the moment breaks.

Brayden thanks Winnie for her time and stands up.

He grabs his coat off the chair and walks out of the bakery.

I tell Sophia I have to go, and then I grab my coat too and run after him. He's already partway across the parking lot when I call out.

"Brayden."

He stops and turns back to look at me. "Leleila, I'm sorry. I was surprised as hell to see you in there."

I'm well aware that lines are being blurred all over the place. I also know that I've never felt this happy before and that my wedding will be upon me before I know it.

"I understand." I fiddle with the zipper on my coat. "So, Dylan wants to set you up, huh?"

Brayden lets out a breath. "Yes. And I don't need his damn help, which I've made clear to him. But my cousin is—and this is something you'll learn if you meet him—not easily deterred. No doubt that persistence helps him out when he's being chased by three-hundred pound linemen."

I laugh. "I'm sure it does."

"But he's driving me fucking nuts. He won't let up, and he's insistent he's going to set me up with somebody if I don't bring my own date."

I swallow. "Well, I'm sure the wedding will be amazing. You'll have fun no matter what."

"I guess so. Dylan and Jasalie deserve an amazing wedding." His hands drop into his pockets.

"That sounds great." I clear my throat. "And I understand if you can't make dance class next week. I know you'll have a lot going on with family and friends in town."

Brayden tips his head back and gazes overhead again like he did last night. My heart lurches, and I feel like it's hanging in the balance as I wait for him to answer me.

"I don't want to back out on you," he finally says as he lowers his gaze to meet mine.

While we're standing there in purgatory, I hear a car start up. I turn my head to see Sophia zipping out of the parking lot.

"Soph!" I wave my hands at her as she passes us. "I need a ride!"

She slows down and her window lowers a crack. "I have to run, Lei. Have Brayden take you home?"

"I have to make a quick stop," he says, glancing at his watch. "It's my parents' anniversary, and I promised Luke I'd pick up the gift from all of us. The place will be closed by the time I bring you home and then go back for it. So if you don't mind an errand..."

"Great!" Sophia throws a hand out her window, now fully lowered, and then she accelerates until she's a cloud of dust.

"Okaa-ay." I shake my head at my completely unsubtle best friend. "I guess I'm going with you."

CHAPTER TWENTY

Brayden picks up the enlarged and beautifully-framed photo of his family at the photo store in the main shopping plaza in Wilcox.

His phone rings as he's setting the gift in the backseat.

"Yeah?" he says as he answers. "She's *what*? How the hell did she escape? There are coyotes all over the damn place at this hour...look, I can be there in about twenty minutes. I have to drop someone...I don't think I can get there any faster. She's on the other side of town from the highway..."

I twist around to catch his eye. "I can sit in the truck and wait for you while you go do what you need to do," I offer. "It will save you fifteen minutes easy."

I can read the conflict in Brayden's eyes from here. He understandably doesn't want to tote me along to his family ranch. Why would he? But at the same time, he obviously is needed immediately.

The desire to help out his family wins, and soon we're driving down the windy road at Wild Ranch, right on the border of Mountainview but in the town of Wilcox.

"Come on inside," he says when he pulls up into the driveway and I make no move to get out of the truck. "It's so dark out here. You can hang with my parents while I help Luke find his damn dog. My twin brothers are out for the night or they'd be the ones running around in the dark."

Meeting parents is normally something I'm fairly skilled at. Meeting Brayden Wild's parents is not something I feel even remotely prepared for. And this mini skirt is never something I would have picked out for a parent meeting. I wonder if there's a way to cover up my legs somehow. Doubtful.

But I feel like I owe Brayden this after everything he's done for me. I take a deep breath, open the passenger door, and climb out.

Brayden grabs the framed photo and leads me down the path toward the gate that leads into the backyard. "They hardly ever use their front door," he explains. "We always go in and out through the kitchen."

He opens the screen door, which leads into a small porch area. Then he opens the wooden door beyond and ushers me in ahead of him.

And suddenly, I'm in the middle of the Wild kitchen. All I smell is chocolate chip cookies. It's so warm and cozy that I take off my coat right away, without even thinking about it. Brayden's behind me, and he takes the coat from me and lays it on the closest chair. Then he puts his coat over mine, and I turn to face him nervously.

"Are you sure this is okay?"

He places his hand on my lower back and whispers into my ear. "It will be fine."

Chills race through my entire body at his closeness, and I work to regain control over my hormones as he calls out, "Mom! Are you home?"

A pretty woman with dark brown hair up in a bun comes hurrying through the swing door that looks like it leads to a dining room.

"Brayden, I can't believe I didn't hear you come in!"

"Happy anniversary, Mom." He hands her the photograph as he kisses her cheek.

She looks at the picture of their whole family, and in the lighted room, I'm able to see too.

Like Brayden, his siblings are all attractive—there's Luke, his handsome twin brothers, and his sister who has long dark hair. To me, of course, Brayden stands out. From his larger-than-life smile to his incredibly bright blue eyes, he's completely gorgeous.

"Thank you, honey. I just love it. Dad will too." She gives him a hug and kiss, and then turns to me. "Pardon my manners. Hello, I'm Edna Wild."

"This is Leleila," Brayden says. "June's sister."

I wish her happy anniversary, and then William, Brayden's father, comes out, and another round of greetings begins. William Wild is gray-haired but very fit, and he smiles a lot. He loves the framed photo, and Edna immediately says they'll hang it up in the living room.

"I think it's great that your sister started a natural grocery store," Brayden's dad says to me as we walk through the swing door and take seats at the dining room table, which is filled with plates of food. There's chicken, salad, and sweet potatoes, and it all looks delicious.

Brayden excuses himself to find Luke, and Edna insists I take a plate of food.

"We've just sat down to dinner," she explains. "Luke and Brayden will be sure to grab a plate themselves when they return."

William takes the chair across from me. "You can never have too many health food stores."

"Yes, that's true," I say. "Brayden mentioned you're interested in healthy eating."

"I love it," he says. "Now, that doesn't mean I don't enjoy my desserts and my nightly glass of wine, though. Nothing can stop me from that!"

Edna brings in a bottle of wine in that moment, and she laughs at the timing. "You can tell we've been married forty years, can't you?" She smiles as she takes a seat next to her husband.

She hands me the plate of chicken first, and I take a piece. It's breaded and moist and so good I could have three helpings worth. Everything is delicious. That's what I tell her, and she beams at me as Luke and Brayden stroll into the room. A large wolfhound trails them.

"Mom, I have to take Leleila home," Brayden says when he sees me seated at the table.

"Nonsense," his mother says. "Leleila has to eat first. So do you. Sit down, boys."

"It's okay," I say to Brayden when he continues to stare at me. "I'm not in a rush. Your mom went to all this trouble, and the food is delicious."

Brayden's jaw relaxes, and he comes over and takes the seat beside me.

"Roxy was stuck in the shed," Luke says as he sits next to his father. "Never barked once until Bray started calling for her." Luke tilts his chin at me. "How's it going?"

I tell him fine, and he slides his gaze between Brayden and me. Just once, but it's enough to know that Luke Wild definitely hasn't changed his mind about Brayden and me sharing something private.

When we finish our meal, Edna brings out the plate of chocolate chip cookies and offers them to me first.

I dig right in. I eat three without coming up for air, and then I tell her they're the best cookies I've ever tasted. Her face flushes with pride, and she insists I have another.

"Did you grow up in Mountainview, Leleila?" William asks me.

I tell him I did, and we all chat for a bit about the small towns in the area.

"Wilcox's football program was always the best in the area," William says. "We lined up in that way with my sons and nephews falling in love with the sport like they did."

I push my glasses up on my nose. "Mountainview's had some decent seasons, but it never fielded a team like Wilcox."

William snaps his fingers. "There were a couple good players like you say. There was a great defensive end—Jones something or other."

"Arthur Jones," I say.

"That's the one. He made the pros for a while."

"Remember there was that drama over the kid who got kicked out of one of the local schools for drugs?" Edna asks. "Was he from Mountainview?"

I choke on my sip of wine and start coughing.

"He was," I hear Luke say in a low tone.

Brayden pats my back. "You okay?" he whispers.

I pull myself together and look up to find Luke's gaze on Brayden and me. He looks thoughtful, and I grip the napkin tightly in my hand.

"Was that kid the one who tried to play for the college in Colorado..." William begins.

I know he's just asking innocently, but the topic is hitting far too close for my comfort.

"Dad, why don't you and Mom show Leleila your dance floor?" Brayden interrupts. "She's learning how to dance."

"Oh, really?" Edna says to me. "That's wonderful. William and I love to dance together."

Everyone heads into a large room at the back of the house, and William opens up an old-fashioned record player. When waltz music comes through the speakers, he takes Edna's hand and they start gliding across the wooden floor.

I glance at Brayden whose jaw is clenched. He appears as uncomfortable as I am.

"Brayden," Luke says quietly. "Can you check on Roxie?"

"Why?" Brayden asks suspiciously.

"Because she prefers you to me, and I want to make sure she's calmed down before you leave."

"I'll be right back," Brayden says to me.

Once he's left the room, Luke steps closer to my side.

"You okay?" he asks me.

"I'm good," I say immediately.

"I always wondered who turned that asshole in," Luke says casually.

I whip my head over and look at him, but his attention is on his parents.

"I just found it strange that the authorities were able to find drugs in his locker that day when no one had ever found them before."

I shift my stance so I'm facing him. "What are you saying?"

He raises his head and his knowing eyes tell me everything. "Whoever turned him in had inside information on how to nail him. And it was personal. That kid was a druggie, sure, but the guy who made sure he was caught? He knew something worse about him than that he dealt drugs. My bet's the kid did something to a friend of his. Someone he cared about."

I will my face to remain blank, but I've never been an actress.

"You looked like you'd seen a ghost at the table," Luke says. "And my brother—let's just say I can read him like a book. He was worried about you. And Brayden doesn't worry over women."

I purse my lips. "I appreciate you giving me your two cents, Luke. I do. But..."

A ghost of a smile hits his lips. "I'm butting out. And don't worry. I'll forget everything I saw tonight."

As soon as Brayden returns to the room, Luke says good night and disappears.

"Brayden, before you leave, take Leleila for a spin around the floor," his father calls out.

"Dad, we're not dancers."

"Well, neither are we," he says as he nearly runs his wife into the fireplace because he's so busy looking over his shoulder at us. "Get on up here and let Leleila practice for one song."

Brayden's eyes are apologetic as he turns to me. "He won't let up until we do it." He holds out his hand. "Just one song?"

I inhale and take his hand. Luke's words are haunting me, and I feel like I'm in a twilight zone as I follow Brayden onto the floor.

As we start to dance, I'm so focused on not messing up the

steps that I don't pick my head up once. I've got my eyes set squarely on my feet, and it's working out all right. Brayden and I haven't run into each other yet.

"Eye contact is the key, dear," Edna says to me. "The connection between partners is what makes a great dance."

I bring my gaze up reluctantly to meet Brayden's.

"Excellent!" Brayden's dad says when the song mercifully ends.

He sounds like a dance instructor. I thank him and step back awkwardly.

And then we say our goodbyes.

Brayden's mother insists on giving me a bag of chocolate chip cookies to take home with me.

"But you should keep them," I protest.

"You appreciate them so much," she says. "It's like you've never had a homemade chocolate chip cookie before! It thrills me to give them to you."

I take them from her and impulsively hug her goodbye. Brayden follows me out the door and down the path to his truck.

I comment on the beautiful garden as we pass it.

"Now that my dad's retired, they have more time to do things like grow a garden." He chuckles. "They used to say all they had time to do before was grow kids and a family."

I get into the truck and bite my lip. My parents' yard is filled with weeds like nobody's ever walked in it. Mom and Dad travel too much to spend any time taking care of the land. And my parents' house felt nothing like Brayden's. It was always freezing because Dad believed that spending money on heat was a waste of finances. He said we were a tough bunch, and if he could live on a beach in a tent with no running water for three weeks, then he could surely live in an insulated home without jacking up the heat just to feed the gas company.

I wait until we're out of sight of the house before I speak.

"Did you tip off the authorities about Noah?"

Brayden's hands tighten on the wheel, and he pulls off to the side of the ranch road.

He puts the truck in park and turns to face me.

"Yes," he says simply.

I stare at him, torn between wanting to kiss him and question him.

"Why?" I ask him. "I was a stranger to you, and it was a risk to alert the authorities. What if he found out you'd done that and tried to get revenge somehow?"

"I made sure my tip couldn't be traced," he says. "And you were never a stranger to me, Leleila. You always felt familiar. I would never have betrayed your trust by telling your story, but I wanted that jerk to be punished for what he did. More than that, though, I wanted you safe."

"So you found a way to get him kicked out of my school and out of town."

Brayden's jaw ticks. "I didn't know your name or where you lived. I couldn't be sure if you went to school in Mountainview. But because of football, I knew who he was. And so I figured if he left the area, he'd leave you alone."

We sit in silence for a moment until Brayden says, "Well, I'd better get you back."

"Brayden." Emotion clogs my throat as I reach out and grab his arm. He turns back, and without thinking about it, I pull him toward me and kiss him quickly on the cheek. I can feel him trembling underneath me, and I rein my lips back from going to his mouth and touching every part of him I can reach.

Instead, I put my arms around him and rest my chin on his shoulder. He wraps his arms around my back and holds me close.

———

When I walk in the door, Phillip is at the microscope.

"I just walked in," he says to me, taking his attention off the lens to greet me. "How was the tasting? I'm so sorry I missed it."

I want to snap at him for skipping out on me again, but I take one look at his bloodshot eyes and keep my frustration to myself.

"It was delicious," I say as I sit next to him. "I was sad you weren't there."

"Me too." He puts one eye up to the lens. "How's dance class going with Brayden? Is it working out okay?"

I stare at his bent head. "Yeah. It's going well."

"Great."

"Phillip..."

"Yeah?"

"Phillip, I really need to talk to you." I wring my hands next to him. "Please give me just one of your eyes while you look into that scope."

He shifts so his left eye is focused on me. "That better?"

"Perfect. Phillip, I met Brayden twelve years ago. Before you and I started dating."

Two eyes are on me now.

"How? Where?" His voice is breathy and tense.

"I was at a party after a football game."

"You don't go to parties."

"I know. But I did—this one time. And I was attacked."

Phillip's head is now fully upright as his attention fixes on me in a way I can't remember him doing in years.

"Tell me everything."

So I do. I tell him about Noah, and how he dragged me into the bedroom, and how Brayden was standing outside it when I escaped.

"He made sure I was all right, and he wanted to kill Noah, but I didn't let him." My voice breaks, and Phillip pulls me into a hug.

"I'm so sorry that happened to you, Lei."

I raise my head to meet his gaze. "Brayden was my first real kiss."

Phillip's arms go rigid around me. "He was?"

"Yes."

"But you didn't...have sex with him?" Phillip's voice is calm. Eerily calm.

"No. You know you were my first."

Phillip's still quiet.

"I would have told you earlier, but I didn't know how to without also telling you about the attack. And I was so ashamed of that. I just wanted to bury it away and never think of it again. Almost like I could pretend it never happened."

"I understand."

"I hadn't seen Brayden since that night. I didn't even know his name before."

Phillip's arms relax. "Lei." He puts his hand on my knee. "I'm not threatened. We don't have that kind of relationship."

No, I guess we don't. But right now, I'm not sure what kind of relationship we do have.

He kisses my forehead. "I saw your painting." He gestures to the easel in the corner of the room.

I back off his lap and return to the couch. "What'd you think?"

"It's a good little hobby, Lei. But you're a scientist, not an artist."

"What do you mean?"

Phillip chuckles. "Well, you're the daughter of two scientists. These paintings are for you, not the public, right? I mean, what you've painted isn't exactly meant to impress, is it?"

I stand up. "That's mean, Phillip."

He keeps chuckling but less loudly now. Less confidently. His gaze meets mine, and it's like he finally sees what I was so certain he'd see weeks ago—something's changed. Everything's changed, really, but I can't expect him to know all of that yet. I'm not sure I even understand what's happening.

That's when it hits me. I got so used to living in Phillip's shadow I grew to believe I couldn't live without him. I lived without him the first sixteen years of my life, but the next ten are filled with memories of Phillip Rowe and all his accomplishments. He's been by my side my entire adult life.

As he finally stops smirking, I realize how devastating it can feel to have somebody you've counted on—somebody you've trusted—crush your dreams and not let you shine. Even though it's unconscious and he means well, Phillip never wanted me to shine.

I turn my back on Phillip and carefully go put my paints away in a trunk. Mom gave me this trunk when Grandma died; she said she used to keep her microscope in there so her mother wouldn't think she was "too much of a nerd." I guess this trunk is meant to keep secrets—and important dreams—safe.

"Lei." Phillip comes over to me as I squat silently in front of the trunk I just closed. "Hey."

"Hi, Phillip." I don't look up at him, though, and he doesn't seem to know what else to say.

"We're going to be okay, Leleila. I'll be away tomorrow night, but in less than two weeks, you and I are going to get married, and everything will settle down."

CHAPTER TWENTY-ONE

The next morning, Phillip has some work to do at the university before he leaves for the conference. Gerry calls and asks if I can meet him for breakfast instead of lunch. That's when Phillip says he'll drive me, and then we can leave together so he can come home and pack.

When we arrive at campus, I wave goodbye to Phillip and walk into Huckman Hall, remembering all the meals I ate here—sometimes with Phillip but often with other psychology students as we hurriedly ate with our textbooks and laptops laid out around us so we wouldn't miss an hour of studying. I don't miss it as much as I thought I would, and my stomach turns into knots of anxiety just going through the cafeteria line with my tray of eggs and toast.

As soon as Gerry and I take our seats at the corner table and he swallows his first bite of omelet, he says to me, "I asked to meet with you because I just found out some news. News that may upset you. But I believe you have a right to know the truth."

Dread shoots through my gut. "What kind of news? Is it about my defense date?"

"Not exactly." He takes a breath and looks me dead in the eyes. "I was talking to a member of the panel—I won't say who because, honestly, it really doesn't matter as they were all involved."

"Involved in what?"

"Leleila, Phillip went to the panel ahead of time and assured them that if they agreed to pass you, he would make sure you fixed your data before sending out your paper for publication. He may have even intimated that you were on board with this idea."

My head starts spinning. "He what? I don't understand."

"Let me back up." Gerry's face contorts with guilt. "I went to Phillip first."

"You. Spoke to my fiancé about my research."

He holds up his hands. "I had good intentions, Leleila. You were so worried about getting your PhD before your wedding, and I thought you needed more time. I asked Phillip if he could talk to you because I was concerned you were pressing to get everything done due to Phillip's timetable rather than your own. He assured me he'd make sure you put in the data you needed for the whole panel's approval. He knew what was needed. But then you presented, and that data wasn't there after all. I couldn't understand what had happened. But now I know—Phillip thought he could persuade the panel to pass you based on his reputation, his merit." He shakes his head. "I'm sure he meant well, but he let his arrogance get the best of him here. Because the panel half-heartedly agreed with his idea, and then they changed their minds once they heard you present. Panels are not known for their loyalty; you know that as well as I do."

My face goes hot. "Phillip was going to help me with my data. But then he said he didn't have time because of his own work. I guess talking to the panel was his idea of a quick fix."

Gerry frowns. "He assured me that he'd take a look at your research. I told him if you stuck with your current data, the panel would most likely fail you. He's experienced enough with a thesis panel to know exactly what I meant. I just never expected he'd go behind my back like that. I'm sorry, Leleila. I just thought you should know."

My heart feels like it's been stomped on. I stand up, leaving my breakfast untouched. "I appreciate you coming to me," I say. "Please excuse me. I have to go do something."

———

Phillip's bent over a microscope in the ecology lab when I barge in without warning. He jerks his head up.

"Leleila. You scared me. What are you doing here?"

I take a seat next to him, ignoring the two other people looking at slides. They take one look at us and immediately get up and walk out, leaving us alone.

"I just had an interesting conversation with Gerry," I say. "He told me everything, Phillip. How you struck a deal with the panel? How could you do that?"

Phillip turns red. "That's true. But I don't know what the big deal is. That committee should have passed you. You were ready. I saw to it myself. They broke our deal. That's on them."

"That committee is what matters!" I say to him. "They didn't think I was ready, and you pushed me. You said I would definitely pass. And you didn't tell me to alter my dissertation, which you promised Gerry you would do."

"You would have passed no problem if the panel hadn't been so idiotic," he says angrily. "You'd have your PhD right now, and we'd both be professors in time for our wedding. We'd be packing our bags for Africa in a month. Hopefully, we'll be able to anyway, but I didn't know there would be another way at the time. So yes, I pushed you to present when you did. But it was all for us, Lei."

"See, that's the thing," I say. "It feels to me like you did it for you. You wanted that grant, and the only way for us to get it was if we both had our doctorates. I was happy to do something together, and of course, I wanted a job at the university. But I didn't want to force the issue if the timing was off."

"No," Phillip protests. "I truly thought you were ready, Lei. You had been preparing for years for your PhD. How was waiting six months going to help?"

"You should have told me Gerry came to you," I say. "I know I was being stubborn, but you should have told me what he said to you."

———

After our talk, which doesn't really end with any resolution, Phillip heads to the airport alone, and I drive to Big Sky Grocer.

I go straight to June's office.

"So ignoring the questionable lapse in ethics between Phillip and the panel, do you think Phillip should have told me what he did?"

"Well, of course I do," she says.

"So why do you think he didn't?" I say.

She purses her lips.

"Because he was trying to protect me?" I suggest. "Or maybe because he really believed in me that much? Or in my data?"

"Is that what you really believe?" she asks me. "That his heart was in the right place?"

I don't answer her.

"Because if you felt that way, I don't know why you'd be locked in a room with your sister trying not to cry," she says as she looks at my face.

"I'm not crying," I say. "I'm too numb to cry."

June reaches out and touches my arm. "I have some good news. People love your mural. I mean, they love it."

I wrinkle my nose, sure she's messing with me.

"I'm not joking!" she says. "I've gotten more compliments on that damn mural than on any products I'm carrying. I had somebody come inside this afternoon to ask about it, saying they saw it from outside. As soon as I told them the artist's name, they asked if you had anything here for sale."

I laugh. "Seriously, that will be a while. I've just started up again."

Impulsively, I quickly text her the picture of the horseback riding painting that I showed Sophia. "Show them this if you'd like."

She looks at the text coming across her screen. "This is great, Lei. You're sure I can show it around?"

I nod. "I guess so."

"Cool."

June makes a circle in the air with her index finger. "Returning to the reason you came by—I love you, so I have to say this bluntly —don't go through with the wedding if your heart's not in it, Leleila." Her words sound suspiciously like a warning. "Don't end up like Mom and Dad, sleeping with a microscope between you. That life works for them because they share a passion for science. But it will never work for you, and you know I'm right. When all you have left between you and Phillip is a microscope, your life's going to feel awfully cold."

"I have to…take some time," I say shakily. "I need to think."

"I know." Her voice is unusually gentle. "But make sure you listen to your heart first and foremost. You know that, though."

"I'm trying." I stand up slowly. "Thanks for the talk. I'll see you later."

Before leaving the store, I stop into the bathroom.

It's while I'm washing my hands that I realize.

My ring's gone.

I peer into the sink in a panic. I pull up the drain plug and look in. I return to the bathroom stall and look all over the tiled floor. I even look into the toilet.

Nothing. No hint of red string anywhere. It's like it vanished into thin air sometime after I said goodbye to Phillip.

I curse myself for not noticing that the knot was loosening. I should have asked Phillip to retie it before he left for his trip. Or I could have put fabric glue on the worn section. But Phillip said it was a forever knot. He promised it was a forever knot, and I believed him. I believed him so much that I ignored the signs—the fraying of the string between my ring finger and pinkie, the way the knot looked different this week than it had during the past six months. It didn't look like it was coming undone, exactly; it just looked...different.

It's not too late. I can go to the convenience store down the street and buy some red string and make a substitute ring. I leave the bathroom hurriedly, only to be waylaid by June asking me to hold the door open while a delivery is wheeled in.

Fifteen minutes later, I finally reach the parking lot and start walking toward my car. Before I unlock my door, I spot a familiar-looking figure standing outside his truck. His head is hat-free, and his dirty blond hair blows lightly in the breeze. His worn jeans hug his ass snugly, and his muscles are lean and hard beneath his thin shirt.

Everything is forgotten. Everything but him.

Impulsively, I walk closer.

"Hey, Brayden," I call out.

He turns around, his eyes lighting up as he sees me. "Hey, Leleila. How are you?"

As usual, he doesn't ask in that cursory greeting so many people use where they don't really want to know the answer. He asks like he's honestly interested.

And for the second time today, I really want to tell someone.

"Do you have a minute?" I ask him.

He holds up the paper bag in his hand. "I was going to eat lunch. I've got a giant turkey sandwich I picked up at the café and a cup of fries. It's plenty for two. You want to join me?"

"Um..."

His bright eyes lock with mine. "Look, we said we'd be friends, hang out as friends until your wedding."

I lick my lips. "Brayden..."

But he doesn't give me a chance to overthink it. The blue in his eyes just gets clearer, and he nods with far more assurance than I have. "Just friends hanging out. You can tell me what's got you looking sadder than usual."

I tug at the strap of my purse. "Sure. Let's go eat."

CHAPTER TWENTY-TWO

We step over the fence separating June's store from Big River Ranch, and Brayden leads me to what he says is his favorite part of the ranch. The pine trees thicken as we walk along the trail, but the path opens out onto a clearing.

I can't help but gasp. There's a swinging wooden bench a few feet away, but that's the only man-made thing I can see. Massive pine trees surround the clearing, and I glimpse a powerful river running just off to the right. I twist my neck so I can stare at the Montana sky, appearing even bigger out here than it does in town, and then I bring my gaze down to where Brayden's watching me.

"Wow," I say to him. "It's incredible here."

We step into the clearing, and Brayden takes a seat on the bench overlooking the rushing river. I sit cross-legged next to him.

It's a breezy day, but the sun is shining, and the comforting Montana sky is a clear blue.

Much like Brayden's eyes when I lower my gaze to meet his.

He points at the nearest tree. "Look at that crazy squirrel chasing the other one around and around the trunk and then high up into the branches. They play all day long sometimes."

I feel the blood return to my face. "Is it easy for you to sit and do nothing?"

Brayden chuckles. "Is that a compliment or something else?"

I smile. "It's a compliment."

"Well, I don't know. Yeah, I guess it is pretty easy. I'm not a list person. I don't have a whole lot of to-dos every day. I try to get the big things done, and that's about it."

I like sitting around, doing nothing, too. I like not having equations and measurements running through my head the way I have with my PhD program and when I help Phillip.

Brayden searches my face. "Do you want to talk about it?"

"Sure. Maybe a male opinion will be different," I say.

When I'm finished telling him about my breakfast with Gerry, I look at Brayden hopefully. "Do you think it's that bad what Phillip did?"

He squirms and doesn't say anything one way or the other, but I see the flash of anger cross his face.

"You wouldn't have done that, would you?" I say.

"I don't..." Brayden begins awkwardly.

"Would you have done it?" I say, my voice barely above a whisper.

"No," he says in a firm tone. "I wouldn't have. And I absolutely wouldn't have kept it from you either. Not that or the conversation he had with your advisor. Especially not if you were the woman I was living with and planned to marry. I wouldn't keep a secret like that from you. It was your dissertation and your data. If he knew it needed to be improved upon before you presented, he should have told you that rather than try to fix the situation himself."

Exactly.

"It sounds like he meant well, though," Brayden adds. "He tried to help."

"He did."

Neither of us adds that his reason for helping had more to do with his own needs than mine. At one point, my needs and Phillip's were the same. But lately, that hasn't been the case. And it's nobody's fault; sometimes you grow out of a relationship.

"We were so young when we got together," I murmur almost to myself.

"How old were you when you started dating?"

"I was sixteen. I met him right after the party where I ran into you. We've been together ever since."

"I'm glad he was there for you."

"Me too. I owe him a lot." I exhale heavily.

"Sounds like that's a burden."

"And yet I'm walking into this with my own two feet and making my own decisions along the way," I say. "I have nothing to complain about."

"Sometimes things feel out of our control." The words come out raw. "Don't you think?"

"Sometimes. I guess sometimes when I'm with my fiancé, I feel like I have to be somebody I'm not." It's the first time I've confessed that out loud to anyone before, and I feel like I'm betraying Phillip just for speaking it.

"Like a scientist?" Brayden asks me.

"Like a saint," I say without meaning to. "Like I have to be exactly what he wants, or else he'll reject me. I guess that's sort of how I felt growing up in my family, so it's a pattern I'm working on changing. Being myself no matter what."

Brayden's warm hand touches my arm. "Do you believe in following your heart?"

"I don't know. I'm not sure I do." I could add that I'm not sure I love Phillip enough to marry him, that I'm not sure I'm in love with him at all, and that I didn't really know any of this until I ran into Brayden again after twelve years of walking through life half-numb.

Like he always does, Brayden finds a way to soothe me. "You want to lie down on the truck bed and look at the sky?" he asks me.

Lying down and looking at the ceiling—or the sky—together has become a bit of a tradition for us. And I love it. I love doing nothing with somebody and having it feel so important.

"Yes," I say. "That sounds nice."

I lie down next to him and shut my eyes. I hear Brayden settle next to me, and I open my eyes and look at the sky.

"Beautiful day today," he says.

"It is. Nothing better than a clear sky in Montana." I point to the lone cloud off to the left. "That cloud looks like a cheetah."

He lets out a low chuckle. "Cheetahs are fast. I'm not sure how I feel about fast."

"You like to take your time?" I say, wondering if that statement holds true in the bedroom as well.

"I guess it depends on the situation. Or the moment." Brayden stops, almost as if he's fighting himself. But then he says in a voice laced with longing, "I'm not that picky if it feels right."

Me neither.

Unconsciously, I reach for my left ring finger.

And I freeze.

I never bought any red string. I didn't even go out to try to find any red string because I saw Brayden in the parking lot and I forgot. I rub at my finger in a panic as if I can bring back the ring magically.

Brayden picks up my left hand and touches my bare ring finger. "What happened to it?"

I jerk my head up to look at him, wondering when he noticed, but his expression is blank.

"It's gone." I shrug. "Sometime between yesterday and today, it disappeared. Phillip had sworn his knot couldn't come undone." I glance down at my bare finger. "But it did."

The loud ring tone of Save the Soil breaks the thick silence between us.

I wrestle my phone out of my coat pocket and answer it as I sit up. "Hello?"

"The test results just came in," Patsy says. "It's bad."

"How bad?"

"As bad as it could be. You know what that means."

"Jesus," I say quietly.

"Where did this soil come from, Leleila?" she asks me. "Because this is no mild toxin here. This is a serious contaminant."

"Give me a little time, and I'll get back to you," I say.

I disconnect the call and turn to Brayden. "We need to talk to your neighbors."

He looks at my face. "The sample results came in. What did they find?"

"In terms of contaminants on a scale of zero to ten? It's a hundred," I say.

When I get home, I go straight to my computer and pull up all my data where I stare at it until I'm dizzy. Remembering Gerry's question to me after I failed, I look at my data more carefully than ever before, and I start to see the flaws for the first time. What I realize, though, is I wouldn't have changed a thing. I believe wholeheartedly in my thesis. I believe I gave it my best shot. I just don't think the panel and I would have ever been on the same page. And that's not Phillip's fault, or Gerry's, or the panel's. It's also not mine. Sometimes, things just aren't meant to be.

I rest my chin in my hand and stare at the screen. I extrapolated one data set after another, but what I never did—not once—was extrapolate why I was really pursuing this degree. I always wanted to help people, but I never stopped to consider another way. A way I could truly be passionate about.

I walk over to my easel and look at the painting I completed. And I smile.

This is what I love to do.

Brayden picks me up for dance class, and as we drive to the store, he lets me know that the ranch owners are going straight to the authorities with the information he provided.

"They wanted to know who helped me," he says. "I gave them your name and the name of your parents' foundation. I hope that's okay."

"Of course," I say. "You did the right thing. Hopefully, they'll be able to resolve this in time before anyone gets sick and the surrounding area risks further poisoning."

We walk into Big Sky Grocer and head upstairs.

Ten minutes into class, Elroy shouts our names in frustration. Brayden and I have been dancing awkwardly since the lesson began tonight. I'm not sure why, but we're behaving more like strangers right now than we have any other week here.

"You two—pay attention now. You seem distracted tonight. You have the basics under your belt. Now take it a step further. I want to feel your heat!"

Brayden leans in and says in a low tone, "Just feel the music. Think of it like an exercise. We can't look like robots, or it won't work."

I nod at him, and we try again. I shift my hips to the music, moving closer to Brayden and then back. I lose awareness of the rest of the class and even of Elroy barking out comments. I just keep my gaze on Brayden's beautiful blue eyes, and I let go of trying to control the moment. The music gets louder, and Brayden and I move even closer together, his chest touching mine as he wraps his arm tightly around my waist. I feel like we're moving as one, and it's amazing.

Elroy applauds heartily and shouts for everyone's attention.

"Today's my birthday," he says with a dramatic pause, which we all fill by clapping and cheering. "Thank you, thank you—so we're going to end class tonight with champagne!"

He reaches behind him for the bottle. "And I've got more where this came from if we run out."

———

An hour and a half later, I stumble out of Big Sky Grocer. Brayden has his arm around me, not in a disrespectful way, more in a "you're going to fall onto your ass if somebody doesn't hold you up" kind of way.

That's right. I got drunk off three glasses of champagne.

Brayden stopped at a half glass and said he'd stay sober to drive me home.

I've never been a drinker, not just at parties but also in life. That feeling of being out of control is one of the worst feelings I can have, and I try to avoid it whenever possible.

But tonight? After the argument I had with Phillip and the way I've felt ever since, not just about him but about my career plans, a glass of champagne was just what I needed.

And a second.

Then a third.

Because the bottom line is—I trust Brayden.

I trust him not to take advantage of me.

I trust him to keep me safe.

And I trust him to be my friend.

My best friend.

I trip as we turn the corner toward Brayden's truck, and he tightens his hold on me.

"Let's stop for a second so you can get your bearings," he says.

I glance up at the sky littered with stars. I can pick out the Big Dipper and Orion clearly, and as I keep looking...

"A shooting star!"

"Cool." Brayden stares at the sky. "Do you know what shooting stars are?"

"They're little chunks of rock in space. The same as a meteor." My drunken mouth won't shut up as I ramble on about how meteor showers happen when the earth passes through the path of a comet. "But shooting stars happen nightly." I tell him how you're supposed to be able to see more shooting stars just before dawn than earlier in the night, "Because we're facing the direction in which the earth is moving at that time. So we intercept more of the stuff in space."

"Do you remember everything that you learned in school?" Brayden teases me. "Or just the questions I've happened to ask?"

"I remember things, but apparently that didn't help with my defense." I laugh. "I'm great at trivia games, though, if you ever need a partner."

Long pause. Then, my tongue still loose from the alcohol, I say what's been on my mind all afternoon and evening.

"I'm thinking of dropping out of the PhD program."

Until I say it out loud to somebody else— somebody who won't judge me—I didn't realize I was that certain about it myself.

Brayden's focus shifts from the sky to my face. "Wow. When did you decide?"

"When I left campus today and I went home..." I stop. "I guess I just realized something felt off."

"Because you don't love it anymore?" he asks me.

"Because I never loved it," I say, and I realize it's true as I say it. "I loved taking tests, and being right, and knowing if I was right that there was a test that would prove it, you know? I loved having a teacher with me, at all times, to tell me what was right and what was wrong. Life felt safer that way. Especially after what happened at the party. I lost trust in my intuition. I guess I felt like I needed a mentor, someone to instruct me on what to do."

Like Phillip. He's been my instructor since I was sixteen.

"Maybe you're still making up your mind about all of it," Brayden says as he watches my face.

"No," I say, and I shake my head. "I think it's made up. I'm not going to go back. I'm going to look for a job, and I'm going to paint, but I'm not going to continue in the PhD program. I'll go see my advisor this week."

We look at each other in silence, and I know Brayden's on my side. It feels strange to not have to justify dropping out, especially when I know telling the other people in my life isn't going to be nearly so simple.

I flick my gaze to his. "My parents will flip out. They're scientists through and through. That world is all they know."

"They must get along well with your fiancé."

"Of course," I say as we start walking again toward Brayden's truck. "Sometimes it seems like they like him better than me."

Brayden squeezes my shoulder. "I'm sure that's not true."

"It is," I insist. "He and my father are like twins."

We reach his truck, and Brayden opens the door for me.

"I can't believe I'm dropping out. I don't usually try new things. I tend to stick with what I'm used to."

"Dance class was brand new for you. And you handled that like a pro."

Impulsively, I reach over and touch his arm. "Thanks for taking the class with me. I don't have a clue what possessed me to decide to dance because this is all very unlike me. I'm more of a book girl normally."

"Maybe you wanted to feel what it was like to have a life partner before your wedding," he suggests.

"Maybe you're right."

The alcohol is still coursing through my veins, and my hand tightens on his arm. He inhales, but he doesn't lean closer to me.

"Do you want to ask me something, Leleila?" His voice is rough. "You can say whatever you want to."

My hormones are awake and dancing. "I want to..."

"What?" The word comes out strangled, almost like he can barely speak. "What do you want?"

His hands are fisted in his lap, and he's clenching his jaw tightly.

I want you.

"I haven't had good sex in a long time," I confess. "Really, ever. And I'm worried I never will. I saw a therapist once about what happened, and she said people can shut down sexually. They lose trust in men and in intimacy."

Shit. Shit. Shit. Why did I just say that? This is exactly why I should never be allowed within a mile of alcohol.

But the light reflecting from the streetlight reveals how the blue of Brayden's eyes darkens even more at my revelation.

He shifts in his seat, facing me head-on. "I understand. I'm sorry. What's been not good about your experience?"

I take my hand off his arm and shrug. "Everything. Phillip doesn't...he doesn't think I'm very sexual."

A curt laugh blows out of Brayden's mouth. "I can assure you, Leleila, that you are absolutely perfect in that department. Maybe your fiancé needs to spend a little more time focusing on you and not trying to get himself off."

"But you've never been with me in bed," I say, feeling how hot my face is. "So you don't know."

"I just spent an hour with my body pressed close to yours on the dance floor." He tips my chin up with his thumb. "You move like sin and honey. You drove me crazy every minute. In fact, if you were single, I'd be worried I would embarrass myself with a..." He gestures to his crotch. "Full mast situation."

I bite my lip. "Seriously?"

"I wouldn't lie to you." His hand cups my cheek. "Okay? I promise I'll never lie to you, Leleila."

"Okay."

A car drives by us, breaking the moment. I pull back, and Brayden drops his hand and starts up the truck.

"You'll be fine," he murmurs, almost to himself. "I promise you'll be fine."

Our drive to my house is quiet. The world around me is spinning, and I'm already getting the beginnings of a headache. Tomorrow morning should be fun.

When we reach my house, he pulls up just short of the driveway as usual.

"Phillip's away." I realize how the words sound coming out, and I fumble to right things. "I just meant—you won't run into him and have to chat about how dance class is going. I know you two don't have much in common."

Brayden's already pulling into the driveway. "If you're alone, I'm going to make sure you get inside okay."

We walk inside with me apologizing for the cold living room.

"Our house is drafty," I say. "We try to keep our heat as low as possible and rely on solar. In winter, though, that's more difficult."

Brayden has me sit on the couch while he goes and gets me a glass of water and some crackers.

When he returns, he gestures to my painting on the easel. "Is that yours?"

I jump up and try to cover the painting with my arms. I don't put them directly onto the canvas because the oils haven't dried yet; I just hang my arms in the air and hope that will do the trick. But Brayden bends his head so he can see underneath.

He turns to face me. "That's amazing, Leleila."

"Thanks." I give up fending him off and step back.

"You can really do this," he says. By the tone of his voice, I can tell he means it. "You have something here."

A weight drops off my shoulders, and I grab my portfolio as we walk over to the couch and sit down. "I appreciate that, Brayden. If you're interested, here's some of my other work. It was a long time ago, but..."

"I'd love to take a look," he says.

As he flips through the pages, I stare at my old paintings. It feels like a lifetime ago, and yet I can still remember how much I loved it.

"I can see you doing this," he says. "You know, professionally."

"Really?"

"Yeah. Not to put pressure on you or anything, I know these things take a lot of work." He furrows his brow. "Maybe you need a job where you have time to paint."

"That would be nice, but it seems unrealistic."

"Flexibility," he says. "That's what you need."

"I do want flexible hours. And I don't want a long commute."

I grab my laptop and open up to a saved tab. "I did find this one job the other day. It's from home. From home could be really nice for me."

Brayden glances at the screen.

"It sounds like it could work," he says. "Why don't you apply for it?"

"I think I will." I lean back against the couch cushions. "When I'm sober. I've thought about painting so much over the years, but I've never done anything about it. Not until I failed my thesis."

"You've probably got a lot of ideas stored up if you've been thinking about it that much."

"I overthink everything." I laugh. "I've thought way too much about learning to dance whereas you're really good at dancing and you've probably never given it a second thought before."

"I've thought a lot about finding the right partner," he says, and I know as soon as the words leave his mouth he wishes he hadn't said them.

I look at him sharply, and he closes his eyes for a second like maybe the moment won't be here when he opens them. But when he opens his eyes, I'm still here, and so is that sentence he just strung together in his head and let out into the open.

I smile at him, his sapphire eyes the only thing I see.

"I remember your eyes the night we met," I say in a soft voice. "They were the first thing I noticed about you."

"You were so beautiful." Brayden's breath goes shallow. "You still are, of course, but I don't usually tell you that." He watches my face as my cheeks heat.

The chemistry is immediate and intense between us, and suddenly we're leaning closer. I stare into Brayden's incredible blue eyes, thinking crazy thoughts like how happy Elroy would be to see our heat. He leans in closer, and I feel enveloped by his masculine power.

He's going to kiss me.

But at the last second, he abruptly shifts back. We stay silent for several more heartbeats, and I can't take the physical closeness any longer. I'm too drunk for this.

I break the gaze and stare down at my water glass that Brayden has hurriedly shoved into my hands.

"I'm worried hanging out together isn't healthy for either of us," he says.

"How come?"

His tone is soft. "Because of the line."

"The line?" I clutch the water glass like it's a lifeline.

"It can get hard to draw the line, Lei," Brayden says so softly I nearly cry. "That's all I'm saying."

"Harder and harder," I murmur.

"I know you were told to find a dance partner for the month." Brayden's voice is so low I have to strain to hear him. "Yet despite your fiancé's laissez-faire attitude, which I personally think is crap, I don't want to complicate things for you so close to...you know, your big day."

I close my eyes and try not to panic.

Brayden's voice is rough and stripped of all pretenses when he speaks again. "Leleila, I think I should leave."

I search his face. His expression is laced with an emotion I can't read, and the pulse in his neck is throbbing. It's like a switch went off inside of him, and he's about to bolt.

He stands up. "If you and Sophia still want to come to the party after Friday's game, you're welcome to."

I narrow my eyes. "You don't want us to come?"

"I do want you to. I just don't think it's going to be your thing is all. And I don't want you doing anything that will make you uncomfortable."

"I thought it was *your* thing."

"It is. It's..." He exhales. "It used to be my thing, and it still is a part of me. You know I don't party like I used to." He practically runs to the door. "Sleep well. I'll see you."

I bang my head against my hand. What a mess. I finish my glass of water, and then I get up and spend the next two hours with a paintbrush in my hand.

CHAPTER TWENTY-THREE

Brayden

Shit. I can't believe I almost fucking kissed her. *That* cannot happen again. I wanted a taste of Leleila's lips again so badly I was shaking. It's been twelve years since I've kissed her, and my need for her tonight was stronger than it's ever been. I had to physically wrench myself away from her and drag my ass out the door.

I've just backed out of her driveway when my phone rings.

I pick up. "Hey, Cam."

"Bray, we're at your house."

Great. I'm in a shitty mood, and I have unexpected company.

"You're already in town for the wedding?" I ask.

"We came early so we could go to the Wilcox game on Friday. Jenson, Olivia, and his sons are here too. Jenson's putting the boys to bed now."

Jenson's the only one of us who's already a father. He and his ex-wife had an unplanned pregnancy when they were in college, and his sons are now six years old. Jenson and Olivia have known each other their whole lives, and they went through a lot of shit to get to where they are now—together and engaged to be married.

"Cool. I'll be home in about ten." I turn right onto Main Street and head for my house.

Cam goes silent, which is unusual for him. He still hasn't told me what's going on, but I know something's bothering him.

"Something's up with you," I say, unable to stay quiet any longer.

"What do you mean?" His tone is sharp.

"Is it Amy?"

He snorts. "Right."

"Okay. So if not Amy, then what?"

Silence.

"Hockey? Your dad?"

"How did you know when was the right time?" he asks.

"The right time..."

"To quit playing football."

I stop at the red light and tap the steering wheel lightly. So it is about hockey. And his dad. The two have always been inextricably linked in Cam's life.

"I knew when I finally accepted that I didn't love playing football the way I would need to if I wanted to make it big. I enjoyed playing, but I didn't love it like I love Montana and the ranch life," I say. "I love to coach and be around the sport as much as possible, but to try to pursue it professionally? That never would have made me happy."

"Yeah." The line goes quiet again.

"My dad says Uncle Tyler always was the most obstinate of all the brothers," I say, referring to Cam's father.

"Oh, yeah? Did he also say my dad was the biggest asshole of the bunch?"

"I don't know. Dylan's dad may have him beat there." I'm not really joking, and Cam knows it. Dylan's nothing like his father, and my dad always says, "Thank God for that."

"I appreciate the input, Bray," Cam says. "I'll see you in a few."

"See you. I'm nearly there."

———

I park the truck in my driveway and head up the steps. Olivia opens the front door before I can and greets me with a hug. Her sleek black hair is up in a messy bun, and she apologizes immediately for, "...letting you into your own house." Jenson and Cam are right behind her, and the four of us walk through the foyer and out to my porch.

We stand in a circle in front of my fireplace with no one speaking at first.

Jenson and Cam don't ask me what I was doing out after midnight or why I look like hell. Like they always have, they accept me without question, without judgment. Besides my cousins and my immediate family, the only other person I've ever met who accepts me unconditionally is across town and days away from marrying somebody else. Someone who's not me. And the more I get to know Leleila Wills, the more painful that truth has become.

I glance at the cup of tea in Cam's hand. "That looks good."

"You want a cup?" Olivia's already heading for the kitchen. "J put the kettle on when we got in. Our flight was freezing cold; the air never warmed up."

We all follow her out of the room and take seats on the kitchen bar stools.

I lean my elbows on the island counter. "Thanks, Olivia. I hope I didn't wake up the kids just now."

"Not a chance," Jenson assures me, pushing an overgrown lock of blond hair out of his face. "Meghan sleeps like the dead, and the kids both take after her." He gets up to take two cups of tea from Olivia, leaning in to kiss her as he does.

As they gaze at each other, my chest clenches with unexpected pain, pain that's all about my own relationship issues. Olivia and Jenson are so in love and their connection so powerful that I can't believe they were able to keep it private for as long as they did. I swallow down my own problems and focus on their long-deserved happiness.

"Congratulations on your engagement, you two." I raise the cup of tea Olivia hands me. "When's the wedding?"

Olivia smiles at Jenson. "We're not sure. I don't want a big formal thing, so we're still trying to figure it all out."

She takes a seat on a stool next to Jenson, and the two of them face Cam and me.

"The happy couple and the last two single Wilds." Cam chuckles. "We make a good pair, Bray."

When I don't laugh with him, he shifts so he can face me head-on. "So, fucking tell us already," he says to me, his mouth twisting in a frown. "What the hell's going on?"

Not sure how much Jenson and Olivia know, I lay out my cards bluntly.

"Her name's Leleila," I say as I clench my hands around the hot cup of tea. "I met her twelve years ago at a party and haven't seen her since. Not until she walked into her sister's store. She's engaged, and her wedding's in less than two weeks."

Jenson raises a blond eyebrow. "That's not simple."

"No. I don't know him so I shouldn't be making snap judgments, but I'm pretty sure her fiancé's an asshole. Treats her like crap. And Leleila's become my best friend." I'm just getting started. "She's free to pretty much do whatever she wants until the wedding. He's not around, and he's not planning to be, not until he's put a ring on her finger and can control her life from there on out."

"Wait a minute." Cam raises a hand to stop me. "When you say she can do whatever she wants, you mean…"

"Not everything," I clarify. "Not anything like you're thinking, so you can pull your dirty mind out of the fucking gutter."

Cam chuckles.

"But outside of that, everything's on the table with this woman, meaning she's free all the time to hang out." I let out a frustrated groan. "Which is weird for me because what started out as friends has turned into me craving her. And she's engaged. So that makes me an ass."

"You're so the opposite of an ass, Bray." Cam's tone leaves no room for argument.

"But wanting her is wrong. I wasn't raised that way. Except I don't fucking know how to stop things between us, other than to just walk away from her. And something tells me that would crush her. She's lonely, and her relationship with her fiancé, from the little I've heard, sounds shitty. You guys are happily engaged; what do you think?" I run my hand down my face and turn to Jenson and Olivia.

Jenson and Olivia look at each other. "Obviously, we can relate," Jenson says to me. "Feeling wrong for the way you feel; knowing you'll never find someone who measures up but thinking she's forbidden."

"Ah, forbidden love." Olivia's tone holds a twinge of bitterness and a fair amount of regret. "I let the rules of others control me for far too long. My father being the mayor, the town's judgment—it nearly undid me to be frank."

"Your relationship didn't have a third person involved, though," Cam says. "How is Bray supposed to handle that?"

"Sounds like you're conflicted about more than morals." Jenson taps the counter, and I glance at him. "From the look in your eyes, I'd say you're also flipping over what you know you'll be losing in two weeks. So you're holding back on telling this woman how you feel."

"You're saying you think I should bare my soul to a woman who's engaged to another man."

"I'm saying don't let her go without a fucking fight, yes." Jenson's tone is certain. "If she's spending this much time with you rather than him, there's a problem in her relationship that she's either not facing, afraid to acknowledge, or she's just plain scared to cut bait. Sounds like her fiancé is fairly controlling."

"She was young when she met him, only sixteen." *And it was after an event that terrorized her, so she was no doubt looking for a lifeline. Someone safe to hold onto.*

But I can't say any of that to them.

Cam exhales. "Getting out of a high school relationship can be tough, man."

Cam's teenage girlfriend wasn't the one for him as an adult. Didn't stop her from hanging on long after it should have ended. And their parents' determination to keep them together made it harder.

"This isn't the same," I say. "This guy's not chasing her around. He's giving her all the space in the world."

"Except maybe she doesn't feel that way," Olivia says. "She may feel like she has to keep doing what he says and playing by his rules."

"That is how we got into this," I say slowly. "He strongly suggested she ask me to be her dance partner because he was too busy to go to class with her."

"Real attentive guy she's got there," Jenson says sarcastically. "Just take stock of all of it. Don't miss something because you're too busy overthinking what's right or what's wrong. She may need to figure this out on her own."

"I get it. That's why I keep backing up. I don't ever want Leleila to feel pressured or pushed."

And I don't want to be hurt.

But I'm pretty sure my world will come crashing down to rubble the moment Leleila and I can't be friends anymore.

"My advice?" Jenson says. "Even though you didn't ask, I would keep fighting for her. You don't want to wake up in two weeks and wish you'd done something more. Maybe she needs a reason to tell him goodbye."

Olivia wraps her arm around Jenson's waist and smiles at me fondly. "A handsome, muscular blond reason with bright blue eyes and a big heart."

I take a sip of my tea. Maybe. Or maybe, I've gotten in way over my head and can't figure out how to swim for safety.

CHAPTER TWENTY-FOUR

Leleila

I spend thirty minutes in the shower the next morning, hoping to cleanse my hangover right out of me. I actually don't feel too badly, probably because I made sure to drink plenty of water before I went to bed.

Once I'm dressed, I check my voicemail. Phillip called while I was in the shower. I call him back, but he tells me he's in the middle of brunch with a colleague, and he asks if we can talk when he gets home tonight. I say that's fine, but then I hear his colleague's voice in the background. It's female. Not only that, I'm surprised by how young her voice sounds. A lot of the professors Phillip rubs elbows with are older than him, but this woman sounds about our age or even younger. Actually, she sounds exactly like...Mindy Cox, the female professor he's been attached at the hip to.

Does Mindy match the sexual fantasy Phillip's always had? The certainty of it hits me like a knife to the heart, and chills race down my spine.

I try to ask him who he's with, but he's already said goodbye. My jaw clenches so tightly it hurts.

Fighting for control, I glance at my text messages. Brayden

sent a text saying he'll be busy the next few days because Cameron, Jenson and his fiancé, Olivia, all came into town early. He said they'll be at the football game and party too. At the end of the text, he added, *Lei, sorry I ran out last night. Let's talk Friday.*

I exhale and call Sophia.

———

Sophia knocks on my window. I walk over to see her face peering through the glass.

"What about knocking on the door?" I say as I let her in.

"That's no fun." She takes off her coat and hat and shakes out her hair. "It's cold out this morning, honey. Feels like fall passed us by all of a sudden."

"It's just a temporary chill. It's supposed to warm up again by tomorrow."

Sophia takes a seat on the couch in the same spot Brayden and I were in last night. I sit down next to her and reach over to take a piece of lint off Sophia's sweater. Her eyes follow my movement, and she shrieks.

"Your ring is gone!"

I raise my hands to calm her. "I know, I know. I didn't take it off on purpose or anything..."

"Well, where is it?" Sophia asks. "Did Brayden rip it off your finger in a moment of passion?"

"Yes, yes he did. He thought it would be really romantic and sexy to forcibly tear a piece of string off my finger. It turned me on so much I just let him do it."

"Ha, ha." Sophia pokes my arm. "You could be into kinky things, who knows."

"I'm not into anything that involves having to explain to Phillip I've lost this ring. I don't have a freaking clue where it went. The thing is, Phillip and I had an argument."

I tell her what happened, and she tsks her way through the next ten seconds. Then she says, "I don't like that Phillip did that.

But what bothers me the most is how much it clearly upset you. You two have always been a team, especially with this whole academic slash science thing you have going on. So for him not to tell you about the deal he struck with the panel—that must have stung."

I nod. "When he gets back, he and I need to talk."

"The Return of Phillip," Sophia repeats. "Sounds like a soap opera, doesn't it?"

"In more ways than one." I look at her. "I think Brayden and I had a moment last night."

"What kind of moment?"

I shake my head. "I don't know. I'm so bad at this kind of thing."

"No, you're not. You're new at this. But this is a very complicated situation." Then she gasps.

"What?"

"I just realized your situation with Brayden might be beyond the scope of my knowledge!" Sophia stares at me. "You may be surpassing me with all this subtle, complex flirting and dance partner crap. Throw in Phillip and you've got a true love situation on your hands."

"You're making it sound so difficult. The truth is, if I just marry Phillip and tell Brayden goodbye, the problem will go away."

"Will it?" Sophia asks me. "I don't think you're being truly honest with yourself there, Lei."

"I don't think I can talk about this anymore right now."

But Sophia ignores me. "Is this really all about Brayden, or does he also make you feel something you don't want to feel? Not just about him but about Phillip?" She narrows her eyes at me. "Do you love Phillip with your head only?"

I look away from her.

"Because love isn't a thinking thing, honey." Sophia taps my arm. "You know what you need to do? You need to get the hell out of your head. Love makes no sense. It's not logical. It's not even always fair. Love just is."

"I don't like illogical. Or lack of fairness."

Sophia makes a face. "I'm talking about raw, animal magnetism. It is what it is, Lei. Get on board, and own it."

After she's gone, I sit by myself for so long that I barely notice when the sun starts to go down. I spend the time thinking and fiddling with the empty space on my ring finger where the string should be.

And as I finally drag myself off the couch to go make dinner, I know what I need to do.

———

Hours later, Phillip walks in the front door, calling out my name. "Lei!" he says. "Are you home?"

"Hi! I'm upstairs!" I call out as I stand in front of the full-length mirror looking at the dress I'm thinking of wearing if I go to Jasalie and Dylan's wedding renewal.

Phillip walks into the room.

"What's that for?" he asks as he stares at me.

I never dress up. Phillip wears suits on occasion but only for his important conference speeches and academic mixers. I bought this dress last year when I was at the mall with Sophia. She made me try it on after she came out of the dressing room and caught me holding it up in front of me. I loved it so much that I let her talk me into buying it. But I put it in the back of the closet behind my old winter coat and never showed it to Phillip. The fabric's cut low in the front, not so low that it reveals too much but low enough to be sexy. It's fitted, and the skirt ends above my knee. It goes perfectly with the black strappy heels I have on, and my hair is pulled up into a loose bun, which shows off the neckline of the dress.

I keep looking into the mirror as I answer him. "Brayden's cousin's wife invited me to her wedding renewal on Monday. I don't know if I'm going or not, but I love this dress, and I wanted to try it on."

I catch Phillip's eye in the mirror. His jaw twitches.

I feel how perfectly the fabric fits my body. I look up at Phillip, and he's staring at me.

For the first time in forever, I feel like Phillip's actually seeing me. But as our gazes lock in the mirror, I don't feel a racing in my heart, and my palms are completely dry. And it's not because we were together for so long and I'm just comfortable with him and not nervous. It's because I don't even want him to touch me. Not in any way other than as a friend. In all our years together, I honestly don't think I ever knew what he wanted from me, and even in this moment, I'm truly not sure.

I turn back and put my arms out. "Welcome home."

He comes closer and hugs me close. "Thanks." He steps back and takes my hands in his. "Honey, I'm sorry I didn't tell you about my chat with the panel, and with Gerry too. It was wrong of me. I promise I'll make this up to you."

I look at him, at the weary look in his eyes, the dark circles underneath them, and I forgive him.

"It's okay." I try to fully unzip the back of the dress but it's no use. My arms aren't seven feet long. "Can we talk?"

His expression shuts down immediately. "I apologize, but I just can't go to the wedding renewal with you. I have too much I have to do. I know you want me there, but Mindy's coming over Monday night, and I promised her we could work together."

I exhale. "Phillip, I'm not asking that. Can we please communicate and have an actual conversation?" I gesture at the back of my dress. "Will you help me with this first?"

As he's unzipping my dress, I connect with his reflection in the mirror. Watching his face carefully, I say the words I've been rehearsing. "Phillip. This isn't working. Us."

Phillip's fingers catch on my zipper. "Lei, you're just confused because I've been so busy. I don't want you to throw away all that we have because of your confusion. In fact, I've already called Gerry. I told him he needs to give you a second chance. I asked him to meet me for a coffee—or an Irish coffee if he prefers—" He grins, but I'm not amused. "I'll make sure he lets you present as soon as possible. Right after our wedding."

I swallow, feeling like, once again, the wave of Phillip has just knocked me senseless and I have no voice to tell him otherwise. To tell him what I really want.

But this time, I charge onward anyway. "Thank you, but I'm not sure that's what's best for me after all. And in terms of you and me, I'm not confused. I know I need a break," I say, trying—and failing—to keep the emotion out of my voice. "A break up, to be more clear. Effective immediately."

Phillip laughs, but the chuckle is condescending. "What do we need a break for? We're getting married in less than two weeks. We've known each other forever. What just happened—this little breach of trust—is nothing compared to that kind of mileage. Trust me."

For the first time I can remember, I don't allow him to seize control of the conversation. "See, that's the thing, Phillip. Mileage or not, and what happened with the panel or not, let's be honest— the most important thing in your life is your work. I'm not saying that's bad. But for me, that's not the kind of marriage I want."

The dress is unzipped now. I spin around and put my hands on Phillip's arms. "This feeling isn't going to disappear in a few days. I've given it a lot of thought."

He steps back until he's sitting on the bed. "Lei. What are you saying?"

I sit next to him. "I'm saying that you deserve to marry *your* person. The right woman who will be by your side because it's what she truly wants. Your perfect match." I swallow. "I'm not that person for you, Phillip. And I've come to realize that marrying you isn't right for me either. I absolutely hate hurting you, and I'm so sorry." Hot tears slide down my cheeks as I say the words.

He puts his hand over mine. "What can I do to change your mind?"

"It's not something you can do. You're wonderful. But you're not right for me. Not as a life partner, and that's not something I will change my mind on. I'm going to move in with Sophia temporarily, and when we're ready, I'll tell my family we've cancelled the wedding."

Phillip stands up. "Let's go downstairs and have some tea."

I change out of my dress and put on a sweatshirt and jeans.

By the time I get downstairs, Phillip's got two mugs of tea sitting on the coffee table, one on either side of his microscope. I sit next to him and we sip our tea in silence for a few minutes.

"What went wrong with us?" he asks me finally. "How did we grow apart?"

I look into his eyes, feeling like I'm seeing them again for the first time in a while.

"I'm not sure," I say, and I'm surprised to feel a thickness in my throat. "I guess it happened gradually."

"I've been married to my job. I can say I'll change, but..." He trails off.

"But you can't make that kind of a promise," I say. "It's who you are, Phillip. And I've always admired you so much for that. I still do."

"Just not as your husband."

I inhale. "Right." I hold up my left hand. "Your ring fell off. I have no idea where."

"That kind of knot can't come undone," he says in a pinched tone.

"And yet it did," I say softly.

Phillip takes my hand in his and rubs my bare finger. "It's so strange to see you without it. And even worse? I didn't notice it was gone."

Pain crosses his face.

"It's okay," I say. "You've been away."

"Does Brayden have anything to do with this?" he asks me abruptly.

I cross my hands over my knees. "In a way, yes. Seeing him again after all this time, spending time together, I remembered some things about myself I'd forgotten. How much I love to paint.

How different you and I really are. I always wanted to make you happy because you've always been so good to me. But I'm not even sure I want to be a professor anymore. I really want to pursue my painting right now." I take a breath and tell him I'm quitting the PhD program. "I'm going to try to sell my artwork in town. That's what I really love."

"I'm sorry," he says. "I'm sorry I didn't support you in that."

"It's not your job," I say. "I was so far down the wrong path I couldn't see my own way out."

"But Brayden gets you." He rubs his eyes behind his glasses. "Shit. I can't believe I didn't see it before. You two look so mismatched. But you two never...these last couple of weeks..."

"No," I say. "Nothing ever happened. And I have no idea what will happen. But you deserve someone who's a match to you and how amazing you are."

When I ask him about Mindy, he smiles ruefully.

"I understand why you're curious. Nothing has happened, but we did really hit it off from the start. I certainly wasn't looking for it to turn into..." He trails off and looks at me. "And I know you weren't, either. I get that. I just want to see everything clearly," Phillip whispers, tears in his eyes. "I guess I was so busy doing that, I stopped seeing you."

I put my arms around him.

As we cry together, I feel like a huge piece of my life has broken off and left me. What's scariest of all, though, is the tiny— but distinct—feeling of relief in my chest. I'm officially single for the first time since I was sixteen years old, and I feel surprisingly calm. For someone who hates change, my reaction stuns me. But it's undeniable.

When I pull back, I tilt my head to the microscope still sitting between us.

"I guess we just outgrew this," I say to him. "We met over a microscope, but things change."

Sometimes you break up over a microscope too.

CHAPTER TWENTY-FIVE

I look for the hundredth time into the only floor-length mirror Sophia has in her apartment. My button-down pink flannel shirt should keep me warm, plus I put a wrap-around black sweater over it, and I like how they match with my holey blue jeans. The jeans came holey, which is not typically my style. I bought them for five dollars, and nothing else fits me this comfortably. I turn around and look at myself from behind one last time before putting on another layer of pale pink lipstick and a second touch of mascara.

I hear the front door open, and I hurry out of the bathroom to meet Sophia.

"Somebody's looking hot." She stands in the open doorway, and a gust of wind comes in with her.

"Soph, shut the door for a minute. It's another cold night, and I want to put on my coat first."

"You better get cozy with the cool weather," she says. "Because if you want Brayden to see that body of yours, you're not going to be able to keep your coat on all night. This is your first night with Brayden as a single woman. You want him to see your body, don't you?"

I cross my arms over my chest. "I'm not sure what I want these days. I haven't seen Brayden since he dropped me off after dance class."

She leans over to give me a hug. "I still can't believe you and Phillip broke up this week. How are you feeling?"

"I..." I almost feel guilty saying the truth. "It's been hard, of course. But part of me feels like a huge burden has been lifted off me. I sound like an awful person for saying that, I know."

"No, you don't, Leleila." Sophia shakes her head. "Phillip's not the right forever guy for you. You're such a bright light, and he's always dimmed your glow. This breakup is supposed to be a good thing."

I fiddle with the buttons on my coat. "Honestly, a part of me was looking for an exit door too. Just like he was." I look at her outfit. "You're going to freeze."

Sophia's long-sleeved sheer top looks like it's meant to be worn in July, not to mention her short skirt. "Slammer will keep me warm. Let's go watch some football, honey."

———

Wilcox High football stadium is loud with screaming fans as Sophia and I make our way through the crowd to the seats she swears Slammer has saved for us.

"So crowded," I say to her. "I forgot how many people come to these games."

"You'll have fun this time!" Sophia calls back to me. "Tonight will heal your demons, Lei."

The idea of going to a bonfire party makes my stomach twist in knots. But going to the party single, a label I haven't had since I went to my last party, shakes me to my core. I feel off-balance, like the foundation I've been leaning on for years is gone.

But I can't deny the sense of freedom I feel. Being able to do whatever I want tonight, with no one to answer to, is a sensation I haven't felt in twelve years.

Sophia stops abruptly, and Slammer immediately pulls her onto his lap. I take a seat next to them and try to calm my nerves.

I'm not prepared for Slammer to start groping Sophia as soon as the game starts, but I should expect no less.

When they're done with that, Slammer insists on getting a beer.

The game is exciting. Wilcox is really good, and by halftime, they're up by three touchdowns. I follow the game, but in all honesty, I spend more of my time scoping out Brayden on the side-lines. He looks so official as he strides along the bench, kneeling down to talk to different players as they come off the field.

"He works with the offense the most," Slammer says to me. "He was a stud when he played."

Brayden stands up tall and scans the crowd almost like he's looking for someone.

Then he locks eyes with me and puts up a two-fingered wave.

And my palms are so sweaty I have to wipe them on my jeans. My heart pounds, and I want him so badly I can hardly sit still.

I wave back tentatively, but Sophia stands up off Slammer's lap and waves both her hands in the air.

"Hey, Brayden!"

"Soph." I tug at her elbow. "Please sit down."

Slammer claps me on the shoulder. "He's a good guy, and he really likes you."

"Brayden's great. It's just complicated," I say quickly.

"What's complicated?" Slammer says. "You like him, he likes you. You have sex."

"Beyond other issues that I won't bore you with, this wouldn't be just sex for me."

Sophia's eyes widen, and she smiles.

Slammer nods. "I get it. Emotional attachment, huh? That's different."

Sophia turns to Slammer. "Do you feel an emotional attachment for me?"

I take a deep breath and try to turn away from them, but the space is very small and cramped.

"Well, you know," Slammer stammers. "We're just starting out. I mean, so far it's all been sex. No attachment for us. Right?"

Sophia takes his half-empty beer and dumps it on his head. "Yeah," she says. "Sure."

She storms off to the bathroom, and I follow her.

"What?!" Slammer calls after us. "What's the matter?"

———

Brayden

As good as the first half went, in the second half, our offense is on absolute fire. Wes only has three incompletions with no interceptions, and he fucking rifles the last touchdown pass through the tightest of windows.

I know what he doesn't know—that there's another scout here from a Division I school. I didn't know until the game had already started, and with the way he was already playing, we made the decision not to tell him for fear of screwing with his rhythm. He's putting on a damn clinic for the entire stadium.

And Dylan came through. I found out this morning that he was able to set up a scholarship through one of his charities, so Wes's dad can move into the assisted living facility in town. He'll be safe and cared for while Wes is in school.

I look up into the stands as the game ends, and we start walking toward the lockers. Leleila is watching me. I give her the thumbs up, and she smiles shyly and waves.

I'd promised myself I would back off, create some distance between us. Tonight, if she does go to the party, I have to keep my promise. No flirting, no touching, and no fantasizing about how much I want to kiss her.

Leleila Wills is getting married soon. And the sooner I get that fact hard-coded into my brain, the better.

———

Leleila

Slammer leaves the game after Sophia tells him to or else.

"I'm sorry, Soph," I say as we wind through the dark road heading for Big River Ranch. "You know you deserve love and somebody who loves you."

"I guess I don't think that," she sniffs. "Or else why wouldn't I have it?"

"I don't think that's always true," I say. "Sometimes it's timing."

"My mother loved the bottle more than she loved me," Sophia says. "So I don't see why anyone else would bother to take the time."

"Of course they would. You're so lovable. And super funny and unique." I touch her arm. "Slammer's just not good enough for you. You need to find somebody who treats you well. I think you're reaching below you, and that's the problem."

Sophia sniffles into her tissue as she drives. "You think so?"

"Absolutely."

———

By the time we reach Big River Ranch, Sophia's brought herself back into party mode. She's certainly resilient.

She picks up speed rather than slowing down on the dirt road, and we careen over it toward the flickering lights in the woods ahead.

"Are you sure about this?" I ask her. "You may be too vulnerable tonight to look for a new man..."

"I'm fully recovered!" Sophia says with a laugh. "You just broke up with someone too, Lei! We're two single ladies going to a party together. We've never both been single at the same time, and I feel great! Better than ever, and I'm so glad that asshole didn't join us."

"Please don't tell Brayden about Phillip," I remind her. "I need to do that myself."

"Of course. I won't say a word," she promises as we see the clearing filled with trucks, people, and a big bonfire in the center. Sophia parks the car and hops out. "Come on, Lei. Come experience being single with me."

I step out of the passenger side, glance around for about three seconds, and then slide my trembling body right back into the car. This is why I never went to another one of these freaking parties. They're scary. I'd rather give a speech for Save the Soil any day then show up at one of these things. I'm happy it's outside and not confined inside a house, but it's still hitting too close to home.

From the safety of Sophia's car, I watch her make her way to the bonfire. Her head's on a swivel as she looks around, probably for her mystery man I involuntarily convinced her would be here. Someone approaches her. Oh God, it's Brayden. They talk for a minute, and then she turns and points directly at her car. I duck down in the seat, hoping he didn't see me and will just give up and go away. I peek through the window a few seconds later. He's walking toward me. I try to think of a reason to tell him why I'm sitting by myself in the dark. When I can't think of any good excuses, I step out of the passenger side to make it look like I'm not avoiding the party. But as soon as I hear the loud music, I disappear back inside the car.

About ten seconds later, Brayden knocks on the window.

I open the door reluctantly, and he scoots in next to me. I try to move over as far as I can, but we're sharing a seat for one.

"Hey." He shuts the door behind him and puts his arm around me.

"Hi, Brayden," I say, trying to sound breezy. "How are you?"

He's wearing jeans, cowboy boots, and a blue sweatshirt that matches his eyes. His jeans don't have holes in them, which will probably keep him warmer than mine will.

"Good," he says. "Is everything all right?"

I open my mouth to tell him about Phillip and me. "Slammer and Sophia broke up," I say instead.

"Oh. I'm...sorry?"

I nod. "It's really okay. It's for the best."

"I don't know how well-matched they were," he says. "Is that why she just told me she's here to find her soul mate?"

I make a face. "That would be my fault. I was trying to be supportive and tell her she can find somebody better than Slammer. I didn't mean at this party, but as usual, Sophia has her own timetable of a zero wait time."

Brayden searches my expression. "So. You coming out?"

"I don't know..." I start to say.

"Come on. I know why you're scared. But I'll be with you the entire time." With his arm still wrapped around me, he opens the door and steps out, pulling me with him out of the car. My feet hit dirt, and I stand up. He keeps his arm firmly around me and we walk slowly in the direction of the bonfire.

"I'm pretty much dreading this," I confess to him.

"I'll be with you the whole time," he vows.

I whip my gaze over to him. He's looking at the party up ahead, but I can feel his focus on me nonetheless.

And I don't think I want to analyze how nice that feels.

"You're going to get through this," he says with a confidence I don't feel. "And when the night's over, you'll know you've let go of the past."

We reach the bonfire, and I can feel people's eyes on me as I walk by them with Brayden.

He leads me over to a truck bed where three people are sitting, one of whom looks familiar.

"Leleila! How are you?" Cam's friendly face peers over the truck at me.

I wave, even though he's right in front of me. "Hi, Cam. Good to see you again."

He hops down off the truck, gesturing to the two people with him to follow.

"Leleila, this is Jenson Beau and his fiancée, Olivia Graham." Brayden's hand squeezes my shoulder. "This is Leleila Wills."

Olivia's jet-black hair is worn loose and falls below her shoulders. Her blue eyes are warm as she greets me. Cam's as handsome as I remember with his dark hair and eyes. I remember Brayden mentioning Cam plays ice hockey, and his broad chest and wide shoulders convey that. Jenson's over six feet, in great shape, and very attractive. He and Olivia make a beautiful couple.

I shake Olivia and Jenson's hands, and then put my hands into the back pockets of my jeans. I stand before them stiffly, sensing they've heard about me already.

But they're polite. The four of them make easy small talk, as Jenson chats about their flight from Philly that was delayed three hours. "Everything worked out for the best, though," he says. He takes his hand off Olivia's back only to brush an errant lock of his blond hair out of his brilliant green eyes before returning his arm to her shoulders. "Because of that delay, we ended up landing the same time as Cam's flight. So the three of us rode to Mountainview together."

"Is this truck one of yours?" I ask, gesturing with my foot to the one they were just sitting on.

"It's Colt's," Cam says. "He leaves it here when he's in L.A. He's got way too many cars as it is. When we were at his mom's last night, she insisted we borrow it for the week."

"Speaking of trucks." Brayden tilts his head to the left where his truck is parked a few feet away.

He gives me a lift, and we sit on the back of his tailgate together. It faces the bonfire; plus, the front of his truck blocks some of the wind, so it's actually quite nice. Some Southern rock band is playing. I only know that because June's ex-boyfriend Sammy listened to this band all the time. This is exactly the type of music I used to say made my skin crawl, but it fits right in here, and the rhythm of the sound soothes me. Once I've made it onto the tailgate and feel somewhat protected from what's going on around me, I relax. Brayden offers me one of the beers he's got sitting on the back of his truck, and I accept. He hands it to me unopened, and I nod at him in appreciation.

I open the beer myself, feeling my anxiety slowly dissipate.

I let my legs dangle over the edge of the tailgate, and I feel like I belong sitting here with Brayden. I feel special.

I want to ask him if he often meets women at these parties.

"I don't normally let anyone sit in my truck," he says as if reading my mind.

I give him a look. "Ri-i-ight."

"I don't," he insists. "I'm not a big dater."

I turn sideways so I can face him.

"I just...sometimes I really don't know why you spend time with me. I mean you could be with any woman you want. And not only do I bring serious baggage, but I'm not that cool or that interesting." I pause. "Or that beautiful. Certainly not beautiful like you are."

Brayden shakes his head. "I think we should steer away from this conversation."

"How come?"

"Because I could show you in a million different ways how beautiful I think you are." His voice drops so low that my heart starts pounding. "But that would be crossing a line." He clears his throat and leans back. "So let's change the subject, okay?"

Before I can fill him in on my break-up, Sophia stops by with a beer in her hand.

"Weren't you supposed to be driving home?" I ask her.

"I've already taken her keys; don't worry," Brayden says. "You guys can sleep out here, like the rest of us, and go home in the morning."

I don't dare look over at him. This is spinning out of hand, and it only took just over ten minutes to get there.

———

Brayden

I've never been so hyper-aware of somebody else as I am of Leleila tonight.

Every conversation she engages in, every person who

approaches her, every time she self-consciously pushes an errant brunette hair back behind her ear, I notice.

I nurse my beer, not wanting to drink much in case she wants me to take her home. Coming to this party is a huge step for her, and I'm not going to let her down.

If she doesn't want to spend the night here, no way will I try to persuade her. But she's on her second beer already and may be in no position to drive herself, so I need to stay sober.

"Hey, Wild!" Jenson calls to me from where he and Cam are standing by the bonfire. "Get over here!"

When I reach them, Cam taps his beer to mine.

"She fits with you," Jenson says to me.

I manage a nod. Fitting with a woman who's engaged isn't my idea of a good time.

"She seems different tonight than the last time I saw her," Cam says, startling me out of my thoughts.

I turn toward him. "How so?"

He shrugs. "Not sure. But something in her eyes...they're different than when we met her at the saloon."

"We've gotten closer since then," I say. "Maybe she's less guarded now."

"She is," he agrees. "But it's something else. You should ask her if something's happened with her situation."

"Her situation?" I say. "I can't. It's none of my business."

"Maybe not," Cam says. "But it is, all the same."

"She'll come clean if something's up," Jenson says. "She doesn't look like she has a deceptive bone in her body."

No, she doesn't. Leleila's not manipulative, one of the many things that attracted me to her. But if something's going on with her upcoming wedding...maybe they decided to move up the date. Maybe she's going to marry him even sooner than she planned.

My jaw tightens, and I take a swig of beer. I'll have to continue to be patient and let her tell me when she's ready.

Leleila

While Sophia is flirting with anyone and everyone, I chat with Olivia. When Jenson calls to her, she jumps off the truck and heads over to him. I watch him kiss her like he hasn't seen her for a year, and the smile that lights up her face when she playfully pushes him away...it makes my heart ache.

I catch Brayden's eye.

"Everything okay?" he asks as he hops onto the back of the truck.

I smile at him. "Yes."

His thumb rubs my ring finger gently. "Still haven't replaced the ring?"

I suck in a breath. "Brayden."

His eyes zero in on mine. "What is it?"

"Phillip and I broke up."

Five words. Five words that hang out there like an announcement in the cool night air.

I can see Brayden's throat working as he swallows hard. "You've got my attention, Lei. Do you feel ready to talk about it?"

His thoughtfulness touches me, and I squeeze his hand tighter. "Yes. No." I let out a quick laugh. "Later."

He brings our hands up to his mouth and lightly kisses my palm. "Later's good."

———

Hours later, Brayden and I are finally alone in the far back of his truck. Some vehicles are just driving off while other people hang out in the remaining scattered trucks. Sophia's already asleep in the back of a truck with a few of the women she partied with all evening.

Cam disappeared with a woman Brayden said, "...is perfect for Cam tonight because she's not expecting him to call her tomorrow. And he needs that right now."

Jenson and Olivia are in Colton's truck, and I can't see them now that the fire's nearly burned out and there are no flashlights bobbing around the field.

Nobody else is close to us, and it feels like we're the only two people in the world. Brayden stretches out his long legs and fixes the blanket so we're both sitting on it. I lean against the wall of the truck bed, trying not to ogle him in his sexy jeans and cowboy boots.

"This has been a good night," I say quietly. "Thank you. For encouraging me to come."

"I'm glad. You deserve to move forward. You know I'm sure not a savior or anything like that." He lifts his arm to gesture around us. "I've got a lot of sides, as does everyone, but partying in the sticks is one of them." His gaze zeroes in on mine. "Part of me thought you'd come, and we'd realize we really were from two different worlds, and that would be the end of it. Kind of like a painless but surefire way to stop this train we're on. Because to be honest, I didn't know how else to stop it."

"You thought that would be best?"

"No." His tone drops. "I think you know what I mean. I'm talking about the fire between us that doesn't want to go out. Because since I ran into you again at Big Sky Grocer, you've been spoken for. I like being with you, Leleila. Too much. And there was a part of me that thought maybe you'd come here tonight, and it wouldn't work out. I figured you'd see me like this and realize how much better you are than I am. I'm no saint, unlike all these people you're related to and hang out with."

"Sophia's a saint? I didn't realize that."

Brayden's lip quirks up. "I didn't mean Sophia. I just thought it would matter to you with somebody like me because Sophia's just a friend. She'll always be just a friend."

"What are you?" I whisper as I lean closer to him.

He swallows and tries to look away. I put my hand on his chin and keep him looking back at me.

"I'm..." His voice is hoarse. "I'm a friend too. A friend who's sometimes wished that he'd re-met you before you were taken."

I could stare into Brayden's beautiful eyes forever. "But I'm not taken anymore."

I'm single. And I don't want to live the rest of my life unhappy. Maybe I've finally decided to sort everything out so I truly do what's best for me.

Brayden's eyes flash, and he leans forward but stops with his lips inches from mine. "What happened, Lei? I need to know before I..." His mouth comes so close I can't believe it doesn't touch me. "Before I do something I'm not supposed to do."

My stomach lurches. "I'll tell you the story," I say as I put my hands into my lap. "But I never want you to think I'm using you for something so shallow as a temporary fling. Because you're my best friend, Brayden. I really, really like you."

Brayden brushes my cheek with his lips. "I want to kiss you, Leleila. No matter how confused things are right now."

I sit back. "I'll fill you in on everything first. I told you how I've been with Phillip since I was sixteen. He's the only guy I've ever dated. He asked me out, and I accepted, and it just kind of went from there. My dad was so happy and proud I was dating him. He thought Phillip would take care of me, I guess. After the way I'd lost faith in myself, Phillip became my rock. And when my parents went to South America for research for most of my senior year, I leaned on him even more." I pause, but Brayden's nods like he's interested. "We were both into our studies, and we both hated the party scene. I thought what I had with Phillip was special because everyone, including me, thought he was so special. But we've drifted in the last couple of years, and I should have been paying better attention. When Phillip kept leaving me for work, at first it felt like it came out of left field. But now, I realize he was calling attention to a much bigger issue."

Brayden straightens up. "He got to you, didn't he? He made you think you don't have a right to be upset?"

"No, I think I have a right. I would be more upset if I didn't feel such obvious..."

His breath quickens. "Such obvious what?"

"Relief." There. I've said it. The emotion that's been messing with me all week. "I felt relieved when I broke it off with him. Free. Maybe even a teeny bit...happy." The last word comes out choppy. "I moved in with Sophia—temporarily, only until I find a place—and even though I'm sleeping on the couch, and have no idea what the hell my future's going to look like, I feel better than I have in months."

Brayden rests his forehead against mine.

I look closely into his eyes. "I've felt broken since that night. Like nothing, and no one, could put me back together again. Until I ran into you at the store."

Brayden's blue eyes darken. "You're putting yourself back together, Lei." He puts his hand on my back and urges me closer to him. "All on your own."

He takes my face in his hands and, with no more hesitation, puts his mouth over mine. He kisses me softly at first, waiting for me to open to him. I do with a moan, and he slips his tongue in my mouth.

Brayden kisses me like his whole life depends on it. He nips my lower lip until I cry out, and he never lets up. It's familiar and new all at the same time. It's safe, and it's scary, only in the best way. It's not just different than with Phillip. It's like I'm brought back to that night twelve years ago but without all the pain that came with it. Back then, Brayden kissed me carefully like he was afraid I'd break.

Tonight, he's all in. He doesn't hold back, and neither do I. My heart's pounding, and my palms are sweating as I let my tongue tangle with Brayden's. He pulls me onto his lap and keeps kissing me, his mouth devouring mine desperately.

When he puts his hands up the back of my shirt and unhooks my bra, shivers dance across my skin. I wrap my legs around his waist as tightly as I can. I don't want to think straight. I don't want to think at all. And I definitely don't want this moment to ever stop because I'm scared I'll never feel this good again.

Our kiss grows wild and out of control. I feel like I could kiss

Brayden forever, and it still wouldn't be enough. I slip my hands underneath his shirt and across his chest, which is solid muscle. He takes his shirt off and I kiss his bare bicep, before getting a glimpse of his tattoo in the moonlight.

"When did you get your tattoo?" I whisper.

"The year I made the varsity football team," he says. "I got it to remind myself of what truly makes me feel free, not the lure of money and fame. I knew I'd lose myself if I pursued playing football as a career. Staying here, in Montana, is what's always made me happiest."

"I can relate to losing yourself in the wrong career," I say quietly.

And then I bite down on his shoulder as Brayden's hands roam up and down my bare back. His touch feels so, so good, even though he keeps them on my back and doesn't wander. But I start to wish his hands would wander everywhere. With a low growl and never taking his mouth off of mine, he lays me down in the back of the truck. He makes sure I'm on top of the blanket, and then he leans over me and slowly unbuttons my sweater.

His darkened eyes lock with mine with each button he reaches. I shiver as his hot breath hits my neck, and then his lips find my mouth again. He increases the tempo of our kiss, and once my sweater's open, he undoes the top button of my flannel shirt. Then he reaches for the second one and then the third.

By the time he's released all the buttons, I've forgotten anything but this moment in time. My body's writhing on the truck bed, begging Brayden to touch more of me. He takes his mouth off mine to kiss my neck, and then he keeps going south, grazing my collarbone with his teeth. A noise escapes my throat as his lips touch the top of my breast, and then he lifts his head back up to kiss me again. Meanwhile, his hands are all over my bare skin, skimming over the curves of my breasts, and pausing to rub his thumb over my pebbled nipple. He groans as his hand drifts purposefully down to my navel and over my hips. He reaches the snap of my jeans, and I can feel his fingers shake as he hesitates.

I tense just enough that he stops.

I drag myself into a sitting position, and Brayden moves away from me, his hands in fists at his sides. I button up my shirt and sweater quietly, but we're both breathing heavily.

He breaks the silence. "Leleila, I think we should go to sleep. I want you to leave this party feeling healed, not confused."

"I'm okay, Brayden. That was...the best kiss of my life."

He looks at me for the first time since we stopped kissing. His lips are swollen and bruised, his blond hair's a mess, and his eyes are filled with such heat that I suck in my breath. We hold the eye contact without speaking until he says—

"Mine too. But I don't want to rush this, and I'll be honest with you. I'm going to fix up the blankets so we can go to sleep because I need to stop putting my hands all over you like I'm dying to do. God knows how much I want to make love to you all night long."

My breath catches in my throat.

I reach out and take his hand. "I'm sorry this has been so messy."

"Don't be sorry that I want you. Or about any of it."

I swallow. "I guess the fact that I'm single isn't enough, huh?"

His eyes find mine. "Not when I want more than one night with you, Leleila. I care about you. I really like you too. And I want to make sure you're more than ready for everything that I want with you. I'm not going to make love to you for the first time in the back of my truck. You deserve better than that."

"Brayden." His name comes out of my mouth in a pained tone. "I'm happy being anywhere with you."

Brayden's hands are on my cheeks immediately. "So let's take our time. You just got out of a long-term relationship, and you're still figuring your shit out. I'm happy to go slow. Okay? I have an idea for our second date."

"When was our first date?"

He gestures from me to him. "It's happening right now. But I didn't know tonight was going to be a date, so our next date will be more official—would you like to go with me to Dylan and Jasalie's wedding?"

I take his hand. "I would. Very much."

"I'll pick you up beforehand."

All I can do is nod before he plants a quick kiss on my mouth and then lets me go. He jumps down off his truck, and I hear him rustling around inside the front of the cab. He taps the glass to get my attention, and I climb off the back and go around to the open passenger door.

"This'll work, I think." Brayden shows me the bed of blankets he's made.

It looks warm and cozy. I never knew a truck could feel so homey.

"It's perfect." I climb up into the truck before Brayden can get out and shut the door behind us. "Bray, I want you here with me. Even if we have to talk all night in order to not touch one another, I want to be with you inside this truck tonight."

Brayden drags both hands through his hair. "Let's start talking then because other parts of me are talking louder than your voice is right now."

And so we do. We talk all night about anything and everything, and eventually, we drift off to sleep with my head on his chest and his arms wrapped tightly around me.

CHAPTER TWENTY-SIX

Brayden

The next morning, I kiss Leleila goodbye inside the truck before telling her I'll see her Monday for the wedding.

"How'd things go last night?" Cam tips his head in the direction of Sophia's car as Leleila disappears inside of it and they pull away.

"I'm in love with her." I didn't mean to say the words out loud, but the sentiment couldn't be more true.

"Shit, Bray." Cam's hand claps my back roughly.

"Yeah." I stuff my hands in my pockets and stare after the car as it gets smaller and smaller, driving away from me.

"Things will work out then," Cam says confidently. "If you feel that strongly, they have to."

I hope he's right.

I simply can't imagine my life without Leleila in it.

———

Leleila

I spend the weekend looking for an apartment. I find a studio apartment on Main Street, just a few blocks from June's store. I'm terrified to live alone, but it's always been a dream of mine, and I figure I can handle a studio. I don't have a lot to bring with me, but I have to start somewhere.

I fill out an application first thing Monday morning. Just as I'm celebrating that milestone, Rona from the at-home job calls to invite me in for an interview this afternoon. She says she knows it's short notice, but they're looking to make a near-immediate hire for the position as they just got a new client, and they need the help right away. Well, I need the help right away too—the help of an income. I make an appointment with her for one p.m.

———

I walk in the door of Sophia's house and she's sitting on the couch.

"I got a job!" I say.

"That's great, but what are you still doing in those clothes?" she asks me.

"What do you mean? I'll change into jeans now."

"Have you forgotten? You need to get into your dress, darling. Brayden will be here any minute."

Shit. The wedding's at four. "I completely lost track of time." I jump up and head for her bathroom with my dress in my arms.

"Ready or not, Lei." Sophia glances out the window. "Brayden just drove in."

I reach the bathroom and slam the door shut.

"Don't let him inside!" I pull off my shirt and pants and begin to apply my makeup. "I need ten minutes." I glance more closely at my face, which looks pale and exhausted. "Okay, maybe twenty minutes."

"Hey, Brayden. Don't you look gorgeous in that suit?" I hear Sophia say. "Leleila's just finishing up putting on her hot dress. Take a seat with me on the couch here."

"This is a nice place, Sophia." Brayden's low voice comes through the door. "You been here long?"

"Five years," she says proudly. "Let's see, how did I find this place? I think it was that guy, Daryl, who I was dating for a while. Well, I wouldn't say dating; I would probably say screwing, you know?"

Sophia giggles, and I hear her flirt button click on even higher. As if telling Brayden how gorgeous he is wasn't enough. *Good Lord.* Why did I not remember what time this wedding was?

Her flirting distracts me so much that I give up on makeup and step into my dress. I zip it up as best I can, but it's just not possible. So I pull my hair up into a twist like I practiced last night, give myself one last brush of rouge and lipstick, and step out of the bathroom and into my heels that are waiting for me right outside the door.

By the time I get them on and look up, Sophia and Brayden are sitting in silence and watching me. Sophia's smiling as I walk over to Brayden nervously.

"Hi," I say. "Sorry I'm late."

"You're not late," he says as he stands up. "I was early."

I stare at his beautiful dark suit and blue tie that matches his sapphire eyes so perfectly. His hair's combed and styled, and his expression is filled with desire. My breath catches in my throat, so much so that I can't speak for a moment.

"Your zipper, Lei," Sophia says for me. "You need help?"

I nod and she turns to Brayden, who also seems to have lost his breath. "Brayden, you want to help Leleila with her zipper?"

Brayden steps behind me. When I feel his hands on my back, I shiver and catch Sophia's eye. She raises her eyebrows at me. Brayden struggles with the zipper at first, and his hand slips, but then he gets it and zips up the back.

"Thank you," I say to him as he comes around to face me again.

"You look beautiful," he says to me.

I smile and grab my fancy purse off the couch. "Have fun tonight," I say to Sophia.

"I will. Don't you worry." She walks us to the door. "You have the key, Lei. If you come back here, that is."

I shut the door on her laughter and look at Brayden as we walk together toward his truck.

"So do you," I say as he opens the passenger door for me and helps me step up onto the cab.

"What?" he says to me.

"So do you look beautiful." I bite my lip.

He steps up onto the cab and kisses my cheek. "Thank you."

During the drive, Brayden's cell phone rings.

He talks for a couple of minutes and then hands the phone to me. "It's an officer from the PD in town," he says.

I take the phone and say hello. The voice on the other end identifies himself as Officer Hayden, who says he sent a team to the ranch this afternoon.

"It was everything Mr. Wild described," he says. "And it's darn illegal I can tell you that. The owners of the property never even knew what was going on; it looks like it was a few of his rogue workmen who set the whole thing up. One of them works two jobs. He was asked to dispose of the container for a wire manufacturing company, and he was to pay the fee and then be reimbursed. Well, he went to find out what the fee was, then told some lie to his company in order to get the reimbursement check anyway, and went and buried the darn container for free."

"Wow," I say.

"He said he didn't think any contaminants would spread when the container was sealed. Of course, there are leaks all through the thing. Our environmental specialist says the darn toxins have been leeching in that soil for weeks."

"That's what I was afraid of."

"But we've got a team together. They'll begin the process of removing the contaminated soil and then containing the rest to make certain there'll be no more seeping of toxins. The cattle will all be tested as well in case any of them ate from that part of the field. The good news? It doesn't look like it reached the reservoir. We have a group of experts coming out to run more conclusive tests, but I think the town is safe. But thank God you two followed up on this. You'll get a lot of press for this one, and well you should. Can you come into the station now?"

I look over at Brayden. "Sure. We have a few minutes."

———

An article will appear about us in the Mountainview Union paper as well as the Montana Times as soon as the reservoir is given the all-clear. There's a reporter at the station who has Brayden and me pose together so he can snap our picture.

"Perfect shot," he says. "Mind if I ask you both a few questions before you leave?"

Brayden picks me up in his arms as soon as we reach his truck outside the station. "This is so incredible," he says. "You're amazing."

"You were the one who found it, who followed your instincts," I say. "I'm happy I could help, and thank God we got to it in time. But you should be proud of yourself."

"And you should be proud of yourself," he says to me. "You're just as much of a real scientist and a genius as anyone in the world. No matter what you do, with a degree or without, you did this all on your own."

He doesn't add "without Phillip." He doesn't need to.

———

When we reach the wedding venue, Brayden goes inside to get ready for the ceremony, and I take a seat in a chair near the front of the outdoor altar.

"Leleila?"

I turn as Olivia slides into the chair next to me.

We chat until the music starts, and Dylan steps out onto the altar. He's certainly eye-catching with that dark head of hair and striking eyes, but I twist around in my seat excitedly to watch as Brayden escorts an older woman down the aisle.

"Brayden's walking with Rosita, Jasalie's former neighbor and still her cat sitter," Olivia whispers to me.

My pulse pounds as Brayden draws closer. His gaze lands on me, and I get lost in the incredible blue of his eyes. He looks gorgeous in his suit and tie. He winks at me as he passes, and I nearly sink into the seat as my knees weaken.

Cam is next, walking next to a curvy redhead. He murmurs something to her, and they both look like they're trying not to burst into laughter.

"That's Lilla, Jasalie's friend and former co-worker," Olivia says.

Ayden and Bella follow them down the aisle. Ayden kisses Bella's temple when she stumbles in her heels, and they walk the rest of the way with his arm around her.

Colton Wild, a huge blond guy with piercing blue eyes, walks hand-in-hand with a slender red-haired woman who Olivia says is his wife, Sky.

Colton's smirking, and Sky gently backhands him in the stomach. He grins outrightly then and kisses her head just as they reach the altar and separate for their respective spots.

Jenson is already coming down the aisle with a tall blond woman.

"That's Jasalie's birth mom," Olivia whispers. "They reconciled after Jasalie and Dylan met. She hadn't seen her since she was a child."

"Wow." I watch as the woman smiles up at Jenson, who keeps his arm around her back.

"Bella said Jasalie wasn't sure she wanted to invite her. But in the end, she decided it would be healing."

Jasalie's mom is visibly trembling as she and Jenson make their way to the front. Jenson has to stop when they get near our row of chairs, and I hear him ask her if she's okay.

"I'm fine. I'm just so happy to be here," she says clearly back.

He escorts her into an open chair in the front row and then takes his place with the rest of the groomsmen.

When Jasalie walks down the aisle alone, I can't take my eyes off of her. She's as beautiful as Dylan is handsome, and her wedding gown is an amazingly gorgeous vintage-style dress. The ivory and champagne colors blend perfectly with intricate neckline beading. The gown has lace trim, long illusion sleeves, and a deep V-neckline.

She looks like a queen.

And Dylan is clearly her king. As they meet at the altar, his entire face lights up with love. Their chemistry together is undeniable, and the minister has to clear his throat three times to get them to look at him rather than each other.

The renewal ceremony is short and casual, a fifteen-minute exchange of vows that reiterate their love for one another. I never thought I was one for romance, especially public sentiment, but Jasalie and Dylan have me mesmerized.

"I promise to be your partner in crime and your biggest fan," Dylan says, his eyes never leaving Jasalie's. "I will love you through the easy and the hard, the joys and the challenges. I promise to create and love a family with you in a home filled with unconditional love and support. I promise to love you forever."

Jasalie's voice hitches as she responds. "I promise to be your best friend and your staunchest supporter. I will love you on the field and off"—Dylan's laugh can be heard through the entire outdoor venue—"If you never again hold a football, or if you never put one down, I will love you and support you. I promise to partner with you, as parents to our future children, in a home where they will grow up learning unconditional love, the ability to solve problems creatively, and the strength to overcome anything life throws in their way."

I wipe my eyes. *Shit*. Now I'm getting emotional at the wedding renewal of two people I literally barely know. Like he knows what I'm thinking, Brayden turns and looks right at me. I stare into the swirling blue of his eyes, trying to beam to him how much I care. How much I want him and need him in my life. I laugh nervously and can't stop.

Brayden

I love you, Leleila.

That's all I want to say right now. All I want to do is jump off the altar, pull this damn tie off my neck, pick Leleila up in my arms, and disappear with her. I'd take her to my family cabin and make love to her for the entire night.

Standing up with Jenson and my cousins, as Dylan and Jasalie renew their vows, is far more emotional than I thought it would be. When Colton and Sky got married, I wasn't in this place. I was single and happy being single.

Because Leleila Wills wasn't around then. She had been once, but that was one night when I was a teenager. Now that she's back in my life, the whole game has changed.

I need to tell her how I feel.

Leleila

Brayden's waiting for me at the edge of the manicured lawn. He takes my hand and leads me away from the crowd of people mingling and grabbing appetizers.

He looks down at my fingers intertwined with his. My left ring finger is bare with any hint of the red string long gone. "How have the last couple of days been for you?"

I inhale and stare past him at the mountains. They're gorgeous —snow-capped and majestic.

I bring my gaze back to Brayden's face. "They've been great, actually."

He sucks in a breath. "I can imagine you're overwhelmed? This is a huge life change, Lei."

I swallow. "I am deliriously happy inside. Outside, I'm still reeling. But I got a job, and I found a place. My first time living on my own. Baby steps. And I found you again."

———

Brayden's parents greet me warmly at the reception hall, and Luke says hello with a wink.

"Heard you and my brother came here together," he says.

I nod. "We did, yes."

He grins. "That's good news."

"I think so," I say with a smile.

If Brayden is breathtakingly gorgeous, Luke is more of a smoldering burn. He strikes me as the kind of guy who dates a lot but doesn't share much of his heart with anyone.

"And how's your friend?" he asks me suddenly. "Ms. Sophia Loren?"

I cock my head and look closely at his blank expression. He's clearly an expert at giving nothing away, but even he can't hide the little flush in both cheeks as he waits for my reply.

"Sophia is great," I say.

He gives me a salute and turns away for the other end of the bar. "Glad to hear it. See you, Leleila."

I order a drink at the bar. I'm still waiting when two muscular arms appear on my left and a set of equally-large arms on my right.

"So you're Leleila."

I turn around and recognize the two men on either side of me.

Dylan and Colton Wild. Their expressions are friendly but curious.

"Brayden told us you're his date tonight." Colton gives me a kind smile, but both his and Dylan's eyes are assessing me the way a brother would look out for a sibling.

"Yes. Hi." I shake Dylan's extended hand and then Colton's. "Nice to meet you." I turn back to Dylan. "Congratulations on your marriage. The renewal ceremony was so beautiful."

"Thank you." His eyes warm. "Jasalie told me she had invited you tonight. She said good things about you."

"She was so kind to invite me," I say. "You two make a wonderful couple."

Colton smiles. "I hope you and Brayden can work things out."

"I hope so, too." I take in a deep breath. "I've brought a lot of complications to the table. I never want to hurt Brayden, ever."

Dylan's expression relaxes. "I'm pretty sure he knew what he was walking into from the beginning. As long as you're always honest with him—he'll be okay."

"Are you two bothering my date?" Brayden says as he steps in next to me and slips his arm around my waist.

Colton grins. "Always. That's what we do."

Brayden frowns and tells me he needs a few minutes alone with his cousins. I wave goodbye to them and go find Olivia, who brings me over to Jasalie, Bella, and Sky.

Sky introduces herself and asks if I've met Colton. I nod, and when I say that Colton and Dylan didn't seem to necessarily trust me, she makes a joke about her husband being a bodyguard.

"You would think these guys are all innocents with the way the others protect them," she says fondly. "None of them knew what to do with me at first, either."

"Really?" Olivia asks.

"Of course. They protect their own."

"I think it's sweet," Jasalie says. "But I never had that growing up. Don't let them bother you, Leleila. They mean well, and once they know you, they'll have your back for life. No matter what."

"In the meantime," Bella says, looping her arm through mine. "We'll get to know you ourselves. Let's go sit at our table."

Brayden

As soon as Leleila's out of earshot, I turn on Colton and Dylan.

"Don't fucking bug Leleila," I say to them.

"Remember how you told me to run Sky off because she couldn't be trusted?" Colt says with amusement.

I scowl. "That's a little harsh. I didn't quite say that."

"You said, 'definitely walk, man,' and that *is* a quote." Colton's smile is even bigger.

I relax. "But I was wrong. So are you."

"Hey." Dylan steps in between us. "We like her, Bray. We were just feeling her out. You tell us you're falling for a woman on the verge of a wedding to another man. Of course we're worried about you. We don't want you to get hurt."

"Not that it's any of your business," I say, knowing they won't let up if I don't fill them in on the updated version of the story. "But she and he broke up. It's over between them."

Colt's blue eyes brighten. "Fuck. That's great news."

I nod. "No more fucking sharing tonight. I've said more than I planned on."

Dylan and Colton chuckle.

"You're the cousin who's going to give us zero heads up that you're thinking of getting married, aren't you?" Dylan says.

"This *is* my heads up," I say. "You meeting her."

Their eyes widen.

"And truthfully, I don't think you've got the right cousin. The guy we've got to worry about no heads up with?" I point my beer bottle at Cam, who's busy flirting with three women at once. "It's that Wild."

"Cam?" Colt spins around to get a better look.

"Mark my words," I say. "He's the wild-card Wild. We all know it."

"Shit." Dylan runs his hand through his hair, effectively ruining the perfect professional styling he'd had done. Luckily, the family pictures are over and done with. "You're right."

———

Leleila

When the dancing starts, Brayden's mom beckons us to follow her and her husband onto the dance floor.

The music is loud, and the band plays lots of different styles, so before an hour's over, Braden and I have waltzed, done the salsa, and danced to Top 40 music. His cousins are good sports, and they try to keep up. Dylan can dance—I'm beginning to wonder what Dylan Wild *can't* do well—and he and Jasalie join us for a while.

When a slow song starts, Brayden pulls me close, and my body melts into his. It's a beautiful song. And maybe it's the song, or maybe it's the way Brayden's looking at me...but I feel like I've opened my heart a little more with each dance until I can't shut it down anymore. I pull him as close to me as possible, and he puts his cheek to mine.

"I didn't plan on falling so hard for you, Leleila," he says in my ear. "But I don't regret one second of our time together. As unconventional a start as it was."

I stop thinking about everything and lean forward and kiss him. My "no PDA" rule flies out the window. I want to touch Brayden so much I don't care who sees.

Brayden takes my face in his hands and kisses me back. The taste of whiskey and cake on his tongue is intoxicating.

CHAPTER TWENTY-SEVEN

Brayden and I leave the wedding reception and walk to the parking lot.

And once we're alone inside the truck, there's nowhere to hide from the sexual tension that's been between us all night.

Brayden turns the key in the ignition as he looks over at me.

He hesitates before he says, "So...is it too soon to ask if you want to come over?"

I instinctively inch toward him. He leans over and kisses me lightly on the lips. His mouth is gentle on mine, but I can feel the urgency behind his kiss. "I don't ever want to push you," he says in a rough tone. "God knows I want you, Leleila, but I can wait as long as you need."

"What about your cousins?"

"They're all staying at the hotel next door. Dylan secured rooms for everyone who wanted them so nobody would have to worry about drinking and driving."

"That was thoughtful."

He lightly nips my bottom lip, and I barely suppress a moan. "It was, but I only had one shot before the ceremony, so I'm safe to drive. And I couldn't think of anywhere I'd rather be than alone at my house with you."

"On your porch?"

"Among other places." His breath ghosts my cheek. "I've imagined being with you in every square surface of my house."

I drop my head to his shoulder as I let out a strangled cry. "That sounds...amazing."

"If you're ready. If not, we'll wait."

I lean closer to him again, hoping he'll kiss me once more, and he doesn't disappoint.

"Yes." I say into his mouth. "I want to come over."

———

I cuddle up next to Brayden on the drive to his ranch. He takes his time on the empty back road, barely going above twenty-five.

"I just want to go slow right now." He kisses my head. "We've got all night."

And it feels like we've waited forever.

———

Brayden's already out of the truck and heading for my side as I grab my purse and open the door. He reaches out and puts his arms around me as I step out. I feel his muscles ripple through his dress shirt, and my anxiety fades as I realize just how much I want to be close to him.

He kisses my neck as he leans me back against the side of the truck. The stars are so bright, and the sky behind them is so dark. Out here on the ranch that Brayden's going to buy one day, there isn't a sound other than the wind.

I close my eyes as Brayden covers my mouth with his own until I get dizzy. When a few raindrops fall on our heads, Brayden picks me up in his arms and carries me up to the front porch before it really begins to pour.

"I heard there's going to be thunderstorms tonight." He puts me down to unlock the door and leads me inside.

I need to pee as soon as we close the door.

While I'm washing up, my phone buzzes. I check the text from Sophia letting me know she'll see me tomorrow, and my finger accidentally hits the news feed.

And I freeze.

"Former Mountainview resident arrested for assault with a deadly weapon. Noah Tate attempted to rob a convenience store last night. He threatened the clerk, stole..."

I shove my phone back into my purse.

Instantly, memories flood my brain of Noah's hands on me. Wrestling me for control of my body. Fighting me for something that was never his to take. Demanding that I give him my innocence.

The fact that I was able to fend him off still amazes me sometimes. It was like I tapped into a strength inside me I didn't know I had, and God gave me the ability to defend myself.

I know not every woman is that lucky.

And I know how much worse it could have been.

But the fear that night instilled in me is back in my mind, and as I leave Brayden's bathroom, I feel the need to be alone.

I make my way to the open doorway of the porch. Brayden's gaze is focused out the window, and he doesn't see me yet. His tie hangs loose around his neck. His hands are in his pants pockets and his jaw's relaxed. He's waiting for me. Two glasses of wine sit on the coffee table by the couch, and two red candles burn by the window.

He turns then and notices me. He picks up a glass of wine and offers it to me. "Come on in, Lei. Why are you standing in the doorway? Do you want me to start a fire?"

I still have my purse in my hands, and I shake my head.

"What?" Brayden catches the look on my face. "What's changed?"

"I saw something." I walk closer and show him the feed on my phone screen.

Brayden reads it in silence. I turn my gaze to the full-length windows leading into his private backyard. I remember every second of the first time I came here. I remember every moment of how Brayden opened up his heart and let me in.

"I think I just need a little air," I say as I turn and head down the hall.

Brayden reaches me just as I open the front door. He puts his arm around my waist and gently turns me around.

His face is filled with concern. He keeps his arms around me, and I lean my head against his chest. I can hear his racing heart, and I hold onto him tightly.

"Lei, you're okay," he whispers into my ear. "You're safe here with me. I'll never hurt you."

"I know." I pull back abruptly and get my two feet out the door. "Just give me a few minutes."

———

Brayden

Shit. I bang my head against the closed door and head back to the porch where I stand with my glass of wine and stare out the window again. I have an active imagination, and images of making love to Leleila in my house have been haunting me since I met her. Against the wall, in my bed, over the arm of the couch—anywhere she'll have me, I'll take her. I want her in every way imaginable, but not until she's good and ready. Because once will never be enough for me with Leleila Wills. I'm kidding myself if I think I'd actually turn her down, no matter how she offers herself to me. If she said she could only do one night, I'd say yes. If she said she could do forever, I'm all in.

Except she just bolted out my front door. Took off without a second glance back. And I'm here alone with nothing but my wine for company.

I will myself to stay put even though every other part of me is screaming to chase her down and rope her back to me where she'll be safe. Because I know she needs to have her space, on her terms, for once. And I'm going to stand here and give it to her.

I know Leleila doesn't want anyone else, even her ex. I saw them together, and Leleila didn't look at him the way she looks at me. Like she wants to tear my clothes off and let me do naughty things to her. Like she trusts me with her life. Leleila thinks she isn't good in bed because of her past, and I know I can change all of that if she'll just give me a chance and let go of the terror.

More than anything, I just want her to feel safe. In the world and with me.

I swirl the wine in my glass and swallow what's left of it in one gulp.

———

Leleila

I run to the small barn on Big River Ranch, straight to the stall where Brayden mentioned Blazer was for the night. The ranch is dark and empty with no one around but me and my demons.

The rain picks up steam as I reach the barn, and I know it's going to be a wet walk back to the house. But Blazer looks up and whinnies when he sees me, and I immediately feel myself relax.

"Hey, boy." I step closer so Blazer can nose my hand. "How are you?"

Blazer's looking for a snack, but unfortunately I came empty-handed. I compromise by hand-feeding him some of the oats from his bucket.

He's so gentle and loving. He would never hurt me.

Just like his owner.

My eyes fill with tears.

I can't blame Noah for the fact that I ran out on Brayden. When I'm truly honest with myself, I realize I'm afraid. I'm afraid to feel as good as I felt when Brayden and I made out after the bonfire party because I've never let myself lose control before.

Especially not in the bedroom. I'm scared to let go the way I think I could with Brayden. My body won't let me forget what it wants, though, and neither will my heart.

I give Blazer one last pat and go stand outside in the pouring rain. Within minutes, I'm soaked. And I'm freezing cold. But I've surrendered. In body and heart and spirit, I've surrendered.

You can't help what you want or what feels right. And if you're smart, you'll listen to yourself and ignore those voices in your head that tell you you're crazy, that tell you change isn't worth the risk. If you're smart, you'll ignore everybody else long enough to make the right choice for you.

I pick up the hem of my dress and turn toward where I just came from.

———

Brayden answers my knock then he puts his arm around me and brings me inside. "You're soaking wet. You must be freezing."

"I went to the small barn to see Blazer." I look up at him. "He's an amazing horse."

"He is." Brayden leads me onto his porch where he puts a thick blanket around my shoulders and goes about stoking the fire. "It should warm up pretty quickly. Do you want tea or hot chocolate?"

I shake my head. "I want you, Brayden. That's it."

His gaze fixes on me, and his crystal blue eyes turn liquid with heat. "Leleila."

We reach for each other at the same time—our lips, our bodies, our hearts. Brayden's mouth is all over mine, his tongue urgent and probing. We pour everything into the kiss—all the emotions we've harbored for the last few weeks, every sensation we've felt but couldn't express. My heart feels like it's going to jump out of my chest, and I cling to Brayden as his heart pounds against mine.

I haven't ever had an orgasm with a man. And while I was terrified initially, now I'm too turned on to slow down.

Brayden unzips my dress and pulls it off my shoulders.

My breasts are now exposed, and Brayden's hands on them are electric. He sucks on one nipple and then the other until I'm pulling his hair. He lifts his shirt over his head in one swift motion, and my hands immediately go to his solid chest. I run my fingers across his torso and around his ribcage, and he groans into my neck. He pulls my dress all the way off and slides off my panties, and suddenly I'm bare to him. I'm making myself vulnerable in a way I never have before, and I don't want to put up any more walls. He continues to kiss my breasts as he murmurs against me how long he's been wanting to touch me. His lips close over one nipple and suck hard, and I nearly come apart. Clutching at his hair, a moan comes up from my throat as Brayden's fingers trail a path down my stomach and between my thighs.

And now my whole body's on fire. Oh, God. Brayden's touching me in a way that I didn't know was possible. Brayden knows exactly what he's doing, and he's so slow and deliberate about it— holy shit. Two of his fingers find their way inside me, and oh my God, I've never been this turned on before.

And oh!—now he's sucking on my nipple even harder as his fingers inside me increase their pace. His thumb presses that spot Phillip never could figure out as if he needed me to draw him a damn map...and oh fuck!, I'm crying out Brayden's name, loudly because...I can't stop. I'm going to come. I am coming. *Holy Christ.*

His mouth shifts from my breast to my lips, and his lips crash over mine as he murmurs, "You are so incredible. So damn sexy. I nearly came in my pants feeling you fall apart on my fingers like that."

"I'm sorry," bursts out of me. "You didn't get a chance to..." I shift so I'm sitting up, and I reach for his dress pants, which are unbuttoned but still on. "Here. Let me take care of you now."

Brayden's eyes widen like I've lost it. He gently pushes me back down on my back. "You just rock my world, and you're apologizing? For having an orgasm? Leleila, what kind of guy do you think I am?"

"Um...I don't know. I thought I wasn't supposed to...until you know, the intercourse."

Brayden breaks into laughter. "God, you really are hard on yourself. And we clearly have to rewrite your bedroom rules. So. Rule number one: there are no rules."

I stare at him. "None?"

His lips meet mine. "None whatsoever. You touch me wherever you want to, however you want to. You let me know what you like and how you like it. And we enjoy the hell out of each other. That actually is a rule: if we aren't enjoying it—either of us—we say something. Deal?"

I nod wordlessly. This is definitely a whole new world that Brayden Wild is introducing me to.

"Now, like I was saying..." He shifts so he can drag his pants down and off his body, and suddenly I'm staring at Brayden in just boxer briefs. Those boxers hug his impressive hard length without a lot of hiding, and I stifle a moan. His face breaks into a grin. "You're staring instead of listening."

"Huh?" I force my eyes up to his, which are filled with amusement. "Sorry. You were saying?"

His lips brush my jaw. "I was saying, now I want to be inside you with a different part of me. But I don't want to rush you if you're not ready."

"We can do that? Have sex after I've come?"

He shakes with laughter. "Not only *can* we do that, but I think you'll find it quite enjoyable."

I reach for the waistband of his boxers, and slip my hand inside. When I touch his erection, we both cry out.

"I'm ready to try." I'm nervous, but I'm definitely ready.

He takes off his boxers and covers my bare body with his own before he starts moving in a way that makes me forget my nerves. Before I know it, he has a condom out. He asks me again if I'm sure, and I tell him yes.

With his mouth latched onto my nipple, causing me to buck my hips in anticipation, Brayden enters me slowly. Inch by inch, he goes deeper and deeper, groaning about how good I feel the entire time. Once he's fully inside me, he stops and touches my cheek with his hand. "Remember our rule—you tell me what you like and what you don't. Promise?"

"I promise."

He kisses me, his teeth sinking into my bottom lip until I cry out in pleasure. And then he starts to move. And shit, I feel like I'm having sex for the first time. The way Brayden stretches me and touches parts of me deep inside that I realize now have never been attended to...I clutch his back like I'll never let him go.

"Lei. Fuck." He drops his head and stares into my eyes. "I'm so close."

I feel close myself, to something I can't articulate. I don't come from intercourse, so I have zero expectations about what can happen.

Brayden's watching me, his breathing uneven and his eyes glazed. "You're ready." His voice is ragged as he drives into me harder. "Let go, sweetheart."

"Bray. I can't." I shake my head like I'm doing something wrong. "I've never..."

"You can." His tone is firm. "You are, babe. Just give in to it. I can feel you about to climax. Give in."

And I do. I was sure I couldn't possibly come again, but I do.

"Oh, God." I shake as my thighs grip Brayden's sides. I lock my ankles together and dig my nails into his back while I call out his name.

I come from a place deep inside me, a place I'm positive has never been awakened before.

Then Brayden falls over the edge with me.

He just made love to me in a way I thought only happened in the movies. It was so profound, and my orgasm was so long, that I'm still crying out after he's finished moving himself.

"Oh, wow," I whisper into his neck as he releases into me. So this is what amazing sex feels like.

Still inside me, Brayden shifts so he can lock eyes with me. He's breathing heavily, and he runs his hand over the small of my back tenderly.

"I have to say two things," he says quickly. "Before our time here is over and you're gone from under this blanket."

I try to interrupt him to tell him that I'm not going anywhere, that I don't ever want to leave him again, but he puts his finger to my lips. "Shh. Just give me two minutes, that's all I ask. First thing I have to say—because I know you were told all sorts of negative crap about yourself in bed—you are so damn sexy, and that was the greatest sex I've ever had in my life. It's never felt like that before for me. Just with you."

I swallow hard, and a warmth fills my chest.

Brayden tips my chin until I'm staring into his clear blue eyes. "Second thing: Leleila Wills, I love you."

A noise escapes my mouth. I may squeal a little.

Brayden's eyes crinkle. "And I'm not saying that because I'm just crazy here from the incredible sex we had. I'm saying it because I do. I love you. I've known for a while now."

"Brayden..." My throat fills with emotion.

"So I guess I should have said I have three things to say." He takes a deep breath. "The third is that I know you were supposed to walk down the aisle in less than two weeks, and I'm not naïve, Leleila. I know what we have could be more of a rebound thing for you, a way to kind of move forward. I want everything with you, anything and everything you can give me. But I don't expect this to necessarily go anywhere permanent, and I won't hold anything against you if it doesn't. I'll wish you well, in your future and in your life, and I'll have no regrets." He kisses me, even as tears cloud his beautiful blue eyes.

My eyes fill too. "Brayden. That was just...shoot." I reach around for my clothes, but I can't find them.

Brayden hands me my underwear. "On my side," he says with a smile. "Maybe I should have held onto them."

I laugh. "Brayden." I kiss him lightly. "I'm crazy in love with you."

His breath hitches. "You don't have to say it just because I did..."

"I'm saying it because I mean it." I kiss him longer. "And what just happened underneath this blanket...I didn't know sex could feel like that. I felt so close to you. I've never even...that was my first time having an orgasm from straight sex. I didn't think I was capable of it."

He lifts his eyebrows. "Really?"

"Really." I put my hand on his cheek. "It's like I've guarded my body and my heart for the last twelve years. I thought it was because I was so scared. You know after the assault, I didn't trust anybody. But now I think it was because I was waiting for you."

I know what Brayden risked by forging this friendship with me. He risked everything, really. Because I could have walked away at any moment, married Phillip, and never seen Brayden again.

I take his hand. "I don't know that I would have been strong enough to listen to my heart if you weren't so courageous with yours."

"Leleila, I don't want to make love just this one time." Brayden strokes my hair. "If it's something you want, when you're ready, I want this to work. I want to love you forever."

I put my arms around him and look into his eyes. "You know I started to fall for you the first time we kissed. As teenagers."

"You hardly knew me."

"I know," I say. "But that was what I felt. And trust me; I'm usually in my head so much it takes a lot—a feeling pretty much has to wave itself in front of my face and poke me to get me to pay attention to it."

He runs his thumb along my bottom lip. "Honestly, I started to fall for you twelve years ago too. Before we even met. The first time we caught eyes."

"Will you stay here tonight?" He kisses my cheek. "I promise I'll make you feel beautiful all night long."

"I'm not leaving," I whisper.

Brayden brushes my bare shoulder with his lips and then kisses his way down my body until he disappears underneath the blanket. His tongue touches that spot he's clearly an expert with, and then it moves further south. When he explores inside me, I clutch at the blanket with both fists. His tongue and lips make love to every inch of me, and I shut my eyes in bliss. Brayden was right. I've never felt more beautiful. I've never felt more loved.

CHAPTER TWENTY-EIGHT

In the morning, I drag myself out of Brayden's bed and into my work clothes. He's already up and has two bowls of cereal out for us. It's not even seven o'clock, and I've had about two hours of sleep.

"I'm sorry about the timing," Brayden says as we sit at his kitchen table and eat. "It's your first day of work. You must be exhausted."

I'm checking my texts. "My mom wants me to stop by. I haven't told my parents about the wedding being cancelled yet. Phillip's parents were on vacation until tonight, so we agreed to hold off on telling any family until everyone can be told. I know," I say impulsively. "You and I can show up for coffee, and I'll tell them about my change in career plans."

"What? Do we ever do anything on a normal time frame?"

"Seems like no." I jump up and bring my bowl to the sink. "Just throw on some jeans. You always look so handsome."

But Brayden doesn't move. "Leleila."

I pour water into the bowl to rinse it. "What?" I say without turning around. "What's wrong?"

"Honey, we look like we've slept together."

I whip around to face him. "Are you serious? How can you tell?"

"It's just...you can," he insists. "We both look tired but flushed. Your lips are pink and swollen and..." He winks at me. "Trust me, we look like we just had incredible sex all night long, and we did." He stands up. "I'll go with you to see them. I'm just warning you—they're going to know. It's all over your face. And mine."

———

Mom's in her bathrobe and no makeup, and she's not thrilled I'm surprising her with someone she barely knows at such an early hour, especially a man. I apologize and say I have job training at eight-thirty and Brayden and I just wanted to say hi.

She invites us in for a cup of tea just as Dad comes around the corner from his office. "Hello, Lei." He looks at Brayden, then at me, and then Brayden again. "Brayden, right?" Dad extends his hand. "Good to see you again."

As we wait for them in the living room on the plastic-covered couch that Mom, clearly flustered, insisted we sit on, Brayden whispers to me, "Did you see your dad's expression? Definitely knows I just made love to his daughter."

I swat at him playfully as Mom walks into the room with mugs of tea. She smiles at Brayden as she sits across from us in a hard-backed wooden chair, and Dad enters and sits in his decades-old armchair.

Dad starts talking quickly. "Lei, we heard that ..." He looks at Brayden and starts to stammer: "Uh...um...Phillip said that you can give your defense in as early as a month."

"Yes, isn't that great news?" Mom gushes. Then she looks at Brayden awkwardly. "I mean, you deserve that opportunity, Leleila. You should have had it regardless. You know, regardless of Phillip's connections."

"Thank you, Mom," I say. I look over at Brayden and then turn back to them. "The thing is, I'm quitting the program. I have to tell Gerry, so please keep it to yourselves for now. And I'm not going into another science program," I add firmly. "It's great for you," I say to them. "But it's just not me."

They try to talk me out of it for a bit, but because there's a guest in the room, they don't press for long.

Finally, Mom shifts her attention to Brayden. "Brayden, you look like you're in good shape."

"Mom!" I say.

"Well, he does." Her gaze travels to his arms. "You must have been an athlete. Were you?"

He nods. "I played wide receiver for Wilcox."

"That's a huge football program," Dad says, his tone rising in admiration. "You must have been pretty good."

"I was okay. It didn't hurt to have Dylan Wild as my quarterback."

"The Super Bowl guy?" Dad's tone gets even higher. "I don't watch sports much myself, and I disapprove of the extreme commercialism of professional sports."

"Dad," I say quietly. "Be nice. Dylan is Brayden's cousin."

"Wow. I didn't know that." Dad sits up straight. "What I was going to add was that I like that Dylan Wild guy. I saw him once in an interview when I was flipping through environmental videos online. He popped up as an ad, and for the heck of it, I clicked on it. Thought he'd come off as a smug know-it-all."

"Oh, my God." I put my head in my hands.

Brayden puts his hand on my thigh. "It's okay," he says softly.

"But he was very articulate and intelligent," Dad says. "He does a lot of work with foster kids, which is a cause I'm not involved in but really admire. He's taking the time to call attention to the foster care system and get people interested in adopting children who have nobody to care for them. He seems like a very good man."

"He is." Brayden speaks with pride. "And playing with him for three years is something I'll always treasure."

"Do you still work out a lot, Brayden?" Mom's eyes have shifted to his chest. "You certainly look like you do."

"Mom," I say sharply. "Filter."

Dad starts talking quickly. "Lei, what are you going to do for work?"

I turn to him. "I actually got hired yesterday. It's a work-from-home job for a consulting firm."

"So Leleila has time to paint," Brayden pipes in.

I shake my head at him.

Mom's eyes widen in surprise. "You're painting again, honey?"

"For fun right now. That's it."

"That's how my research started," Dad says. "I picked up a microscope one day for fun, just for the heck of it." He chuckles. "Haven't put it down since."

"Leleila's really got a talent for painting," Brayden says.

Mom's eyes brighten. "You know," she says as she peers at me, "I think that's wonderful."

"Really?" I say.

"I do," Mom says.

Brayden smiles at me and then quickly turns his focus to his tea as Dad's eyes lock in on us. I smile casually at my father, who looks like he's dying to ask me where the hell Phillip is right about now.

I bring the mug of tea to my mouth.

———

I work all morning and then stop into Big Sky Grocer for lunch.

Brayden sees me and immediately grins. He comes over and gives me a hug just as Sophia calls out to us.

"Hey! Fancy running into you two here."

June comes running down the aisle and nearly crashes into me. "Lei!" she says with a smile.

I look at her suspiciously. "You never get this excited," I say. "What do you want?"

"I don't want anything," she says, still smiling. "But somebody does. Guess who was just in here asking who painted that mural on the wall?"

I shrug. "Who?"

"Gus Newton, owner of Perks Coffeehouse. He's the one who puts up local art in his shop. He wants yours, Lei."

I shake my head. "I don't get it."

"Oh my God!" Sophia yells. "Those paintings that are hung up in there? They're all for sale," she explains to me. "Some of them sell for hundreds of dollars."

"Really?" I say.

"I'll tell him you're interested," June says. She hands me his card. "Call him yourself, actually, and you can figure out a timeframe."

Brayden grins at me. "That's awesome."

"So June, did you hear your sister and Brayden are about to be the town heroes?" Sophia says.

She fills June in on the soil development, and June is so impressed she suggests I tell Mom and Dad, "...so you can brag. Hey, how come Phillip didn't help you with the testing?" she asks me suddenly.

"Phillip didn't believe it mattered," Sophia says airily. "Phillip was too busy trying to save the world in his head rather than the one he's living in."

Brayden gives Sophia a look, but June thinks it's hysterical.

Sophia bumps June with her basket by mistake and June looks at what she's bought. "Your breakfast?" she inquires.

"Bananas with a donut," Sophia says as she turns to Brayden and me and gives us both a knowing look. "One goes perfect with the other. What else do you need, right?"

Brayden grins at her. "You just don't have any shame, do you?"

"None whatsoever," she says with a look over at me. "I think others could learn from me, actually. Life is supposed to be fun, after all. And if it ain't fun, what's the point?"

Brayden kisses me goodbye by my car. "Good luck this afternoon," he says, and I know he doesn't just mean my job. "I know you need to take some time to get your feet under you, so please..."

He cups my cheek in his hand. "Take it, okay? However long you need. I'm not going anywhere. Take the time for you, Lei."

I kiss him back. "I'll be thinking of you the whole time."

On my way to work, the leasing agent calls to tell me my application was approved and that I can move in this afternoon if I want.

"Yes, that's perfect," I say to her. "Thank you very much."

———

While Phillip's teaching class, I pack up all my stuff. It doesn't take long; most of the furniture is his from before we moved in here, and I'm not going to try to share things we bought together. Cut the couch in half? I don't think so.

I pack what is really and truly mine, and I leave the rest. If Phillip wants help later to sell some of it, I can do that. Because I know he may want to leave this house, too. All the memories here are of the two of us, and I think we both need a fresh start.

I reach for the phone then. I need help moving, and Sophia's at work.

"Hi, Leleila." Mom answers on the second ring. "How are you, honey?"

"I'm all right." I clear my throat. "I'm sorry to have surprised you this morning like that. Phillip and I officially broke up. I had to wait to tell you until he could reach his parents. It's all for the best, for both of us, and I've never been happier."

"Oh, honey." After making sure I'm definitely okay, Mom says she likes Brayden. "I never knew, Lei. And that's my fault. But I never knew someone like Brayden could work so well with you."

"It's not your fault, Mom," I say.

"No, it is. I pride myself on knowing the facts, and the fact is you're different than your father and me. You know I was so different from my own parents, too, and I feel like I should have seen this. Good for you. I'm proud of you."

"Thanks, Mom," I say. "Um, is Dad there? I need him for something."

———

It takes three trips to get my stuff from the house to my new apartment. Between Dad's economy car that barely fits a human being in the back seat, and my sedan, we could do better. With Brayden's truck, it would have been one easy trip, and we probably would have gone to dinner afterward and celebrated and then made love to christen my new place. But I can't call Brayden for this. I want to start my official relationship with him on the right foot, not moving out of the house I shared with my ex.

"Are you okay, honey?" Dad asks me as we unload his car in the parking lot and start toward the elevator.

"Yeah."

"You sure?"

"Yes."

"It takes a very strong, brave person to change course, you know." He stops to shift the boxes in his arms. "You moving out, taking up painting again—that takes courage."

"But you always said to stay the course."

"I meant if you love the course you're on. If you don't, I think changing course takes just as much conviction," he says. "You know you're doing the right thing."

"Yes. Thanks, Dad."

We finish unpacking, and I wave goodbye to my father as he pulls away. Then I walk into my new apartment alone. I stand in the middle of the tiny studio, completely clueless about what to do next. I'm definitely scared. I'd been dutifully marching along in place by Phillip's side, and Brayden was like a wake-up call, the best wake-up call I've ever had in my life. But I've never been a woman without Phillip by my side. I grew up with him.

I reach for the phone to call June.

"I live near your store now," I say.

"What do you mean?"

"I live on Main," I say. "I moved out on my own. Like you did a hundred years ago? Well, I'm just now catching up to my little sister."

I can practically hear her mind racing, trying to figure out what's going on. "Are you saying..." she begins but doesn't finish the sentence.

"I'm saying Phillip and I broke up, and I'm head over heels in love with somebody else," I say.

June screams. Three times. When she finally comes to, she says, "I wondered why Brayden looked so tired today. He didn't sound sick. He looked pretty satisfied, actually."

"Enough," I warn her.

She laughs. "Leleila, I'm happy you're happy."

"Thanks."

"And I've cleared some space in the front corner of the store, by the way. It's going to be for your paintings. I'll sell them, and maybe then I can pay you back for the new business your sign and mural sent my way."

"That's awesome," I say to her. "But you don't owe me anything. Actually, I was wondering about that empty suite next door to you?"

"The dusty, peeling paint suite?" June asks me.

"Yes," I say. "That one. How much do you think it leases for?"

"Not much," she says. "The building owner begged me to incorporate it into my store. Said I could have it as part of the same lease price. She just wants to see it being used."

"I want it," I say. "I'll turn it into a painting studio, and I can hold a mural painting class there too."

"That's a great idea," she says. "I'll call Jodie and tell her to hold the suite. You can call it Big Sky Painting."

"Actually, I'm going to call it Painting Big Sky," I say. "Oxymoronic, right?"

"But it works," she says.

When I hang up with June, I get a joyful phone call from Mom and Dad together. I guess the town newspaper came out this morning, but they just saw it. Brayden and I are on the cover with the title "Town Heroes" above our heads.

"Oh no," I say. "Brayden's going to be so embarrassed."

"He should love it," Mom says. "It's wonderful. And what a lovely picture of you both. Brayden looks so handsome."

I finally get them off the phone with a promise to bring Brayden over for dinner so we can tell them the whole story. "Every detail," Mom insists, "Especially the parts where you and Brayden take that romantic trail ride through the woods. And did he lift you at all?"

"Lift me?" I repeat.

"In his arms," she says. "You know, over a stream or something fantastic like that. It's always in the romance novels that way."

"Mom, I had no idea you read romance novels," I say. "I thought that was beneath you."

"Oh, who doesn't love a little romance now and again?" She giggles. "Right Fred?"

Dad chuckles, and I hastily tell them goodbye.

Then I take a deep breath and call Gerry. I have to leave a voicemail, but he calls me back within the hour and agrees to meet me at Huckman Hall for tea.

———

Gerry sits quietly until I'm done telling him my decision and my reasons behind it. He reacts in silent surprise—I only catch it in his eyes—when I tell him Phillip and I ended our engagement, and then he says, "So what are you going to do? Because I know you couldn't have made either of these decisions lightly."

"No," I say. "Not at all. Actually, there is something..." I tell him about my painting.

"I saw the mural at the store," he says. "And I wondered who did that. It's quite eye catching, you know." He smiles. "I'm proud of you, Lei. I admire what you're doing very much."

"Thank you for always trying to guide me in the right direction even when I was so far off," I tell him.

"And you and that guy in the paper," he says with a twinkle in his eye. "Your partner in heroism...he wouldn't have anything to do with your future, would he?"

I smile at him innocently. "Why would you say that?"

"Just a hunch," he says. "Pretty impressive stuff that you two sleuthed out, by the way. You don't need to be tenured to see that."

I smile wider. "No, I guess not."

I leave Sophia a message that I'll call her later, and then I take three days alone. I work, and I paint, and I enjoy my own space. I need to make it mine before I invite him into it. I also do something I've been avoiding.

I call a therapist in Missoula, someone a colleague mentioned she saw and highly recommended. I make an appointment with her for next week to discuss my past trauma and how to get a handle on it. If I ever run into Noah again, I don't want to feel like I have to hide. And if I'm going to be in a healthy relationship with Brayden, I want to feel strong and in control of my life, not like I'm running from old demons.

I also can't avoid Sophia. By the end of day two, she's called ten times, and when I do return her calls, she insists on meeting me at the café.

"Okay," I tell her. "But I'm still figuring my life out. I'm not sure I'm ready for an outside opinion."

———

Sophia stares at me as I walk through the doors.

"What?" I say as I sit across from her at the table.

She blinks and then shakes her head. "Nothing," she says, and I'm almost disappointed. "I just had this crazy thought the other day when we saw each other, but then you left the store so fast to get back to work. And then, when I saw you walking through the door just now..." She stops as she stares at me again and gasps. "Holy fuck! You lost your purity ring, didn't you?"

I shush her. "Quit yelling. I'm not sixteen. Or religious."

She lowers her voice. "But did you? Did you have sex with Brayden?"

I nod and try not to smile any wider than I am.

"And?" she starts to ask. Then she looks at me closely again and surely notices the sparkle in my eyes and the happy glow in my face, a glow that hasn't disappeared despite the days apart. "I don't even need to ask you. Congratulations on having amazing, life-changing sex, Lei."

"It's not just that. I mean, yeah, that's great. But I love him. A lot."

"I know you do. It's so awesome!"

I keep smiling.

———

The next evening after I finish work, I drive to the ranch. I get out of the car slowly and walk up the steps to Brayden's house. I knock, my stomach doing cartwheels.

"I moved out on my own," I say as soon as he opens his door.

His eyes brighten. "Are you sure you're okay?"

I step inside and shut the door behind me.

"Yes. I'm finally okay." I reach out and hug him, resting my cheek against his soft blue t-shirt. "I live on my own for the first time in my life. And I officially dropped out of the PhD program."

I step inside and shut the door behind me. "Plus, I'm going to lease the empty business suite next door to June's and do my painting there."

"That's awesome," he says.

"And I'm seeing a therapist."

He takes my hand. "That's great, Leleila. I'll support you with that in any way I can."

He leads me out to his porch and lies down on the rug in front of the fire. I join him, and he stretches his legs out, his blue jeans still hugging every part of him to perfection. He points at the cracks in the ceiling paint. "It's a sun. You see it?"

I look where he's pointing. "I do," I say, and I feel the blood coming into my body after my day of work.

Brayden reaches over and takes my hand in his.

"A lot of changes, and they're all good," he says. "So let's celebrate."

I turn to face him, and my stomach clenches. "What do you mean?"

"I mean"—Brayden turns on his side and kisses my neck—"I want to spend quality time with you indoors at last with no interruptions." He stands up to draw the shades and then lies back down next to me. "What do you say?"

I feel like I'm going to explode if he doesn't touch me right now. I say yes.

"All day?" I reach for the buttons on his jeans.

"And night," he says as he kisses me.

"I love you, Brayden Wild," I say. "You're my best friend. You're the best thing that's ever happened to me."

Brayden's sapphire eyes are clear and brighter than ever as he looks at me. "I'm so in love with you, Leleila. I can't picture myself with anyone else. No matter how many obstacles seemed to be in our path, all I've wanted is to spend every day together. I've never loved a woman like I love you. This feels like I never want it to end. I'm forever yours. And hopefully you'll be forever mine."

Forever sounds good to me now. When it's with the right person, forever sounds perfect.

EPILOGUE

Brayden

I watch as Leleila heads toward me down the cereal aisle of June's store. Same beautiful woman with the striking green eyes, coming to meet me in a store aisle. But everything else is different. She's different.

The tension that always coiled around her, that look of almost near-pain she would wear, is gone. Leleila Wills is happier now. And of course I'd love to take all the credit, but I'm just one piece of the puzzle. Her dream of painting is becoming a reality. She sold a few pieces to a couple of stores on Main Street, and she's going to hold her first showcase at her studio early next year.

Phillip and Mindy started dating and moved out of Mountain-view and into Missoula so he could be closer to campus. Leleila said she didn't care either way, but I know it was a relief for her to not have to run into them in town all the time. We still see him and Mindy occasionally at Big Sky Grocer, and the four of us are friendly. But they don't come to town often.

After a year of dating like "normal" people, Leleila and I finally decided to move in together. I had purchased Big River Ranch six months earlier, and Leleila said she couldn't imagine finding anywhere she loved as much.

We've already discussed how much we want to start a family together someday in the near future. And that's why I've got this ring burning a hole in my pocket.

When Leleila reaches me, I put my hands on her waist. "Come walk with me," I say as I give her a long, sweet kiss.

"Where are we going, Bray?" she asks me as I pull back. Her eyes are dazed and slightly unfocused like they always are after I kiss her.

"It's a surprise." I take her hand and lead her out to the street.

When I stop at the door to CeeGee's Bakery, she squeals. "I'm starving! I would give everything for a cupcake right now."

"Well, you don't have to give anything because here we are." I open the door, and we walk up to the counter.

We do our usual routine of taste testing the new flavors of cupcakes available today. Leleila settles on a peanut butter cup while I go for the double dark chocolate ecstasy.

We sit down at a booth in the back, and when she's not looking, I slip the ring out of my pocket and onto the top of her cupcake like a cupcake topper.

She lifts her head from where her gaze was staring into her purse and turns to her cupcake. My pulse is pounding as I watch her go from about to swipe a bit of frosting off the top and then lick it off her finger, as is her custom, to the moment she sees the bright diamond glimmering on the dark sugary top.

"What the heck—" Her fingers close around the ring and she lifts it out of the frosting gingerly. Her gaze flies up to meet mine. "Brayden. What is this?"

I leave the booth and sink to my knee in front of her. "Leleila, I love you more than anything. I want to spend the rest of my life with you. Will you marry me?"

The hand holding the ring goes to cover her mouth, which has dropped open. Her eyes widen as she stares at me without speaking.

"Lei? I know you went through an engagement once before and

it didn't turn out the way you'd dreamed. If this is too soon, please say so. I'll wait for you. You know I will."

A mischievous glint fills her emerald eyes. "No substitute dance partner required?"

"No substitute dance partner allowed," I say firmly. "Ever. I don't want to share you with anyone. And I don't ever want to be with any woman but you."

Her mouth turns upward in a beautiful smile. "That I can get behind." She throws her arms around my neck and leans down to kiss me hard on the lips. "Yes, I will marry you, Brayden Wild. I love you."

I slide into her side of the booth, and then I slip the ring onto her finger. She holds her hand up to the light. "It's so perfect," she says of the square-cut stone in the center of a circle of diamonds. "I couldn't have picked out anything better for me."

I lock eyes with her. Neither could I.

CAMERON

As the youngest cousin, Cameron is the only Wild still single...but not for long. Order your copy of CAMERON now!

Take a peek at CAMERON:

Savannah

Every day is the same. I go to the Climax Coffee Shop, and then to the hockey rink where I've worked since I was a kid.

But today, a cocky guy cuts me in line. A dark-haired, sexy guy with laser eyes and a perfect body.

I can't ignore how hot he is, and I especially can't ignore how he's the only man to ever make me *want*. Like really want.

By the time I walk into my office, I'm completely thrown off by the Hot Stranger.

Then my boss tells me a new player is joining our ice hockey team and it's my job to do whatever it takes to make him comfortable.

Only one problem: the new hot shot is the *Hot Stranger*, and the rulebook says I'm forbidden to score with team members.

My boring life just got a lot more interesting.

Cameron

Savannah McMann has fierce green eyes and a temper to match.

But she's shy and skittish whenever I put my eyes on her. I can see she's wounded but I can't tell what kind of jerk hurt her.

And why the hell do I care anyway? I'm on this team to get my stats up, not to score with the coach's assistant.

But my head keeps finding reasons to end up in Savannah's office, while another part of me dreams of being in her pants.

She's got a strong defense, so I've got to play it slow or I'll end up flat on the ice with my stick in my hands.

One thing's for sure: I want her. I like her. And I'm ready to take a few body checks to show her I'm the real deal.

READ CAMERON AND SAVANNAH'S STORY IN *CAMERON*, AVAILABLE NOW!

ALSO BY MELISSA BELLE

Boston Boys Series

BOSTON BILLIONAIRE

BOSTON LOVE

BOSTON ESCAPE

BOSTON ROOMIE

WILD MEN Series

WILD MAN

COLTON

DYLAN

AYDEN

JENSON

BRAYDEN

CAMERON

Sign up for Melissa's Newsletter to receive alerts and updates on upcoming book releases.

ACKNOWLEDGMENTS

Thank you to:

J. Dylan for your time and brilliance;
D. Yacovetta for all the detail-catching;
J. Hunter for your creative ideas;
My husband for exploring Montana with me;
And to my amazing readers!

ABOUT THE AUTHOR

Melissa Belle writes contemporary romance novels in a style that's sexy, sweet, and steamy. She lives in New England with her family, and often works through her story ideas while hiking with her husband, or hanging out with her two rescue kitties.

When she's not writing love stories, Melissa Belle loves to travel. Her first novel was written while riding through Europe on the train.

To receive an email when Melissa releases a new book, sign up for her newsletter!